THIS SIDE OF MIDNIGHT

#4 TILDAS ISLAND SERIES

TAMSEN SCHULTZ

Copyright © 2021 by Tamsen Schultz

Cover Design by Paige Alley-Payne
Edited by Rebecca and Woody Fridae

Print ISBN: 979-8594125476

All rights reserved.

No part of this book may be reproduced in any form or by any electronic or mechanical means, including information storage and retrieval systems, without written permission from the author, except for the use of brief quotations in a book review.

To my community of Winters, CA – your generosity of spirit as we recover from the devastating LNU fire is more inspiring than you know. We may not be a perfect town, but no one can say we don't pull together when the chips are down.

ACKNOWLEDGMENTS

This is the penultimate book in this series and it's been so much fun to write. Part of that joy has come from the fact that it's set in the Caribbean, and during this time of COVID, when travel isn't such a great idea (if even possible), having the opportunity to visit the islands every time I sit down to write has been a welcome respite.

If you've read the other books in the series, you might remember that in *A Fiery Whisper*, I mentioned an image on the cover that pays tribute to the history of the Virgin Islands…did you see it? The same images have made appearances on all the book covers and it even has a tie to the name of the series. If you think you know what the image is and how it ties to the series, send me a quick email and let me know. And, just for fun, the first correct answer I receive will get a little prize.

As always, thank you to my PA, Stephanie Thurwachter and my editors, Woody and Rebecca Fridae. I also want to thank my family by choice, Angeli and Sarah – being able to see you both (and the rest of the fam) for the month of November meant more to me than you know. And last, but not least, to my Ladies of Letters…you've been keeping me sane this past year (and, let's be real, probably longer than that).

PROLOGUE

DECEMBER

Dominic leaned against the wall and tried to strike a pose that conveyed both confidence and calm. The hospital had done its best to disguise the odor of antiseptic and anxiety, but that particular scent had worked its way into his nostrils, and now he was pretty sure that every time he smelled it from this day on, it would bring him back to this moment.

He glanced over at his family. His mom and dad sat side-by-side, gripping each other's hands, his mom's head resting lightly on his father's shoulder. His two sisters and their husbands sat in remarkably similar tableaus. He was the only one standing. The only one alone.

The clock on the wall clicked over a minute and Jeremiah, his oldest sister's husband, leaned down and spoke quietly to Pamela, his wife. With her head resting against his shoulder, Pamela nodded, then sniffled. Jeremiah pulled a tissue out and handed it to her.

Dominic's gaze traveled to where his other sister sat, her hands intertwined with her husband's. Pamela was older than he was by five years, but he and Katherine were only eighteen months apart. They'd been close as kids, but when he'd left home to join the Air Force and she'd gone on to law school, they'd let the distance—and their respective jobs—be an excuse to drift apart.

He stifled a sigh and glanced at the clock. He'd come home to Louisiana for what was supposed to have been a couple of weeks of R&R from his job as part of a special FBI task force stationed on Tildas Island in the Caribbean. What he'd walked into was a nightmare—a possible cancer diagnosis for his mother, the matriarch, and center of their family.

His eyes traveled to his mama. He hadn't lived in Louisiana for more than a decade, and it was true that he and Katherine had drifted, but his family was tight. They always had been and always would be. That love, that loyalty, and that bond had come from his parents, and in particular, his mom.

She'd been a stay-at-home parent for most of his early years, while their father, a professor, had taught at the nearby university. Even managing three kids and supporting her husband's career, she'd had dreams of her own, though. Dreams she'd made come true when Dominic had been ten and she'd opened her first restaurant.

Dominic still remembered his mother's smile the day she opened the door to her home-style breakfast cafe and the way his father had teared up at her achievement, so moved to see the woman he loved so happy. Now, twenty-five years later, Korryn Burel was one of the most celebrated chefs in the state. It was well deserved, and no one—and he meant *no one*—could cook like his mama. But to him, she'd always be the one who prodded him to do—to be—better, the one who'd bandaged his scrapes while dispensing life lessons, the one who held the family together with her love and light and drive to make the world a better place every day.

And now they were waiting to see if she'd die.

Dominic blinked and looked away. When would the damn doctor arrive?

"Dominic, baby, why don't you sit down?" his mother asked.

He met her gaze, and in her dark eyes he saw the mother he'd always known. She was the one who might be getting the cancer diagnosis, and yet here she was taking care of him.

"She's right, son," his dad said. "Why don't you have a seat?" As George Burel spoke, he patted the empty chair to his right.

Dominic switched his attention to his dad. Other than Dominic's bright green eyes that he inherited from his mother, he was the spitting image of his father—tall with a lean build, smooth, dark skin, and a killer grin. While Dominic deployed his smile to influence and encourage witnesses and suspects alike, the elder Burel had used his to sway and inspire students. After almost forty years of teaching, he'd mostly retired from his professorship of Literature at the university, but that hadn't slowed Papa Burel down. He still played tennis three times a week, helped out at the restaurant when asked, and his world still revolved around his family. He'd aged, though. In fact, the amount that his father's black hair had turned grey since Dominic's last visit had been Dominic's first hint that all was not well.

Dominic shook his head. He didn't want to sit. He wanted to stay standing, he wanted to stay alone on his side of the room. Perhaps it was childish, perhaps he was being weak, but if the doctor gave them the news none of them wanted, his mom would have his dad, Pamela would have Jeremiah, and Katherine would have her husband, Michael. He needed the steady wall at his back to offer cold comfort because he had no one to lean on and he wasn't about to burden his family with his grief when they'd all be struggling with their own.

The shuffling of feet in the hallway and the garbled words of a quiet conversation happening on the other side of the closed door drew everyone's attention, and the question of whether he'd sit or not became moot. His sisters straightened in their chairs and in almost identical moves, Jeremiah and Michael wrapped an arm around their respective wives. His dad leaned over and kissed his mom's head. It was a sweet gesture, but Dominic saw the man's eyes close for a moment and in that moment, Dominic's heart broke. His father was being faced with the reality that the love of his life might be taken from him.

The door swung silently open and the doctor entered. Dominic's family all leaned forward a touch, as if bracing themselves for an assault. He pressed his back to the wall, hoping it would hold him up if his world collapsed around him.

The doctor was young, close to his own age, and she wore a gentle smile.

"Mrs. Burel, thank you for coming in today, and I'm glad your family is with you," she said.

Dominic hated that she'd led with that ambiguous statement. What did that mean?

"Dr. Joachim," his mom said, her voice wavering.

Dr. Joachim's eyes quickly took in the room, then landed back on his mother. "It's good news, Mrs. Burel. The tumor is benign. Once we remove it, you should have no further symptoms and, after a short recovery, you should be able to resume your normal life."

A beat passed, a flickering moment in time when everyone in his family held their breaths as they absorbed the words. Then everything erupted. His sisters curled into their husbands and tears and words of relief flowed. His parents simply held each other though Dominic knew they'd be praying, giving thanks, in their silence.

As for him, the wall he'd hoped would hold him failed, and he sank to the floor. Acknowledging how close a call they'd just had, a string of four-letter words flowed through his head, releasing some of the pressure of the past few days. Knowing that his mother wouldn't appreciate him letting off steam in that way, though, he kept his special embodiment of relief to himself. But he didn't stop himself from crying. He couldn't remember the last time actual tears had fallen from his eyes—maybe when he'd been ten and dislocated his shoulder? There was no shame in them now, though. Fuck no. His mama was going to be okay.

Then just as quickly as the tears of joy started, laughter followed. First his mama, then his dad, then soon, his sisters and their husbands had joined in. Dominic smiled, too, as he looked up and watched his family. Watched them hug their partners, then hug each other, then come together in a group hug.

The room filled with love. His sisters held on to their husbands and his parents stayed wrapped in each other's arms. Gratitude and grace coursed through his body. But from where he sat, alone on the floor, he wondered if maybe, just maybe, something was missing from his life.

CHAPTER ONE

DETECTIVE ANIKA ANDERSON stood in front of a wall of windows and looked out at the banquet room and all the faces staring back at her. Her good friend, Mike Hague had invited her to speak at his Rotary Club lunch meeting this week, and though she'd had four weeks to prepare, she wasn't entirely sure what she was going to talk about.

Oh, she had a ton of information—everything from crime stat trends to what was happening with the new traffic circle in town—but she wasn't sure what would interest this diverse group of people. Forty faces, ranging in age from mid-twenties to somewhere close to a hundred, politely waited for her to begin. They were all professionals (or retired professionals) in some industry or another, so perhaps talking about the community policing program the department had recently kicked off was a good place to start? It was aimed at keeping the more touristy parts of the island safe and fun, and since the majority of the island's economy came from the tourist industry, surely that would touch on all their interests?

"I have a few topics I can cover today," she began. "But I thought I'd start with the new Community Policing Program the department kicked off in January. It's been running for ten weeks, but even in that short time, we're seeing a decrease in petty crimes and—something many of you may be interested in—an increase in good social media reviews of our restaurants, shops, hotels, and parks."

When all the faces lit up with smiles and a few chuckles filled the room, Anika relaxed, safe in the knowledge that she'd picked the right topic. She spent the next twenty minutes talking about the new program, then several more minutes answering questions, before Jack Jones, the club president, had to close the meeting. Speaking at community outreach events was a department mandate, but unlike many in the Tildas Island Police Department, she never minded doing it.

"Detective Anderson?" A tall, svelte woman approached Anika. The waitstaff had come into the room to start cleaning so Anika nodded to the woman, then gestured to a spot where they wouldn't be in the way.

"I'm Chris Williams," she said, extending her hand as they came to a stop in a corner.

The window was still at Anika's back, and the morning heat radiated from the pane.

"I manage Mother's House," Chris continued, referring to the non-profit that provided assistance to homeless and at-risk pregnant women. Anika knew of the program, it had a good reputation and despite the dollars the tourists brought to Tildas, there was a much larger population of homeless and at-risk than most people thought.

"Of course," Anika said. "It's a great program." Something flashed through the window and Anika glanced outside. There was a construction crew on the hill behind the hotel where the meeting had taken place and the sun was reflecting off the window of a large crane.

"Here," Anika said, moving to the right so Chris could turn away from the window and not get blinded by the reflection.

"Thank you," Chris said. "I wanted to ask you if the department might be interested in donating…"

Anika continued to listen to Chris solicit a donation for the House's annual fundraiser even as something caught her eye. As she moved a little closer to the window, her gaze zeroed in on a dumpster that sat in the unused parking lot behind the hotel below where she stood in the second-floor conference room.

"Detective Anderson?" Chris asked.

Anika pulled her attention from the dumpster to Chris. "Yes?"

"Do you think the department would be willing?"

Anika's gaze darted back down to the dumpster before she answered. "Here," she said, pulling a card from her pocket. "Email me the details, and I'm sure the department would be happy to help."

Chris took the card and beamed at her. "Thank you. It says a lot to have the support of our police."

Anika gave a distracted nod, then Chris shook her hand and took her leave. Before she was three steps away, Anika was once again staring at the dumpster.

"What's got you so fixated out there?" Mike asked, coming to stand at her shoulder. Mike had been a cop in New Orleans before retiring twenty years earlier to Tildas Island. "My granddaughter likes to ogle the construction crews, but you don't—"

"That," Anika answered, pointing out the window toward the dumpster.

Mike inched closer and craned his head to follow her direction. A beat passed. "Is that…"

"Yeah," she said on an exhale. "That's a body."

Dominic glanced at the clock on his computer. A quarter to five. In another forty-five minutes, he'd be meeting Anika at the community center. He'd started a little two-on-two basketball program for the young men who used the center as a way to escape their living situations, and Anika was kicking off her third, six-week program in self-defense for women.

"You at the Center tonight?" Alexis Wright, another of the agents on their five-person FBI task force, asked.

"Yep. You want to join?" he asked. They both sat at their desks in the FBI office in Havensted, the main town on Tildas Island. The other three members of the task force were offsite—Damian Rodriguez and Benita (known as Beni) Ricci were at Hemmeleigh Resort running security scenarios with the resort security, and Jake McMullen was meeting with the transportation authority of Tildas Island. The Summit of World Leaders would kick off in less than two months and ensuring the smooth passage from the airport to the resort of the 150 attendees was not an easy feat.

The Summit was the reason for the task force. Just over eighteen months ago, when the steering committee had selected Tildas Island for the event, the US government had realized that although Tildas had been a US territory for over a hundred years, it knew very little about crime or security in the region. They'd quickly appointed FBI legend Sunita Shah as the director of the task force, and she'd hand selected the five members. It was hard to believe that their eighteen-month stint on the island was nearly over.

Alexis shook her head in answer to his question. "I'll join next week, but I have a few things I want to get out the door tonight. Nothing urgent, but some of my calls went a little long today and I didn't get as much done as I needed to."

Shah had assigned each of the five agents to thirty different leaders, and, as part of that task, they acted as the security liaison between the event coordinators and the security teams for their assigned leaders. The liaison role included weekly calls with each leader's security team and both he and Alexis had spent the majority of the day on the phone.

Dominic nodded and resumed typing up his summary of the last call he'd had with the team from Australia. He'd just hit save when his cell phone buzzed. Glancing at the screen, he couldn't help the smile that tugged on his lips.

"Hey Anika," he said, answering the call. "You ready?"

He could hear a lot of background noise, and when she sighed, he knew their evening plans were shot.

"I caught a case," she said. "Suspicious death out at the Lookout Hotel. Any chance you can ask Alexis or Beni to take my class for the night? It's going to be a while before I get out of here."

A flash of disappointment speared through him, but she had a job to do—a job she loved and was damn good at. "Alexis is here, I'll ask her. Don't worry about it, we'll get it covered. Drinks tonight if you can?"

She sighed again then covered the phone and shouted out an order to someone before uncovering the phone and returning to their conversation. "I may need it after this afternoon, but not sure how late this will go. I'll text you when we wrap up and we can decide then?"

"Sounds good. Go kick ass."

She chuckled. "Thanks, Burel. Talk soon."

Dominic ended the call and looked over to Alexis who was already watching him.

"Everything okay?" she asked.

"Suspicious death over at The Lookout. Any chance...?"

"Of course I'll step in," Alexis answered without hesitation. Because that was how his team rolled—all for one and one for all, and all that. It didn't matter that Anika wasn't an actual member of their team because over the past five months, she'd become a de facto one.

"Thanks," Dominic said. "I'll forward you the attendee list and the basic structure of the class that Anika uses."

Alexis smiled and rose from her seat. "Sounds good. I'll go grab my workout bag from my car. I'll change then we can head out in twenty minutes?"

"Perfect," Dominic answered. He watched Alexis leave and while he was grateful that she'd been able to jump in so quickly, a little part of him—okay, a big part of him—wished it could have been Anika.

CHAPTER TWO

"Joseph Taglia," Officer Rosey Parkhurst said, handing Anika a folder when she walked into the station the next morning. Rosey had been a member of the Havensted Police Department for almost as long as Anika had been alive and was always the first to know everything. For the most part, Anika appreciated having her as part of the detective division, at least until she nosed around Anika's private life. Thankfully, this morning, they had more than enough work to keep them busy.

"Fingerprint confirmation?" Anika asked, opening the folder and scanning the contents.

"And dental," Rosey confirmed.

Joseph Taglia was a resident of Los Angeles and had arrived on Tildas Island three days prior to his death. Whether his visit was a vacation or business, Anika didn't know, but at least they had a name now and could start finding answers to all their questions.

"Have you started digging yet?" Anika asked, taking a seat at her desk and powering up her computer.

"Was just about to," Rosey replied. "All the usual, I assume?"

Anika nodded. "I'll look into family to see who we need to be notifying, but if you could start looking into the rest—employment, reason for visiting the island, and all that, that would be great."

"What would be great?" Detective Mateo Garza, the senior detective, asked, as he walked into the room.

"The victim is Joseph Taglia of LA," Anika said, handing him the folder Rosey had given her. "I'm looking up family, Rosey is looking up everything else."

Mateo looked at the contents of the file much the same way Anika had moments ago. After a beat, he nodded, closed the folder, and handed it back. "I'll go check in with the Medical Examiner and see if he has anything yet. Once you've notified any next of kin, let's head over to the hotel to take a look at his room. Assuming he was staying at The Lookout," he added.

Anika gave a mock salute. "I'll call the hotel and confirm. If he wasn't a guest there, I'll find out where. I should be good to go in about an hour." She hoped. Finding the family of a deceased person wasn't generally too difficult, but occasionally, the process could get complex.

Thirty minutes later, it was clear that Taglia was going to be one of those complex ones. To the best of her ability, she'd found no family—no spouse, no kids, no siblings, and his parents were also deceased. With a frustrated breath, Anika sat back in her chair and tossed her pen on the desk.

"Do you have a place of employment yet?" Anika asked Rosey.

"Loose Ends Studios," Rosey answered. "He's an accountant in the tax division. Started there a little over three years ago."

"You have an HR contact by any chance?"

In response, Rosey leaned closer to her computer, typed in a few keys, then sat back. "It's on its way to your inbox. You think this is a suicide?" Rosey asked. Anika was used to the woman's abrupt changes of topic, but this one made her pause before clicking on the email that had just arrived in her inbox. Neither she nor Mateo had speculated with anyone other than each other whether it was suicide or murder—or even an accident. It was too early to tell and neither had wanted to make any judgments that might impact the trajectory of the investigation.

"Is there something that makes you think it's suicide?" Anika asked.

Rosey shrugged. "Mateo mentioned it last night. He said it's still classified as suspicious, but he also said it looked like suicide to him."

Anika frowned. When she and Mateo had talked about it, she'd been leaning toward murder, and while he hadn't agreed, he definitely hadn't indicated that he was leaning toward suicide. After all, who committed suicide by jumping off a five-story roof into a dumpster? There were much easier ways to do it, especially on an island with a lot of cliffs.

"Not sure," Anika answered. "Hopefully, we'll know more once we get into his hotel room."

Not wanting to discuss it further, Anika clicked open the email Rosey had sent and picked up her phone. Five minutes later she was connected to Alicia Cortez, the Chief People Officer of Loose Ends Studios.

"This is Alicia Cortez, how may I help you?"

Anika introduced herself then relayed the reason for her call. When she'd finished, there was a beat of silence before Ms. Cortez sucked in a breath.

"Joe is really dead?"

"I'm sorry to say, he is," Anika answered.

"He was such a nice guy. How did it happen?"

"We're looking into all possibilities and aren't prepared to make a determination yet."

"Of course," Ms. Cortez responded, though Anika got the sense she wasn't sure what she was saying "of course" to. "How can I help you?"

"We haven't been able to locate any family for Mr. Taglia.

Can you tell us if he's listed any next of kin on any of his paperwork? Maybe a beneficiary of his 401K or something?"

"I...Yes, I can do that. Not at this moment as it will take a little bit of time, but I can look into it right away and get back to you."

"Thank you," Anika said. "Do you know what brought Mr. Taglia to Tildas?"

"Yes, yes I do," Ms. Cortez answered. "It was a contest we ran at the studio for all employees. It had to do with updating our branding. Employees submitted ideas and the winning idea won an all-expense paid trip to Tildas Island for a week."

"And Mr. Taglia won?"

"He did. He was excited about it. Said he'd never been to the Caribbean before. God, this is terrible. Poor Joe."

Anika's mind flashed to an image of Joseph Taglia lying in the dumpster. Yes, poor Joe.

"Is there anything else you can tell me about him?" Anika asked.

"He was a nice man. Very kind and considerate. It was a little bit of a leap for him to come to the studio since he'd spent most of his life in the tax department of some bank in DC. He loved living on the West Coast, though, and with no immediate family, he took advantage of everything LA has to offer."

"In what way?"

Ms. Cortez's voice carried a thoughtful tone when she answered. "He didn't have anyone else's schedule to consider, so he'd often take off for weekends and go hiking or exploring. He was also learning to surf, though he laughed about that more than anything else—said a fifty-year-old man had to have some ridiculousness in his life. He enjoyed it here; he liked the sunshine and the food and going to places like Joshua Tree. He was a nice man," Ms. Cortez said. Sadness had crept into her voice and Anika knew the reality of his death was starting to sink in.

"Thank you, Ms. Cortez," Anika said. "We'd appreciate it if you could keep this to yourself to the extent you can until we find out if he has any next of kin to notify."

"Oh, of course. It's just so awful," she said.

Anika gave the woman her contact information then ended the call as Mateo walked back in.

"You done?" he asked.

"You get anything?" she countered.

He rolled his eyes at her. "Yeah, I got something. Not a lot, but the ME is starting the autopsy in about an hour. I'll fill you in on the way."

"I still need to call the hotel. I couldn't locate any next of kin so just got off a call with his employer. I'll fill you in on the way," she mimicked. "As soon as I confirm he was a guest at The Lookout," she added.

A few minutes later, she had the confirmation she needed, but Mateo had gotten distracted by something on his computer, which meant they wouldn't be leaving for at least another ten minutes.

"Rosey, can you run down to transportation and see if you can get the details of his flight?" Anika asked. Mateo's eyes flickered up, but he held his tongue until Rosey had left.

"What's that about?" he asked.

"You told Rosey you think it's suicide?"

Mateo shook his head. "Maddox was in here last night after you left," he said, referring to their chief of police. "*He* was pushing the suicide theory. I just said it was possible."

"Why would he do that?"

Mateo shot her a "get real" look. "Because a murder, or even an accident, is bad for tourism. Though of the two, an accident would be better."

Anika gave a disgusted shake of her head. She had a lot of issues with the leadership of the police department, and this wasn't the first time their chief had tried to get them to let what was or was not good for the island tourism dictate an investigation. However, this was the first time he'd done it with a potential murder.

"What *do* you think?" she asked. Mateo had a lot of swagger in him that sometimes made it hard to take him seriously, but he was, despite all that, a good detective.

He sat back in his chair. "Hard to say. There were no signs of a struggle on the roof where we think he fell from, and there's no reason we know of that he should have been up there in the first place, given that the rooftop bar is closed for construction. Kind of makes me think it might be suicide or an accident, but I'm not willing to rule out murder. Not yet anyway."

Anika agreed. All signs *were* pointing to suicide or accident, but something felt off; something that held her back from committing to either of those.

"What do you think about bringing Dominic in?" she asked. Mateo and Dominic had met several times. The two weren't exactly bosom buddies, but they had a begrudging respect for each other.

"Why would we do that?"

"Because he's seen more of this kind of stuff than we have. Other than the occasional domestic violence or drug overdose, when was the last time we had a murder? Or at least one like this?"

"We don't know if it's murder," Mateo countered.

"Exactly," Anika said. "It's suspicious. Dominic might see things we don't. Also, given that the victim is from LA, it might be good to have someone from the FBI involved to cover any multi-state jurisdiction issues."

Mateo considered her argument. It wasn't that she thought she and Mateo couldn't do it on their own, but she didn't want to take the chance of missing something. The jurisdictional issue was a real one, too. Again, there were protocols to handle it and they didn't *need* the FBI, but it couldn't hurt.

Mateo exhaled dramatically. "I don't love it, but let's see if he's available. It can't hurt to have them in the loop, especially if we need some assistance in California."

Mateo was one of the few men on the force who treated her as something close to an equal, but even he had an ego and if she made big deal of bringing the FBI in, he might change his mind. So rather than comment on Mateo's reluctance, Anika pulled out her phone and texted Dominic.

"Any chance you're free for an hour or so?" she wrote.

Little bubbles appeared then a few seconds later, a text. *"Sure. I have to be to Hemmeleigh by lunch, but other than that, I can rearrange some things. What's up?"*

"That body from yesterday. Still a suspicious death, we could use your eyes. And your jurisdiction. He's from LA."

"The Lookout, right? I'll meet you there."

She typed out a quick thanks, then shut down her computer and rose from her seat. "He'll meet us there," she said to Mateo. "Now, you going to tell me what you have?"

"Patience, young cricket," he said as he, too stood.

"You're three years older than me," she shot back, falling into a familiar banter.

"Biologically," he pointed out as they left their office headed toward the parking lot. "In maturity and experience—"

"You're twelve."

"Harsh, Anderson."

"Says the man who couldn't figure out the new coffeemaker for three weeks."

"It was complex."

"There were printed step-by-step directions posted right above it."

"Get in the car, Detective."

Anika chuckled and slid into the department issued SUV. Despite their teasing, Mateo *did* have more experience than the three years between them might suggest, but only because he'd risen to the rank of detective much quicker than she. It wasn't something she dwelled on often, and it certainly wasn't Mateo's fault, but from the time she'd passed her detective exam to when they couldn't put off her promotion any longer, four years had passed. Their chief had not been keen on elevating a woman into the position, but now that she was in the role, she gave it everything she had, every day.

"So, what do you have?" she asked as they departed the parking lot and headed toward the hotel.

"Not much, but the blood work came back with a few anomalies. The doctor didn't have the specifics yet, but there were definitely drugs in his system."

Five months ago, her familiarity with the local drug scene had taken a dramatic shift. She'd been pulled into a case—the very one where she and Dominic had first met—that involved some scary-as-shit designer drugs. The drug, and its effects on people, wasn't something she'd ever forget, but she was pretty sure the FBI task force had shut that operation down. Still, she wondered if there could be a connection to Taglia.

"What about alcohol?" She wanted to know more about the drugs, but if Mateo had had more details, he would have said.

"Yes, but not a lot. Like a couple-of-drinks-with-dinner amount."

Anika looked out the window while she went through what little they had on the victim: a seemingly successful tax accountant, on an all-expense paid vacation, with not a lot of alcohol in his system, but some unidentified drugs.

"Committing suicide while on vacation seems like kind of a weird thing to do," she speculated.

"Yeah, but so does cheating on your spouse when you're on your honeymoon, and we've seen that, too."

Mateo had a point with that one—they did see people do some weird shit when they came to play on Tildas Island. It was sometimes like they left their morals and good sense at home.

"Fair enough. I'll withhold any judgment until we get a better picture of Mr. Taglia."

"It could have been an accident, too," Mateo said. "That rooftop bar is closed for renovations now, but it's not hard to access. Maybe he's a photographer, and he went up to take some pictures, got a little too close to the edge, and went over."

The bar *did* have great views. It was hard to imagine how a guest who'd never been to the island before would know that, though, since it had been closed for several months.

Anika made some non-committal sound to acknowledge Mateo's point, and the rest of the drive was made in silence. When they pulled into the lot, Anika immediately spotted Dominic. He was leaning against his car, his arms crossed, and his head tilted back, studying the hotel. There was no mistaking her reaction to the man. He was handsome as sin with his chiseled features, smooth, dark skin, emerald green eyes, and a body that had been honed by his years in the military.

But Dominic was a player through and through. The kind of man she stayed far away from when it came to matters of the heart—or even matters of simple lust. So, while her body might have a reaction to him that she couldn't control, she'd become an expert at ignoring that reaction and controlling her response to it. Surprisingly, over the months she'd maintained her tight control, he'd become a good friend—someone she could count on and someone she respected.

"There's your boyfriend," Mateo said, pulling into a spot a couple over from where Dominic had parked.

"And there's your girlfriend," Anika shot back, pointing to an iguana sunning itself on the sidewalk.

Mateo considered the reptile, then laughed. "Her claws are shorter than those of the last woman I dated."

Anika laughed, too, as they exited the car. The sound must have caught Dominic's attention, and he turned to face them.

He had his aviator sunglasses on so she couldn't read his expression, but his lips quirked into a little grin.

"Garza. Anika," Dominic said once they'd approached him. "Nice to see you both. Too bad the circumstances are what they are."

She and Mateo both muttered their agreement, and the three made their way inside. After a quick conversation with the manager, they were given a key card to room 214, and a few minutes after that, the three of them were standing in Taglia's room, taking everything in.

Although there wasn't much to take in. The cleaning crew had been by the day before—before they'd known of Taglia's death—but if Anika's initial impression was anything to go by, Taglia was a very tidy man.

A book was opened and resting on the bedside table next to a water bottle. Three pairs of shoes were neatly lined up against the wall by the dresser, and when she opened one of the drawers, Anika found a tidy stack of folded T-shirts. Opening the other three drawers, she found them in much the same order, but holding his shorts, boxers, and socks.

"He was definitely a tidy man," Dominic said, walking toward the bathroom.

Mateo opened the closet and found a couple pairs of pants and a few dress shirts hanging inside.

"Anything in the safe?" Anika asked.

Mateo bent down to examine the small device then shook his head. "Nope, it's open and unless someone broke into the room, opened the safe, and emptied it, I don't think he used it."

"He's got some medications in here," Dominic called from the bathroom.

Mateo motioned with his head for her to check them out.

When she entered the sizable room, Dominic was leaning down, reading the labels but keeping his hands to himself. "That's a blood pressure medicine," he said, pointing to one.

"And that's one they give to people post-cancer treatment, but it could also be for something else," he said, pointing to another. "I don't know what the other two are."

Anika joined him and studied the bottles. All were prescribed to Joseph Taglia, and all appeared to come from the same pharmacy in LA. "We'll bag them and get them to the lab," she said. "Anything else in here?"

She let her gaze sweep the room. It looked much the same as the bedroom—tidy and relatively sparse. A comb, a toothbrush, and toothpaste were positioned on the right side of the sink, and a razor, shaving cream, and fingernail clippers were on the left.

Her gaze lingered on the left side.

"What are you thinking?" Dominic asked, surprising her. She hadn't been staring at the items for *that* long.

"What makes you think I'm thinking anything in particular?"

He smiled—his real smile, not the one he deployed late at night after a few drinks. "You get this far off look in your eyes when you're mulling things over," he said.

She frowned. Did she?

"You do," he said, as if reading her mind.

With a little shake of her head, she pointed to the items. "I'm curious, when you travel, do you bring nail clippers?"

Dominic's attention immediately went to the left side of the sink. A beat passed, then he answered. "Not usually, no. Not for a short trip."

It was an oddity, to be sure. But that wasn't what was tugging at the back of her mind. She tried to catch the illusive thought that was teasing at the edges of her memory, but when it proved too slippery, she turned and rejoined Mateo in the bedroom.

He was on the phone, calling in the evidence collection team. When he was done, he slid his phone into his pocket. "St. George, O'Clare, and Hernandez are about ten minutes out. I'll oversee the collection. You want to go talk to the manager again and see if we can get any CCTV recordings?"

Anika nodded. "We'll take a trip to the roof, too. We saw it yesterday, but I want Dominic to have a look."

Mateo's gaze flickered to the agent, but he nodded in agreement. Without another word, she left the room, Dominic trailing behind her. They headed back down to the main level where she took a few minutes to convince the manager to send over any CCTV recordings of all the areas Taglia might have been the night he'd died. She'd hoped to get footage of the rooftop, but since it was under construction and they'd wanted to save some money, the hotel had disconnected the cameras in that area.

"What's your initial impression?" she asked as they ascended to the top. So far, Dominic had been mostly silent, but by the way he'd studied the room and the questions he'd asked, she didn't need to be a detective to know he was already forming his own opinions.

"Tell me about the victim," he said.

By the time they reached the roof, she'd given him the sparse details they had. She paused after stepping through the doors and surveyed the scene. The construction was mostly done, and with the exception of a few odd boards lying around, some handheld tools stacked on a utility shelf, and general construction site litter, the space looked ready for guests to enjoy.

Dominic walked over to the edge of the building and looked down. Anika studied him as he examined the drop. His arms were crossed again, and his lips tugged down into a small frown.

"What are you thinking?" she asked, mimicking his earlier question as she joined him at the railing.

"That was the dumpster where his body was found?" he asked, pointing to a blue dumpster positioned below them.

"Not the exact one," she answered. "We had that moved yesterday, but it's the same location."

"What was his time of death again?"

"Between twelve and four in the morning."

Dominic turned and leaned his back against the railing. The side of the building rose two feet above the floor level and then two rails, each about a foot apart, were bolted onto the top, bringing the overall height from the bottom to the top of the wall to four feet.

"It's a weird place to commit suicide," he said.

"Or even to have an accident," she said, tapping the top railing.

"But as long as we're on that track, if it was murder, why here?"

"Maybe he was up here and there was a fight of some sort?" she suggested.

"Possibly. Any signs of that on his body?"

"We don't have anything back from the ME yet and his body was a little messed up when we found him. It was hard to tell," she answered.

"Did he know anyone on the island?"

She shook her head. "We don't know that yet. We just got confirmation on his ID this morning and haven't been able to track down any kin. I'll spend this afternoon looking into that, but I do know this was his first trip to the island. He sounded like an amiable guy when I spoke to the representative from his company. Maybe he met someone here?"

"An amiable man who meets someone and in just a few days they hate each other enough to get into a fight that results in one of them being dead?"

She inclined her head. "You're right. Probably not likely. His pants were all pulled up, too, so we can forgo speculation that he fell in the middle of having sex with someone." It might have sounded like an unusual leap of logic, but during her first year as a detective, a woman had died after falling over the railing of her hotel room balcony while having sex with a man she'd just met. The story had become something of a department legend.

"Probably not likely," Dominic agreed, "But also not something to ignore because I think we both know that weird shit happens all the time. If someone else was involved, maybe they didn't even know each other. Or maybe Taglia saw something he shouldn't. Or maybe he hit on some guy's wife or husband. At this point, who knows?" With that, he turned again, and she followed suit. They both stood looking down at the dumpster.

"Were there any signs of a struggle at all?" he asked.

"I'll talk to housekeeping today. They would have cleaned his room yesterday before we knew he was dead. Up here, though, it looked just like…"

That same thought that had danced in her mind while in the bathroom, flickered again. Only this time, it took hold and coalesced into something solid.

"What?" Dominic asked.

She held up a finger to silence him then pulled out her phone. Tapping into a secure app, she pulled up the crime scene photos. Flipping through a dozen pictures, she found what she was looking for. Zooming in, she caught her breath at what she saw. Without a word, she held it up to Dominic to see if he saw the same thing or if maybe she was just gazing at shadows.

He took the phone and slid his sunglasses to the top of his head. After a beat, he zoomed in on the photo even more.

"He has three broken fingernails," he said.

Anika nodded.

"Why would a man have three broken fingernails if he has a nail clipper?"

She let out a small sigh of relief. The nails were an oddity and perhaps it meant nothing, but it meant *something* to her that Dominic had noticed the same thing and hadn't dismissed her observation.

"So maybe there was a struggle," she said.

Dominic inclined his head. "But here or in the room?"

Without another word, the two of them started scouring the rooftop. She and Mateo had looked the day before, but with no obvious signs of a struggle, they'd left further investigation for later. With evidence now suggesting that there *might* have been an altercation, she switched from looking for the obvious to looking for the subtle.

Forty-five minutes later, Mateo joined them on the roof just as she and Dominic finished their detailed search of the area.

"The team is wrapping up in the room. There's not much to go through. We've collected everything, but since housekeeping was in, we didn't find anything obviously out of place. How about you guys?" Mateo asked.

Dominic looked to her to fill her partner in, but something held her back from telling Mateo everything.

"There are potential scuff marks here," she said, pointing to a three-inch section of the wooden deck. Mateo sank down on his heels to look.

"Could have been from a dropped tool or something, but we'll get the team up here to get some pictures when they're done with the room."

Anika glanced at Dominic, but it was hard to tell what he was thinking with his sunglasses back on.

"Anything else?" Mateo asked.

"Some scuffed paint on the railing and a handprint on the door of the elevator," she answered.

Mateo rose and his head swiveled around to take in the scene. "Good work. It probably won't amount to anything, but I'll send the team up. You want to stay and direct them and I'll take housekeeping?"

Anika nodded. "Sounds good."

"You sticking around, Burel?" Mateo asked.

"If Anika's not tired of me already," Dominic replied.

Anika rolled her eyes at him, and Mateo's gaze bounced between the two. After a beat, Mateo nodded and said to Anika, "Text me when you're done up here. I'll meet you downstairs and we can head back to the station."

Dominic turned away, a small smile on his face, but Anika ignored him and confirmed the plan with Mateo. Once her partner was on his way down to housekeeping, she turned to her friend.

"What was that about?" she asked.

"What?" Dominic asked with all sorts of mock innocence.

"That snicker." She crossed her arms and waited.

"I didn't snicker, but your partner does *not* like having me hang around. Or more to the point, he doesn't like that you don't mind having me around."

She rolled her eyes again. "I have no idea what you're talking about. Now can we get back to work?"

"He has the hots for you, Anika. Everyone—except apparently you—can see that. What I want to know, though, is why didn't you tell him about the fingernails? It was a good catch."

Anika walked to the railing and leaned her hip against it. "He doesn't have the hots for me. He's friends with my brothers, he feels the need to look out for me. As for the nails, I don't know why I didn't tell him."

The thing with Dominic was that he wasn't just another pretty face, and in response to her comment, he simply stared at her, then shook his head. "If you don't want to tell me why, then don't tell me, but don't lie to me, Anika. You never do anything without a reason."

She both loved and hated this part of her relationship with Dominic. He didn't let her get away with a lot of shit. She appreciated the fact that he both knew her well enough to call her on her bullshit and cared enough to do it. What she didn't like was how vulnerable that made her feel.

Finally, with a sigh, she answered. "You saw how quick he

was to set the stage to dismiss what we found. He doesn't completely ignore my input, but if I point out something that isn't something obvious—like the scuff marks—he's always quick to come up with some reason why it probably isn't important. It's like I'm only allowed to notice the things that anyone who has watched more than two episodes of CSI would catch. After that, I have to work twice as hard to prove that whatever I've found is worth looking into."

"And as for the nails, it's easier to hold that one close to the vest since there isn't anything you can do about it right now," Dominic finished.

Anika nodded. "We already have pictures of Taglia's hands, and we've collected the nail clipper. Unless we find the actual nails, there's not much anyone can do to prove or debunk their relevance."

The sounds of the ocean filled the silence that followed along with the occasional gleeful shout of a child playing at the beach on the other side of the hotel. It would have been a peaceful moment had their reason for being on that rooftop not hung over them.

"I'm sorry it's like that for you," Dominic said.

Anika lifted a shoulder. "It could be worse."

"It could also be better. It *should* be better."

She turned, leaned against the railing, and lifted her face to the sun. "It could and it should, but it is what it is for now."

This side of Dominic—the side that listened to her, the side that was more than a joke and a good time—was becoming more and more common in their interactions. Oh, he still flashed his trademark smile more than he should, but there was also a part of him that he showed her that was something different—very different—than the player she'd first met.

"You're a good friend, Dom," she said.

He let out a rueful chuckle. "I'm learning."

Before she could ask him about that cryptic comment, the

three officers arrived to take photos of the potential evidence she and Dominic had found. It didn't take long, but through it all, Dominic stayed out of the fray, his back to the team, as she did her job.

She wasn't entirely sure, but she had a sneaking suspicion that he'd positioned himself that way on purpose. With his back to them, the three men to whom she issued orders didn't have the opportunity to look to him for confirmation; because despite the fact Dominic had no authority, they would have done just that.

Yeah, Dom was right. It *should* be different. But for now, it was what it was.

CHAPTER THREE

Dominic trailed after Mateo and Anika as they made their way through the lobby. Evidence collection was done, housekeeping had been interviewed, and the three of them had held a small debrief. Dominic didn't have much to add, but he did weigh in to agree with Anika that whatever had happened to Joseph Taglia, the setup for any scenario—murder, accident, or suicide—was odd.

He paused under the portico to take a call and when he saw it was from Jake, he waved Anika and Mateo on. She and Mateo had a lot to investigate, they didn't need to wait for him. Besides, she'd already agreed to meet him at The Shack, his team's go-to bar and restaurant, later that night, and he'd have a chance to catch up with her then.

"What's up?" he asked, answering his cell.

"Good news or bad news?" Jake asked.

"Good, then bad."

"The runway repairs and updates will be done in two weeks, so we'll have some time to make sure they hold before everyone arrives."

"It's always good to know that planes aren't going to hit any potholes at takeoff or landing. Now what's the bad news?"

"We ran the background checks on all the new hires at Hemmeleigh and four came back with flags. I know you're headed out there this afternoon. Any chance you can take a look at the original paperwork?"

"Of course. Send me the names, and I'll look into it. How bad?"

"Not good. One was implicated in a murder, one has connections to a Russian crime family, and two were employed by Blackstream."

"Blackstream? That tech company that went under after it came to light that they were using their security contracts to spy on the DoD?"

"The very one."

"Hm, well that's interesting."

Jake chuckled. "Yeah, Alexis and I thought so, too. Where are you now?"

As he walked through the parking lot, Dominic filled Jake in on Joseph Taglia. "I'm just leaving The Lookout," he said, stopping at his car. "Anika and Mateo are on their way back to the station, and I'm on my way to Hemmeleigh. She's meeting me at The Shack tonight to catch me up. Mateo agreed to bring me in as an extra set of eyes, but I think Anika would rather use me to bounce ideas off of than really get me involved in the investigation."

"Yeah, I don't blame her. The department's not bad, but it's got to be a pain in the ass to always have people questioning your ability."

Anika and Mateo pulled out of their spot, but she wasn't looking at him, so Dominic didn't wave goodbye. He watched them leave and once they'd turned onto the road, a white rental jeep pulled out of a spot at the end of the row and followed them. Dominic paused, his hand on the door of his car. The jeeps were standard issue rentals, but something about the timing of it leaving, and the direction in which it turned, caught his attention. Unfortunately, he was too far away to see the license plate.

"Dom?" Jake said, bringing his attention back to the call.

"Sorry, got distracted. Did you say something?"

"Yes, Nia and I will meet you at The Shack tonight. What time?"

Dominic frowned. Nia and Anika were tight, and Jake was his closest friend on the island—probably in life, too, but since they'd met less than eighteen months ago, Dom hadn't officially given Jake that title yet. Still, he hadn't planned on meeting anyone other than Anika and the thought of sharing the time with his friends and colleagues didn't sit well.

Then again, what had he expected picking The Shack as the meeting place? After Isiah, the owner, had started dating Alexis, the mountaintop bar had become the team's version of *Cheers*—someone from their task force was there five out of the six nights a week that it was open. He made a mental note to suggest something a little more out of the way next time he wanted to hang out with Anika. Or he could just fail to mention it to anyone—that would work, too.

"We agreed on six-thirty, but you know Anika, it will probably be closer to seven. Especially since she's got this case." When they'd first met, Dominic had assumed that Anika's perpetual lateness to social gatherings had something to do with not wanting to spend much time with him. But in the last few months, he'd realized that her internal clock ran about thirty minutes later than everyone else's. Now her tardiness was kind of charming and he just planned around it.

"Sounds good. Nia's out on the water today so that timing will give her a chance to shower and change."

Jake's partner was a marine biologist who ran the Caribbean Marine Research Center on the island. She was also one of

Dominic's favorite people and he'd been almost as happy as Jake when the two of them finally got together. Seriously, it didn't get much more fun than hanging out with Jake and Nia. Except when he got to hang out with Anika.

After agreeing to invite Beni and Damian to The Shack, too, they ended the call and Dominic climbed into his roasting car. He had four significant employment flags to look into, a key card system to test, and several other security protocols he needed to run through at Hemmeleigh that day. He had plenty of his own work to occupy his time. Yet somehow, as he drove the winding roads to the north side of the island, his mind couldn't let go of the strange death of Joseph Taglia.

"Sorry I'm late," Anika said as she walked out onto the veranda at The Shack a few minutes after seven.

"Where's Charlotte?" she asked, as she greeted the others with hugs.

"She left for Switzerland yesterday. Short trip though. Only a couple of days," Damian answered, standing to give her a kiss on the cheek. Charlotte was Damian's newly minted wife—having married her earlier in the year in a small, but lavish ceremony on the island—but she was also some big-time economist. Anika wasn't exactly sure what she did, only that it necessitated several trips a year to locations all over the world. As much as Anika liked the idea of traveling, the thought of jetting to Switzerland—which had to be at least a twenty-hour travel time from the island—for four days held no appeal. Then again, she didn't travel all that much and couldn't imagine going anywhere off island for less than a week. She loved Tildas, but it was *not* the easiest island to travel to and from.

"Can I get you a drink, Anika?" Isiah asked, joining them on the veranda. She glanced around the table and, not surprisingly, everyone else already had a beverage. She tried to be on time, really she did. And she was always on time for work. But when it wasn't work, well, she was grateful that this group of people didn't particularly mind that she was perpetually at least thirty minutes late.

"A beer would be great. Thanks, Isiah," she said, taking a seat between Alexis and Dominic.

Isiah returned a few minutes later and set a pint of local IPA in front of her before taking a seat on the other side of Alexis.

"Heard you had an interesting day today," Isiah prompted before taking a sip of his own beer.

"I filled them in this morning," Dominic said. "Not sure what more you learned this afternoon?"

Anika glanced around the table. Neither Isiah nor Nia were law enforcement of any type, though Isiah was a retired SEAL. Talking about the case in front of them would definitely be frowned upon. Then again, her chief had changed his tune and was now dead set on Taglia's death being an accident, and she didn't doubt that in the next day or two, he'd push Mateo into making that the official cause of death. She had her own doubts about that determination but didn't have any evidence to back those doubts up—not even after what they'd uncovered during the afternoon. If it *was* an accident, though, then there was no reason she couldn't talk about it. She was picking and choosing facts to suit her needs, but she'd reconcile that with her conscience if she ever felt the need.

"He has no next of kin, and his closest friend appears to be his eighty-year-old neighbor." Anika paused and smiled, remembering her conversation with the woman. "She's very cool so I can hardly fault him for that. She was a movie star in the fifties, had all sorts of crazy stories. Anyway, she confirmed he had no family."

"How'd you find her?" Beni asked. Anika glanced at the agent. Beni was the least personable of the team, but Anika had a secret professional crush on her—Alexis was pretty badass, too, but there was something about Beni's no-nonsense, take-no-shit confidence that Anika admired. She'd never admit it to anyone, but there had been a time or two in the past few months where she'd even channeled Beni when going toe-to-toe with her leadership on a few issues.

"She's listed as the beneficiary of his life insurance and 401K. She's also all over his social media," Anika answered with a grin. "She acknowledged that it's unusual that she's the beneficiary given that she and Taglia met less than three years ago. She said Taglia asked her to put the money into the foundation she runs since he had no family for it to go to."

"Foundation?" Jake asked.

"She runs an organization that supports people who worked in film before the days of unions and retirement and such," Anika answered.

"Generous of him," Beni said. Anika almost laughed at the cynical look on her face.

"Believe it or not, Beni," Jake said, "people, on occasion, aren't complete asshats, and they can be genuinely generous."

"I didn't say anything!" she defended herself, making the table laugh.

"Anyone want anything to eat?" a woman asked from the threshold between the bar and veranda, interrupting the conversation.

Anika looked over but didn't recognize the newcomer and she cast a questioning glance at Isiah.

"Anika, meet Serena. Serena, this is Detective Anika Anderson. Be nice," he added, giving Serena a stare that probably would have intimidated his SEAL team back in the day.

Serena no-last-name glared at Isiah, then shot Anika a toothy smile. "Ignore Isiah, he's mad because I told a customer not to ask me for a menu recommendation. It's a dumb question to ask someone you don't know, don't you think?"

Anika wasn't quite sure what to make of the comment though the more she thought about it, Serena had a point. Why did people ask waitstaff for their personal recommendations? For all the customer knew, the waiter's favorite meal could be boxed mac-n-cheese.

"Just tell Huck to make us a bunch of stuff," Isiah answered. Serena rolled her eyes at him but turned and left. "And stay behind the bar," Isiah called after her retreating figure.

"Uh, who's that?" Anika asked, pointing to the now empty doorway.

"Long story," Alexis said. "Let's just say she's a former CIA operative that's having a hard time letting her former life go."

Anika swiveled her head in the direction of the bar, not that she'd be able to see Serena. She'd never met anyone who worked as an operative for the CIA before. At least not that she knew.

"Isn't there some saying that once in, always in?" Anika asked.

"She's not totally out," Isiah said. "But she's out for now while she figures some shit out."

Anika wasn't sure what to make of Isiah's cryptic comment or the fact that he randomly hired a former operative. Then again, his primary sous chef, Huck, was a retired SEAL and also former CIA *analyst* so maybe The Shack was becoming the place to go for downtrodden members of the intelligence community?

"Okay," Anika drew the word out.

"What did the ME say?" Dominic asked, bringing the conversation back to the case.

"And did anything come of what the evidence team collected?" Alexis chimed in.

"Cause of death was severe head trauma, likely caused by the impact with the dumpster. He had negligible alcohol in his system, but he had high levels of a sleeping aid," she answered.

"Was that one of the medications we found?" Dominic asked.

Anika nodded. "Recently prescribed by the same doctor who prescribed the other three medications. We haven't had a chance to talk with him yet, but we have a call in to his office."

"What were the other three meds?" Damian asked.

"One for high blood pressure, one that Dominic recognized as being prescribed to patients post cancer treatment, and the third was a mild blood thinner."

"Did he have cancer? Could that be a cause for suicide?" Dominic asked.

"The Medical Examiner didn't find any, but we need to talk to his primary doc to get any history. The ME *did* say, however, that that medication is also used as a general anti-nausea medication and Taglia's neighbor said he suffered from motion sickness. It's possible that's what it was prescribed for."

"So, it's still up in the air whether it's murder, suicide, or an accident?" Dominic pressed.

Anika took a sip of her drink and considered her answer. There was no evidence to contradict the answer her chief would want her to give, but...

"Just tell us what you think," Alexis said.

Anika's gaze flickered around the table, taking in the interested expressions on her friends' faces. "I think my chief wants it to be an accident, and so far, there's no reason to think otherwise, but it doesn't feel right to me," she said.

"What doesn't feel right?" Alexis pushed.

"From talking to his neighbor and tracking his movements since he arrived on the island, he seems like a cautious, though friendly, guy. He took a sunset cruise one night, took a guided hike another day. Ate dinner at the hotel each night, though his credit cards have him eating lunch at a few places in the tourist part of town. He doesn't strike me as the kind of guy to wander too close to the edge of a building in a location that's currently closed to the public."

"How high was the concentration of sleeping pills in his system?" Dominic asked.

"Not high enough to kill him, but high enough to make him a little out of it," she answered.

"Taking more than prescribed, but not enough to do lasting damage sounds planned to me. But if he just wanted to be a little out of it to give himself the courage to jump, why not take the whole bottle and be done with it?" Dominic posited, finishing her thought.

"So, it looks like an accident or maybe even suicide but probably isn't?" Nia asked.

"I don't want to commit to that yet, but the thought did occur to me," Anika answered.

"I don't like the sound of that," Jake said as Huck and Serena returned to the veranda carrying two large trays piled with platters of food.

The group stayed silent as the food was set down on the table along with plates and silverware for everyone. "Anyone need another round?" Huck asked, once his tray was empty. Serena hadn't bothered to wait and had already disappeared back into the bar.

When everyone nodded, Isiah rose and joined his friend in getting the refills while the rest of them piled their plates with everything from peas and rice to jerk pork to fried plantains and papaya. The scents mingled and filled the air around them, and as Anika sat back and admired the spread, she gave a small prayer of thanks for having fallen into the orbit of this group of people—they were good people, but they also ate damn well.

"If it was a murder made to look like an accident or suicide, what kind of person would do that?" Nia asked.

"Someone with an intense grudge against the victim. Someone who would go to the lengths needed to plan such a thing," Damian answered.

"Which again, doesn't make sense," Anika said. "If someone

had that kind of grudge against Taglia, why wait until he's traveled here to do the job? Wouldn't it have been easier to reach him in LA?"

"I agree," Alexis said. "If this really is murder, there are two other options I can think of. The first is someone who planned the killing, but then waited to find the right victim."

Anika's stomach turned at that. "So, it doesn't really have anything to do with Taglia himself, he just fit some killer's idea of the right victim?"

"We've seen it before," Alexis continued. "And if you're a killer looking to enact a specific kind of murder, Taglia wouldn't be a bad victim. He was older—though not too old—and was traveling alone on an island he'd never been to before."

"So, basically a serial killer. Or at least one in the making, is what you're saying," Anika said.

Alexis grimaced. "Basically, yes."

"What's the second option?" Dominic asked.

"A professional hit," Beni chimed in and Alexis nodded.

The table was silent, then Dominic spoke. "I can see that. If it is murder, this could definitely be a professional hit. Regardless, we still come to the same question…why Joseph Taglia?"

"I think that's what Anika and her team will need to find out," Beni said.

"So long as my chief keeps the case open long enough to let us do that," Anika said on a sigh just as Isiah set another beer down in front of her.

She picked up the pint glass and took a sip. The next few days were going to be rough—no way would her chief even consider the possibility of a professional hit or a potential serial killer. The weight of it all—the investigation, the fact that she'd be pushing up against her own colleagues—settled on her shoulders. Then her gaze wandered over all the food set out on the table before flickering up to take in the view and the company around her. Yeah, it was going to be a long few days, but that didn't mean she couldn't enjoy these quiet, almost stolen, moments. So, with that thought—with that lifeline—she put everything that had to do with Taglia in a mental box then dug in.

After saying goodbye to Anika, Beni, Jake, and Damian in the parking lot, Dominic paused at the entrance of The Shack and inhaled a deep breath. As they inched closer to summer, the night air seemed to be getting heavier with each passing week, and though Dominic didn't love the heat, he did like the scents it brought out.

Just as he was about to step back into the bar, a white jeep drove toward him. The Shack sat at the start of a small point of land on the southeast side of the island with nothing but residences beyond it. A car coming from the direction of those residences wasn't unusual. There was a familiarity to it that caught Dominic's attention, though.

He watched the jeep drive past, the tinted windows giving nothing away about the driver other than he—or she—appeared tall. This time he got the license plate, though. He had no idea if it was the same jeep as the one he'd seen earlier, but it couldn't hurt to check it out.

He was watching the taillights recede as the vehicle made its way up the point and toward the main road, when Alexis joined him.

"Everything okay?" she asked.

Dominic's gaze lingered on the road though the car was nowhere in sight. "Just saw a car that looked like one that followed Anika and Mateo from The Lookout today. It's probably nothing since it's the standard jeep rental, but it struck me."

"You get the license plate?"

He nodded but didn't say anything. Was he crazy to think someone could be following Anika?

"Dom?" Alexis asked, drawing his attention.

He looked at his teammate as she studied him, then he glanced down the road again and shook his head to clear it of his wayward thoughts. It didn't make sense for someone to follow Anika, she wasn't the lead detective on the case. He was probably just being paranoid.

Turning back to Alexis, he smiled. "I was coming back inside to see if Isiah needed any help with clean up." He was no stranger to the chores it took to run a restaurant and was never shy about offering to jump in at The Shack. Isiah almost never took him up on it, but still, Dominic offered.

"He's got Huck, Marty, and Serena tonight. He's fine. Give me a lift home?"

Dominic eyed her, not because he wasn't willing to give her a ride, but because Alexis Emelia Wright definitely had something she wanted to talk to him about, and he doubted it had anything to do with Joseph Taglia or the upcoming World Summit.

With a sigh, he gestured to his car, and they climbed in. "You've got five minutes before we reach your house so whatever you want to talk to me about, know you have a time limit."

Alexis laughed. "Nonsense. I can sit in this car all night and you won't kick me out."

Unfortunately, that was true. He'd never bodily eject any of his teammates from anywhere unless it was for their own good.

"But Isiah will be home eventually, and you'll want to tuck in for the night. You're down to four minutes, now," he added.

She laughed again, then sobered. "What happened when you went home at Christmas?"

He jerked at the question he hadn't been expecting. He hadn't told anyone about what had happened during that trip, mostly because he was still processing it himself. Coming so close to losing his mom had brought all sorts of questions and feelings to the surface, and yes, he was working through them, but no, he did not want to share them with Alexis or anyone else for that matter.

"What do you mean?" he countered tentatively, well aware that with her psychology background Alexis could easily lead him to divulge things he had no intention of divulging.

"You came back different. The same in many ways, but different, too. I want to know why."

He considered his options before answering then tried to stick closest to the truth. "It had been a while since I'd been home, and I realized while I was there that I needed to change that. Our time on this island is limited, and I'm starting to think about what's next."

Alexis didn't say anything as they pulled up to her gated property. Mac, her head of security—because she had her own personal security thanks to her superstar parents—opened the gate and waved them on.

"Hmm," Alexis said as he pulled under her portico. "Why does that sound like a reasonable, yet incomplete answer?"

Dominic flashed her a smile. "Probably because it is."

"You have friends, Dominic. You know we're all going to be facing the same thing. It might be worth talking about."

"I know you all are more than just my teammates. That's never been in question. But sometimes we need to work things out on our own."

"Like figuring out how you feel about Anika?"

And there it was. She'd lured him into thinking he might not have to discuss that topic. He should have known better.

"Some things definitely *do not* need a group conversation."
She grinned at him.
"Seriously. They don't," he said.
She winked.
"Stop that shit, Alexis Wright. Stop it right now."

She laughed, but thankfully, she also opened her door and put one foot on the paved drive though she didn't get out. He almost thought he'd gotten away without hearing any more on the subject, when she turned back around. "For the record, we've all noticed that you're not manwhoring around as much since Christmas. I don't know if something happened or you've come to your senses about Anika, because let's face it, she's had you by the balls since you first met—in a good way—but you've changed in subtle ways. In good ways. It's like all the good parts of you are even better."

"And the bad parts?" he couldn't help but ask.

She lifted a shoulder. "We all have demons, Dominic. You're just not feeding yours as much as you used to."

And with that, she leaned over, brushed a kiss on his cheek, then slid from her seat and shut the door. Without so much as a wave—or a thank you—she turned and walked into her mansion.

Dominic caught a brief glimpse of her two dogs—Red and Howdy—dancing around on the tile floor, before the door shut behind her. The conversation had been what he'd thought it would be, but he also knew he'd dodged a bullet. Alexis had let him off easy. Sort of.

As he pulled away from her property and started toward his apartment, her words echoed in his mind, raising more questions and giving no answers. He *had* changed, she'd been right about that. In many ways—most ways—it hadn't been intentional. He hadn't woken up and thought to himself that the next time he went out drinking, he *wouldn't* go home with a woman. No, it was more like that behavior just didn't appeal to him. Not the sex, of course, sex was always appealing, but the fun, physically gratifying if emotionally hollow, encounters weren't all that interesting anymore.

Was it because he wanted more with Anika? Or was it because his mother's near-death experience had shaken him up more than he'd let himself contemplate? Or maybe it was the vague sort of dissatisfaction that had settled over him with respect to his personal life after seeing his sisters so close with their partners.

He pulled into his apartment complex and parked the car. In the still of the dark night, he let out a long breath. Perhaps Alexis hadn't let him off so easily after all.

CHAPTER FOUR

Some days Anika woke up knowing they'd be shit days. Maybe that made her a little bit psychic, but she tended to think it had more to do with her ability to read people and situations better than most. As one of four women on the forty-person police force and the youngest of five siblings, four of whom were her older brothers, she'd spent a lot of time while growing up just watching.

So, when she rolled over in bed the morning after meeting Dominic and his colleagues at The Shack and felt that little flutter of foreboding in her stomach, she knew the day would not be a good one. Most likely because unless she and Mateo found something concrete to point to Taglia's death being a murder, their chief would probably push for them to officially call it an accident and close the investigation.

She switched off her alarm and stared at the ceiling, her fan going round and round. She debated whether or not to go for a run, but opted to tear the Band-Aid right off and head into work. Well, that, and she hated running. Hated working out at all, if she were being honest. Then again, hitting the in-house gym had become easier in the past few months since she and Dominic had learned they lived in the same complex.

It was a huge piece of property—by island standards—with five apartment blocks, two restaurants, a beach cafe, and several other amenities, including three gyms. She and Dominic had started meeting at the main gym three times a week. It made working out somewhat—but only somewhat—palatable. Unfortunately, today was not one of their designated meet-up days and he was scheduled to be out at Hemmeleigh early in the morning, so an impromptu session was also out of the question.

With a grunt of annoyance, Anika tossed her sheets off, rose from her bed, and dragged herself into the shower. Once the spray woke her up, she turned it off and grabbed a towel as she pondered what tactic her chief would take today. She and Mateo still had a lot of work to do, including getting in touch with the doctor who'd prescribed Taglia's pills, but that wouldn't stop the chief from doing whatever it was he decided to do.

Pushing those thoughts aside, she wiped the mirror down and hoped it would stay fog-free for more than the two minutes it took her to put on a little powder and mascara—much more than that wasn't worth it in the tropical climate since it all melted off anyway.

After running a brush through her white-blond hair, Anika slipped into her robe and made her way to the tiny kitchen. Her routine was to let her thick hair dry while she made coffee and breakfast and then she would wrangle it into some sort of bun to keep it off her neck for the rest of the day. She often thought about cutting it, but in the end, it was the only real vanity she had. She was decent looking enough, if not a little on the short side, but her hair was the only part of her physical appearance that she felt any particular fondness for.

Forty minutes later she was on her way to the station, mentally making a list of what she intended to accomplish that day: Check in with the ME, go over the evidence reports, get in touch with Taglia's doctor, and see what Mateo's thoughts were about the scuff marks. She didn't hold out much hope for a positive response on the latter, so she left that as last on her to do list.

She'd just hung up with the ME when Mateo walked in. "Late night last night?" Anika teased. His shirt was rumpled, and his dark hair stood up on end and pointed in a variety of directions.

He shot her a look that said more than he seemed able to muster verbally and sank down onto his chair. He stared at his computer, then raised his gaze to meet hers.

"Anything new on Taglia?"

"Tox screen details are in, but not much more to report than what we had before. Sleeping aid levels were high, but not enough to kill him, and unless he had some pre-existing condition, nothing in the combination of things he had in his system would have killed him either."

Mateo rose and walked to the coffee pot. "You talk to the doctor yet?"

"It's only seven o'clock in California. I was going to give it another hour then call," she answered.

Mateo gave an absent nod, his attention on the coffee he was pouring.

"I was going to pop down to the lab and pick up the evidence reports. Want to come?" she asked. He swung his head her direction. His eyes were bloodshot, and he really did look like hell. "Never mind. I'll pop down and bring back anything interesting," she said.

Mateo mumbled a thanks then shuffled back to his desk and dropped onto his chair. Anika shot him one last look then rose and headed for the elevators. She'd just stepped into the hall when the doors slid open and Rosey strode out. Rather than make a dash to catch the car before the door closed, she slowed her steps and met Rosey.

"You going down to evidence?" the officer asked.

Anika nodded. "Mateo's looking a little rough this morning, so I was hoping you could look into something for me?"

"Name it and I'm your girl. Or woman, as the case may be," she said, drawing a smile from Anika.

"Can you call Loose Ends Studio and get some more details about that contest Taglia won? It might be nothing, but it strikes me as weird that a numbers-guy would win a marketing contest."

Rosey shrugged. "Sure, but maybe he had a secret creative side. Might not be as weird as you think."

Anika grimaced. "I know, that's why I'm asking you and not running it by Mateo first. I think we both know the chief wants to call this an accident, but there are a few things that aren't adding up. At least not yet."

"I got your back," Rosey said. "Who the hell knows what the chief will do, but until we know, I'm all yours."

"Thanks," Anika said with a smile. "I'm going down to grab the reports. I'll bring them up and we can all go through them. So long as Mateo doesn't have to move, he'll probably be okay."

Rosey rolled her eyes and shook her head but said nothing more before turning and walking toward their little corner of the open office. A two-minute wait later and Anika was descending to the basement of the station where the lab was located. It wasn't a large facility and didn't have many of the most up to date pieces of equipment, but to date, it had served the department well.

"I was wondering how long it would take you to get down here," Angela Parmenter said, maneuvering her wheelchair around the lab tables scattered around the room. Anika often thought there should be a better way to organize the lab to make it a little easier for her colleague, but after working in the lab for twenty years, Angela liked things the way they were.

"How'd you know I was here?" Anika asked, taking a seat on a stool; the ancient piece of furniture squeaked and groaned with her weight, as slight as it was.

"Your car is parked next to my accessibility spot, which means you must have gotten in early to claim that prime real estate."

Anika chuckled. "You'd make a good detective, Dr. Parmenter."

Angela shook her head but smiled as she reached for a stack of folders. "I don't like people enough to do what you do. I much prefer the cold, unemotional machines I work with."

They both knew that wasn't the entire truth. Angela had had to deal with a lot of people on her journey to obtaining her Ph.D., and she also had a husband and two teenagers. She was far from the cold woman she liked to portray.

"So, what do you have for me?" Anika asked, holding out her hand.

Angela placed the folders in her palm, but Anika didn't open them yet. She'd go through them with a fine-tooth comb, but she wanted to hear Angela's thoughts first.

"Not much there. The paint on the railing wasn't quite dry and there was some on the victim's shoes. The most interesting thing about that, though, is that it was on the tops, not the soles."

"Like someone tipped him over the side and his feet scraped the top of the railing?" Anika asked.

"Or like he was climbing up to either jump or get a better view, and he slipped and caught his feet."

Anika made a face. "So, 'inconclusive' is what you're trying to say?"

"Afraid so."

"What else?"

"We didn't get anything from the scuffing on the deck except that whatever caused it was traveling in the direction of the ledge the vic fell from."

"But no splinters or anything in his shoes?" Anika asked.

Angela shook her head. "No, but the grain of the wood wasn't really broken, just stretched, if that makes sense."

"Bent, like in building a ship, but not broken?"

Angel nodded.

"Okay, so no splinters. Last but not least, the handprint?"

"Definitely the victim's. A full handprint. It's in the file along with the reports from the contents of his room. There's still not much to go on, but it is interesting that the prescription for the sleeping pills was filled the day before he arrived on the island while the others are a few weeks old."

"What about the contents of the bottles?"

"The pills are what they're supposed to be, but if you go by the prescribed date and recommended dosage, the quantity in two of the bottles is off. Of course, that doesn't really give you anything since he might have gotten refills before he ran out of his last bottle or, in the case of the nausea medicine, he'd only need it when he needed it; it's not one that needs to be taken regularly."

Anika let out a long sigh.

"Sorry," Angela said, giving her a sympathetic look. "Not that it means anything, but I'm with you on this one. Everything hints that it was either an accident or suicide, but nothing says it's definitely one of those. Evidence will always trump the circumstances, but the circumstances are weird. Who the hell climbs onto a five story hotel roof to commit suicide or, if not suicide, for some other reason where you'd accidentally fall? It's fishy, but I haven't been able to prove anything one way or the other."

Anika's gaze lingered on the "Confidential" stamp on the files, then she let out another sigh. "Something *does* feel off, but we can only do what we can with the evidence we have on hand," she said, sliding off the stool, the seat cushion sucking in air as she stood.

"You know where to find me if anything else comes up," Angela said, turning her chair around and heading to the microscope she'd abandoned when Anika had arrived.

Anika thanked her then headed back upstairs. When she walked into the office, both Mateo and Rosey were on the phone, though Mateo's call looked a little more serious. He nodded and scribbled something down on a piece of scrap paper, then after a beat, he said something else before hanging up.

"Play time is over, Anderson," he said, rising from his seat.

"I missed playtime?" she replied with a grin, setting the files on her desk.

"We have another body," he said, already walking out the door. "Up in the canyons. I hope you have some hiking shoes."

Well, shit, the day kept getting better and better. At least she hadn't taken a run that morning.

"The evidence team is going to have a field day with this," Anika said as they rounded what she hoped would be the last turn before they reached the body. She hadn't been on this hike since high school as it was mostly flooded with tourists heading to the iconic waterfall during the day and high school kids looking to get drunk and party at night. Technically, the trail was closed after sunset, but generations of kids had always ignored that specific rule and partying at "the falls" was a tradition.

"The responding officers shut the trail down and are trying to clear it, but yeah, between the hikers and gawkers, today is a good day to be a detective rather than evidence collection… relatively speaking, anyway," Mateo answered as they came out of the tropical forest and into the basin at the bottom of the waterfall.

Two officers were standing guard over the body while three more were making a valiant effort to move a group of five tourists back down the trail. The officers' arms were akimbo, gently pushing the tourists back, but it was impossible to keep the crowd from snapping photos.

"Lockhart," Anika called. The man in the middle of the three craned his head then nodded in acknowledgement. "Collect their phones and tell them you'll start arresting them if they aren't on their way out of here in the next three minutes," she said.

Harry Lockhart grinned. "You got it, Detective." By the time he turned back around, the tourists were already backing away. The officers advanced on them, holding out their hands for the phones. A few minutes later, Lockhart and his crew had the group well out of sight and the phones bagged and tagged.

"Chief's not going to like that. Threatening tourists and all," Mateo muttered as they approached the body.

"That's someone's son, maybe brother or husband or nephew," Anika said, gesturing to the body. "I don't want any of those pictures getting out before we can reach next of kin. If the chief has a problem with that, I'll deal with it."

Mateo made some indistinguishable sound, and she wasn't sure if he was backing her up or calling her crazy. Either way, she didn't much care, she'd done the right thing and was comfortable with her decision.

"So, what do we have DeLaney?" Mateo asked as they came to a stop at the feet of the young man lying on his side, one arm stretched out under his head, the other tucked up against his chest. If they hadn't known he was dead, he'd look like someone who'd lain down for a nap.

"Young male, perhaps late-twenties. No signs of struggle, no blood, and no obvious wound," Kim DeLaney answered. Kim was a ten-year veteran of police work, but a relative newcomer to the island. She'd moved down from Louisiana with her husband when he'd taken a job at the island hospital seven months ago.

"Is the ME on his way?" Mateo asked, kneeling beside the young man.

"He is, sir. As is the evidence team," DeLaney answered.

"Who found him?" Anika asked, circling the body, looking for anything that might indicate the man hadn't just lain down and died.

"Pippa and Morgan Cates," DeLaney answered, nodding to a couple who sat on a fallen tree forty feet away. "Got an early start this morning and made it to the top of the falls for sunrise. They found him on their way back down."

"They didn't see him on their way up?" Anika asked, looking to the top of the falls. It was another thirty-minute hike to the top from the basin.

"No, they passed this way and swore he wasn't here," DeLaney answered.

"And how long were they up there?" Mateo asked.

"Thirty minutes."

"So, within the time it took them to get up, have their Kodak moment, and get down, this young man died," Anika said, more to herself than anyone else since she wasn't saying anything they wouldn't have already figured out.

Mateo rose from where he'd been crouched. "And with the density of the forest and roar of the waterfall, I'm going to take a gamble and guess that they didn't hear or see anything?"

Both Delaney and the other officer shook their heads. Anika's gaze lingered on the second officer. He was a newbie to the force with only eighteen months experience and was trying to avoid looking at the body without appearing to be avoiding looking at the body.

"Harris," Anika said, drawing the attention of the young cop.

"Why don't you take the Cates down to the station and get an official statement. We'll wait here with Officer DeLaney for the ME and evidence teams."

The young man's eyes narrowed, but then flitted down to the body. She'd pricked his pride by sending him away from the crime scene, but he also looked begrudgingly relieved. "Yes, ma'am," he said, then moved away to gather the couple.

"You're winning fans and friends all over the place today," Mateo said, shoving his hands into his pockets. There wasn't much any of them could do at this point but wait for the ME and the evidence team.

"I think we both know I'll never win any popularity contests," Anika said. "But he looked like he was about to puke, and I figured I'd save him from that embarrassment at least. If he doesn't see it that way, that's on him."

"I don't know, you seem pretty popular with that FBI crowd," he said. She swung her gaze to him, and he shrugged. "My brother was at The Shack last night, saw you with them."

"They're friends, Mateo. You should try having a few every now and then."

"I have friends."

"You have family and women you sleep with," she corrected. DeLaney's gaze rose. Mateo came from one of the big, old, insular families on the island—the kind that had so many cousins that non-blood related friends weren't really invited into the circle.

"Family are friends," he countered.

Anika held her tongue. In some ways Mateo was right, but in others? He didn't have a clue. He'd been born with the privilege of a built-in circle and didn't have a clue what it was like to get thrown into situations where he didn't know anyone and had to learn to survive. He didn't have a clue what it was like to have to get to know someone, to take the time to decide if they were trustworthy or not.

"What do you think?" Mateo asked, thankfully changing the subject.

Anika frowned. "Heart attack maybe? Seems young for that, but I suppose it's possible."

"Or maybe an aneurysm? I've heard of those happening to younger people."

"That his water bottle?" Anika asked, pointing to a metal bottle lying ten feet away.

"We think so," DeLaney answered. "Without prints, it's hard to tell since it's not in his bag or his hand, but we made the assumption it was and left it there."

Anika glanced at Mateo who nodded in response to her unasked question. She withdrew her phone and began taking pictures, being sure to capture the position of the bottle relative to the body. When she had a good twenty shots, she pulled on some gloves and picked up the bottle. Twisting the top off, she looked inside. It was about two-thirds filled with what appeared to be water. Raising the bottle to her nose, she sniffed.

"Smells like water, maybe with some of that electrolyte flavoring in it," she said. They'd get it tested, but for now, it didn't shed any light on the situation. Had it been alcohol or one of those high caffeine drinks, it was possible it could have been a contributing factor to whatever happened to their victim. But water?

Recapping the bottle, she placed it inside an evidence bag, sealed it, then placed it back on the forest floor.

"Any ID?" she asked DeLaney.

"I didn't look, didn't want to touch anything after we ascertained he was, in fact dead."

It had been the right decision, but now that she and Mateo had seen the body, so long as they didn't move it before the ME got there, they could at least try to find an ID. Kneeling beside the young man, Anika reached a finger into the back pocket of his hiking shorts and felt nothing. She did the same with the front pocket she could access without moving him and it, too was empty. Deciding to take a gamble and see if she could finagle opening a zipper or two on his backpack without moving him, she reached for the smallest compartment first. It was the least safe place to keep an ID since it was the most accessible to pickpockets, but sure enough, the top of a wallet came into view as the zipper slid open.

Reaching inside the compartment, Anika gently pulled the thin canvas wallet out and flipped it open.

"Nothing," she said, turning to show Mateo the empty wallet. There was no ID, no credit cards, no pictures, nothing. It was as if he'd just bought it and slid it into his backpack for the hell of it.

"Why carry an empty wallet?" Mateo mulled over more than asked.

There were so many possibilities that came into Anika's mind that she pushed them aside. Maybe it wasn't his, maybe he hadn't wanted whoever found his body to be able to ID him. Whatever reason, it wasn't something they were going to be able to figure out on the side of a trail three miles from the main road.

As she slid the wallet back into the backpack, the sounds of people making their way up the trail echoed around them. Assuming the officers at the trailhead had done their job and kept everyone else out, there was only one group of people that could be. Rising from her crouch, Anika walked to stand beside Mateo to greet the ME and evidence team.

"They sound like the Seven Dwarves hiking up here. If they burst out into 'hi ho hi ho, it's off to work we go,' I'm not responsible for my actions," Mateo muttered.

Anika chuckled at that; the group *did* sound a little happily chummy to be hiking to a potential crime site. "As long as it's not *Let it Go*, I think we can hold it together."

Mateo laughed, too. He had more nieces and nephews than

she could count, and she had no doubt that whether he wanted to or not—and, knowing him, he most definitely did not—he would know every word.

"Fuck, now I'm going to have that song in my head all day."

She grinned. "That's what partners are for," she said, then hummed a few bars, eliciting a scathing look from her companion.

"Ah, my least favorite sight this early in the morning," the ME said as he came around the bend and stopped in front of them.

"You live for dead bodies," Mateo shot back.

"I'm pretty sure he means us," Anika said, flashing Dr. Rasmussen a grin. Rodney Rasmussen had been the ME on the island for as long as anyone could remember. She had no idea how old he really was, but he had more energy than most people her age and was definitely fitter than the evidence team who trailed behind him.

"We'll get out of your way then," Anika said, stepping to the side and giving Dr. Rasmussen his first unimpeded glimpse of the scene.

For a moment, the ME stood there, observing the scene. Then he motioned for an evidence tech to start taking pictures. Less than ten minutes later, the doctor was kneeling beside the body.

"No signs of injury," he said after he conducted a cursory examination. "Help me get his backpack off." A tech stepped forward and together, they gently removed the bag from the young man's back.

Without needing direction, the assistant handed the bag to Anika as Dr. Rasmussen rolled the body onto its back. Once the tech had set an evidence bag on the ground to protect the backpack from the dirt, Anika set it down and immediately started going through each of the three compartments.

She already knew the first held the empty wallet, but

confirmed it was otherwise empty. The second, middle compartment, held two protein bars and a bag of trail mix. She left them in there rather than bag each one separately. Like the contents of the water bottle, the contents of the backpack would be tested.

Opening the third, she found another water bottle, only this one was more like a thermos. When she unscrewed the cap, steam rose from the contents. Upon looking inside, the liquid appeared the color of coffee with cream, but when she sniffed it, the scents of cardamom, cinnamon, and ginger filled her nose. Tea, or chai to be more precise. Resealing the thermos, she set it on the plastic and continued her perusal.

She pulled out what looked like a breakfast burrito wrapped in tinfoil and set it beside the thermos. Then the bag shifted, and she caught sight of something very interesting. Reaching in, she pulled out two pill containers. Neither had a label and one bottle had two pills in it while the other had one.

Holding them up, she gave them a little jiggle and the rattling sound caught Mateo's attention. "What'd you find there?"

She lifted a shoulder. "Hard to say when they don't come with labels." She held one in each hand so Mateo could see.

"Well, that's an interesting twist," Mateo said as another evidence tech appeared at her side with two evidence bags. She hadn't bagged anything else from inside the backpack, but everyone knew that between a breakfast burrito and two unlabeled pill bottles, the latter had a greater probability of shedding some light on the situation.

"Anything else?" Mateo asked.

Anika shook her head. "Nothing as interesting as that," she said, zipping the bag then rising. The same tech picked up the clear plastic evidence bag that had been placed on the ground and held it open for her. She lowered the backpack inside and watched him seal it before she returned to Mateo's side.

They both knew better than to question Dr. Rasmussen while he worked, so they stood in companionable silence while he and one of his assistants poked and prodded the body. Another twenty minutes passed before the ME rose and gestured for the team to bag the body.

He walked toward them as he stripped off his gloves, his assistant trailing behind with a collection bag. Dr. Rasmussen stopped in front of them, then turned to his assistant and placed the gloves in the bag, before waving him away.

"Dead about three hours, which, from what I hear, aligns with the timeline you have from the hikers who found the body. No signs of foul play, no obvious injuries, but, as I always say, we'll know more when we get him back to the lab."

"Any chance it was an OD?" Mateo asked.

Dr. Rasmussen looked at Mateo the way a kindergarten teacher might look at a troublesome student. "We'll know more when we get to the lab. There's no point in speculating at this time; it's a waste of my brain power."

Mateo looked to be getting ready to say something else, but Anika cut him off. "Your team need any help? We'll have the officers accompany you down so you don't run into any trouble."

Dr. Rasmussen nodded. "Thank you. We've got everything under control, but the escort would be nice. I know the trail was emptied, but once we get to the parking lot, I suspect there will be quite a few gawkers, and it would help to have your people there."

Anika nodded, then stood to the side and gestured for the doctor to lead the way. She and Mateo moved even farther off the trail when the evidence team came by, one carrying a box of bagged items and the other two at either end of the stretcher carrying the body. She and Mateo had done a cursory look for shoe prints, but on a popular hiking trail, it was a fairly useless task, so evidence collection had been relatively quick.

Once Dr. Rasmussen and his team were safely in their vehicles and on their way to their respective labs, she and Mateo headed to the police station. The ride was mostly silent, both of them lost in thought. Anika wasn't sure what was going through Mateo's mind, but she'd bet it wasn't all that different from what was going through hers. Tildas Island didn't have a lot of violent crime or suspicious deaths. That two of them had occurred within days of each other was, well, unusual.

After parking the car, they crossed the street and passed through the metal detector at the entrance of the station. Anika mulled over the two pill bottles as they rode the elevator up in silence. She was still pondering the potential implications of the bottles when they stepped out onto the third floor and came face to face with the chief.

"I hear you have an OD on the waterfall trail," he said. Cyril Maddox was an imposing man. At six-feet-three inches tall, he towered over Anika and often used that to his advantage. Or tried to, anyway. She didn't love having him in her space, but by now she was used to it.

"Dr. Rasmussen is looking into it. He said he'd be able to get to the autopsy later today, but until then, we have no conclusive cause of death," she answered.

His dark eyes narrowed at her, and she noted—rather randomly—that Cyril Maddox had gray hairs growing out of his ears. The man was in his early sixties, not particularly old, but his black hair—and apparently even his ear hair—was heavily shot through with gray.

"We did find two pill bottles in the backpack, but we don't know what they are or if they have anything to do with the man's death," Mateo interjected.

Chief Maddox shifted his attention to her partner and Anika let out a quiet breath. He didn't really intimidate her, but she didn't really like him either. He was a misogynist and one of the island good ol' boys. If he'd been just an officer, it wouldn't have been so bad. But because he was the chief, he set the tone for the rest of the department, and Anika had little doubt that a lot of the resistance she came up against in her job was a result of the chief's attitude.

"A young man with unidentified pills? I think we both know what that means, Detective," the chief said. When it became obvious that Mateo wasn't planning on responding, the chief glared at them both then walked away. He was nearly to his office, when he turned back.

"And that body from The Lookout Hotel?" He waited for both of them to nod before continuing. "Unless you have hard evidence otherwise by the end of the day today, I want it declared an accident." He didn't wait for a response after that order, and instead, he walked the remaining few feet to his office and closed his door—not quite a slam, but hard enough to make it clear she and Mateo had pissed him off.

"He's such an asshole," Anika said.

Mateo chuckled. "Three more years until he retires. Then again, if you look at the contenders for his position, at least those in the department, you might be better off with Maddox."

Anika grimaced. Mateo was right. Unless they hired from the outside, the truth was, the politics—and culture—of the department weren't going to get any better.

She let out deep sigh. "I'm going to focus on the two bodies we have. It's *way* more productive than thinking about what the next thirty years of my career might look like."

CHAPTER FIVE

The sun was beginning its descent behind the hills when the call from the ME came. Dr. Rasmussen had been remarkably speedy with his autopsy, but because they'd made so little progress on either case, the hours between when she'd returned to the office and when the call had come had felt interminable.

"They are still running fingerprints through the database, but there was enough ketamine in his system to fell an elephant," the doctor said without preamble.

"So, to be clear, that was the cause of death?" Anika asked. It might sound like a dumb question, but when she'd been a rookie on the force, they'd pulled a body from the ocean that they'd presumed had drowned in the ocean. He *had* drowned, but in a bathtub in his hotel…with the help of his greedy son. Ever since that case, she never took it for granted that what might be the obvious cause of death was, in fact, the actual cause of death.

"Yes, that's COD," Dr. Rasmussen said. "No other signs of foul play. He was in excellent shape otherwise."

"Can you send me the reports?" she asked.

"On their way," he answered, then ended the call.

Anika set her phone down and tapped the back of it with a fingertip, her mind going to the two empty pill bottles.

"Suicide or accidental OD?" Mateo asked, sitting at his desk across from hers.

"I'd rule out accidental OD. Most people who become addicted to ketamine start small. The doc said he had a lot in his system. If he was a user, his body would have shown signs of that, and according to Rasmussen, it didn't."

"Okay, so not a habitual user so likely not an OD. Suicide?"

It was logical, but once more, something felt off to her. Then again, maybe she was reacting to the chief's earlier directive about Taglia's death and just rejecting the obvious out of spite.

"I'm going downstairs to see if Angela has tested those pills we found in the backpack," she said, rising from her seat and grabbing a notebook. "Once I get back, I'll try Taglia's doctor again, I haven't been able to get ahold of him yet."

Mateo gave her a vague nod as his attention fixed on his computer, and without another word, she headed for the elevators. As she waited for the car to arrive, she pondered what life would be like if police work really was like the movies with instantaneous lab results and obvious suspects. But unfortunately, her life was not a movie. How could they identify suspects if they didn't even know who one of the DBs was and the other didn't seem to have any connections to anyone on the island? And as for labs, well, hopefully Angela would have something for her.

"The pills were ketamine," Angela said as soon as Anika set foot in the lab, fulfilling at least one of her movie-based fantasies. "Two different dose levels, but the same manufacturer."

Well, maybe it was suicide after all and *that's* why they didn't have any suspects.

"I assume they are available by prescription only, so probably off market?" Anika asked, leaning her hip against a table.

"The dosage in those pills is required to be administered in a hospital under supervision, so yes, definitely a street-buy," Angela confirmed.

"If you were going to commit suicide, would ketamine be a good way to do it?" Anika asked.

Angela regarded her. "It would be relatively painless and depending on how much you took, fast. It would have been a challenge, though, to get the purity and strength of those pills. Not insurmountable for someone committed to the act or someone who had access to the drugs, like a pharma rep or doctor, but it's not like getting a prescription for sleeping pills."

A tech walked in, waved to Angela, and flashed a smile at Anika. Greg Whitman was new to the lab, but a Tildas Island boy, through and through. He'd been two years behind her in school. After graduation he'd taken off for the mainland but had returned a year ago. He'd been trying to get her to go out with him ever since.

"Hey, Anika," Greg said.

She acknowledged him with a nod but turned her attention back to Angela. "What about fingerprints?" Anika asked.

"The only clear sets we found were the victim's. You know who he is yet?"

Anika shook her head. "Still running the prints through the system."

"There was a smudged print on the water bottle, though," Greg said, joining them.

"Not the victim's?" Anika asked.

Greg shook his head. "Not the victim's, but it's also not clear enough to run through the system to look for a match."

Anika straightened. "Was it smudged like it would have been if someone had handled the bottle then tried to wipe it clean, but missed a print?"

Greg cast Angela a look, and she gave a small jerk of her head in Anika's direction as if to tell him to go ahead.

"Well?" Anika demanded.

"It's possible," Greg said. "Actually, it's likely. That's all we can say, though. We don't know if it was wiped on purpose or by accident. For all we know, it could have been the housekeeper at the victim's hotel who picked it up to clean underneath it, then wiped it down."

Damn, he was right. There were any number of reasons a partial print might be on a water bottle. Angela would have told her straightaway if the water had been laced with ketamine. So, if the bottle hadn't been the delivery method, then there would have been no reason for the murderer to touch it. Assuming it was even a murder, which Anika wasn't sure of at all.

"Ugh," Anika said, in an uncharacteristic show of frustration. "These cases are driving me crazy."

Angela gave her a ghost of a sympathy smile, and Greg looked about to try to swoop in and make an offer to cheer her up.

"It's early days for both. Especially the one from today," Angela pointed out.

"The chief wants us to call Taglia's death an accident," Anika said.

"We talked about that yesterday. You have to admit it's a possibility. Maybe even a probability," Angela responded.

"He'll want to call this one a suicide. I'm sure of it," Anika continued.

"And it might well have been," Greg said.

Anika shot him a glare. Both he and Angela were right, but she liked Angela too much to glare at her. Greg, well, the jury was still out on him.

"Why don't we grab a drink after work, and you can walk me through what's bugging you," Greg offered.

Angela glanced at Anika and then rolled her eyes and gave a little shake of her head. Angela knew Anika had no interest in Greg *like that*, but there was one person she respected and with whom she could talk all this through. Someone who wouldn't hesitate to tell her if she was way off base, and, more importantly, someone she'd listen to.

"Thanks, but not tonight," Anika said.

"Or any night," Angela muttered just loud enough for Anika to hear.

"I'm meeting a friend later," Anika continued, ignoring Angela's comment. After eliciting promises from both Angela and Greg to have the reports sent to her, she said her goodbyes. Pulling out her phone as she left, she dialed Dominic's number, and, opting to take the stairs, walked toward the stairwell.

"Anika," Dominic answered, a hint of his Louisiana accent coming through in his voice and making her smile. "To what do I owe this pleasure?"

For the first time since she'd woken up that morning, the weight of everything lifted from her shoulders a little bit.

"How about I meet you at Toto's tonight and tell you in person? I'll buy," she said.

Dominic chuckled. "You don't have to ask twice, but I'm buying. See you there at six," he said, then hung up before she could protest his comment about paying. She paused at the landing between the first and second floors and looked out the window and onto the streets of Havensted. A cruise ship was in town, its stacks just visible over the tops of the buildings. The palm trees in the park on the corner swayed in a gentle breeze. A dark cloud hovered to the south threatening an evening shower, but tourists still filled the streets.

She smiled at the view. Despite the issues with her chief, the culture of the department, and these two troublesome cases, all in all, Tildas Island was not a bad place to live. Especially not when she had fish tacos and time with Dominic on her calendar.

Dominic grabbed a table with a view of the Caribbean stretching out as far as the eye could see. He'd always loved the water but growing up on the bayous and swamps of Louisiana was a little different from the tropical paradise he now called home. Well, it wasn't entirely paradise—groceries were more expensive than on the mainland, choice was somewhat limited whenever he needed to buy something, and no, most retailers didn't ship to Tildas without outrageous international shipping fees tacked on to the price. The fact that Tildas Island was a US territory didn't seem to sway anyone. On top of all that, there was poverty—not anything different from what he was used to seeing on the mainland, but when it was juxtaposed against the backdrop of the island as a playground for the rich, it seemed starker.

Even so, he loved it. He didn't want to stay here forever—no, with his mama's close call in December, he was thinking that he'd look for a position closer to home once The Summit was over and the task force disbanded. But in the meantime, he was damn well going to enjoy it.

And the woman who just walked in.

She was a complication, though. He recognized that. He also knew that he'd figure out what to do about that complication before he left. He had to. She was the only thing that gave him pause when he thought about leaving in three months' time. He'd wanted her in every conceivable way since the first time he'd laid eyes on her five months ago. And before he'd left for that fateful trip home in December, he'd flirted and toyed with her like he'd done with other women dozens of times.

She was attracted to him, too. Or at least physically her body responded to his—he saw it in the way her eyes followed him and how her breath shifted when he stepped in to her space. In the first months after they'd met, he'd tried to take advantage of that attraction and had laid all his tricks and skills on her in an effort to move from the 'professional acquaintance' category to the 'lover' category. But he hadn't ever succeeded. In fact, the harder he'd tried, the more distant she'd become. She hadn't ever been rude. No, instead, she'd just backed away from him—physically and mentally—and shut down. He'd hated it, and like a child, the more distance she put between them, the harder he had worked to get her attention.

It wasn't until he'd gone home and been faced with the reality of how quickly life could change that something shifted inside him. No, scratch that, it wasn't the possibility of losing his mama that had changed things—hell, as a member of an elite Air Force pararescue team, he knew damn well how fast life could change. What had changed was seeing his mama and dad and his two sisters with their husbands. Seeing the connections between each couple in their time of crisis—their loyalty, their strength, and their love—had changed something inside him. They all seemed so much stronger, so much more grounded, than he ever felt. He didn't think everyone needed to couple up with someone else in order to be happy, that wasn't it at all. But for him, someone who *did* want family, someone who *did* want what his sisters had...well, he'd known something had to change. He'd decided on his flight back to Tildas that if he wanted what his sisters and parents had, then maybe he should start being a man who could *offer* that to someone if he ever found the one he wanted to offer it to.

With that realization, things had slowly changed, and as he'd changed, not surprisingly, so had his relationship with Anika. It wasn't that they didn't still have fun together, but he didn't toss empty compliments at her, he didn't try to get her into his bed with every sentence he spoke, and most of all, he did what he said and said what he did. She wasn't a woman who trusted easily and before January, he'd never given her a reason *to* trust him. She trusted him now, though.

And in that trust, he'd discovered a woman who was not just beautiful, but one who was smart and funny, one who struggled with her job, one who loved her family, one who, with the right person, understood that to be vulnerable was to be strong. He'd discovered a woman he wanted—hoped would be—in his life for longer than the few short months he had left on the island.

But until he knew what he planned to do after The Summit, he had no intention of doing anything about it. He didn't know if she'd even be interested in having a relationship with him, but what he did know was that when the time came—if it came— when he handed her his heart, he was going to be all in. What she did with that would be her decision, but he wasn't going to give her only pieces of him.

"Dominic," Anika said, approaching the table. After pausing to kiss his cheek, she slid into the seat across from him. "Thanks for meeting me. I really appreciate it."

"Anytime, darling," he said. He couldn't drop old habits *entirely*. At least now, instead of withdrawing from him, she just shook her head and smiled. "I ordered us a couple of beers," he added as the waiter made his way to their table. "I held off on the tacos though since you seem to alternate between the fish and the shrimp, and I wasn't sure which you'd want."

"It's definitely a shrimp night," she said. They both leaned back as the waiter set two pint glasses of the local IPA down on the table.

"You ready to order, then?" the waiter asked.

Anika placed her order, and Dominic chose the fish. That way, if Anika changed her mind, they could share. When the waiter retreated to the kitchen, Dominic picked up his glass. Anika did the same, and they clinked the edges.

"To a beautiful night in the tropics," he said, taking a sip and leaning back in his chair. The ocean breeze flowed gently through the open-air restaurant and he watched as Anika took a sip, then closed her eyes to savor the moment.

She smiled and opened her eyes again. "That was a way nicer

toast than what I was going to propose, which was a sarcastic one about two dead bodies and a bottle of ketamine."

"That sounds like the beginning of a bad joke," Dominic said.

"I wish."

"Another body today?" he asked.

She nodded. "It's part of the reason I wanted to talk with you. The chief wants us to rule Taglia's death an accident, and we've been able to push it off, but now we have another body. Died this morning on the waterfall trail."

"Of a ketamine overdose?" Dominic asked with a frown. After Jake and Nia had stumbled into a massive designer drug operation back in October, he and the team had been keeping a pretty close eye on the drug scene in the area. So far, Special-K, as it was called on the streets, hadn't shown up on their radar.

Anika nodded. "There were pills in his backpack, and the ME said there was enough in his system to fell a horse. Well, he said an elephant, but you know what I mean."

He did. Ketamine wasn't a drug you messed around with. "Are you thinking suicide or an OD?"

She told him what she and Mateo had discussed that afternoon. She also told him that, as with Taglia, the chief had already determined the cause of death, only this time it was a suicide rather than an accident.

Ketamine would be a relatively painless way to go, but... "Did you say there were pills in his backpack?" he asked.

Anika's gaze held his and she nodded. "Two bottles. One had one pill in it and the other had two. The lab tested both and they were the same manufacturer, but different doses."

"Two bottles. Both with lids on tight and in his backpack?"

She nodded again.

"Top or bottom of the bag?"

"Bottom, under the breakfast burrito," she answered.

He sat back and started to say something, but the arrival of the waiter with their food stopped him. When the waiter was back out of earshot, he leaned forward again. Anika did the same.

"I've seen my share of suicides. Being in the service then getting out of it and having to adjust to civilian life isn't a walk in the park," he said. "Don't you think it's weird that he took enough pills to kill himself but then decided to leave three? And then on top of that, he closed the bottles back up and put them back in his backpack?"

Anika blew out a deep breath, her bangs fluttering in the draft. "I thought so, too. The chief obviously disagrees, and Mateo isn't weighing in one way or the other, but at least it's good to know I'm not the only one who thinks the setup was a little, well, quirky."

Dominic picked up a taco but didn't take a bite. "Was the backpack zipped up?"

"Zipped, tidy, and he was still wearing it."

He took a bite and shook his head. Waiting until after he swallowed before speaking, he said, "That's definitely weird. It's possible that's part of his personality, like some OCD or something. Absent that, though, the set up you described does *not* sound like a suicide."

"So, I now have two deaths that *look* like an accident and a suicide, but if you look closer, are probably something else. You guys suggested the possibility of a professional hit last night, and I don't discount it, but it seems a little far-fetched. Can you think of any other reason someone would want to set up this kind of scenario?"

She took a bite of her food as Dominic shook his head. "I know it's far-fetched, but right now, it seems the clearest option. Talk to me about what you know about Taglia and this new dead body. Do you even have an ID on the guy from this morning?"

Anika shook her head.

"If you found a connection between the two, I'd say *then* it would be worth looking into the professional angle. In fact, if there is a connection, I'd give good odds it is a professional. *Why* they'd do the hit here on Tildas, I don't know, but if you find a connection, you might figure that out, too."

"And if there's no connection?" Anika asked, then took a drink of her IPA.

"We could be looking at the serial killer theory Alexis suggested."

Anika's lips flattened and she turned her gaze to the ocean. She didn't speak for a long time, but Dominic didn't intrude on her thoughts. He just picked at his meal and watched her. Finally, she sighed.

"So once again, we're looking at a professional hit or a serial killer. Welcome to Paradise, ladies and gentlemen."

CHAPTER SIX

Anika took a seat at her desk the next morning, dreading the day. Not so much because of what she had to do, but because the chief would no doubt be aggressively set on having Taglia's death declared an accident. She and Mateo had been able to put him off the day before, but that reprieve would be short-lived.

"I've got an appointment to talk to the Loose Ends Studio folks at eleven this morning," Rosey said, swiveling her chair to face Anika.

"An appointment?" she asked.

Rosey nodded. "Turns out they didn't feel comfortable talking to us and wanted their lawyers present."

"Hmm," Anika said, taking a sip of the coffee she'd brought from home. She hadn't had a sip of station coffee since her first week on the job. "You think there's something there?"

Rosey cocked her head. "Hard to say. It's LA, they could just be being cautious."

Anika considered Rosey's words. Her co-worker was probably right. After all, one of their employees did die on a vacation the company paid for.

"You have your questions ready?" Anika asked.

Again, Rosey nodded. "I have a few. Then I have some more depending on how cooperative they are being."

That drew a laugh from Anika. "Meaning if they start jerking your chain, you're going to draw it out and cost them thousands in attorney's fees?"

Rosey grinned. "You know how much I like to chat."

"About what?" Mateo asked, striding into the room.

Anika waved off his question with a vague gesture. He eyed her as he removed his suit jacket but didn't say anything until he'd taken a seat.

"What's the plan today?" he asked.

"Ideally?" Anika half-joked, half-asked. "We get an ID on the DB from yesterday and clear evidence that points to how he died and then we get the same for Taglia and then we close both cases in a blaze of glory. I don't think anyone has ever closed two suspicious death cases in one day in the history of the department."

The look Mateo leveled on her made her grin. Once again, he wasn't sure quite how to take her comments. Something she was way more amused by than he was.

He sighed and stood. "I assume, from your comments, that we still have no ID on the body from the trail yet?" he asked, making his way to the coffee machine.

"I got in five minutes before you and haven't had a chance to turn my computer on yet," Anika answered, leaning forward to do just that. She logged into the system as Mateo doctored his coffee. Sure enough, there was an email from the lab.

"Hameed Khan," she called out to him. Then she started when Mateo leaned over her shoulder, one hand on her chair, the other holding his coffee cup and resting on her desk.

"Thirty-three years old. Hmm, I would have guessed much younger than that," he said, reading the brief report.

Anika *had* placed him much younger than that. She'd thought him closer to twenty-five. "An auditor from a company based out of New York," she said, reading the report out loud. "No spouse, and just a surviving father and sister."

"You want to do the honors?" Mateo asked, straightening from the desk.

What she wanted was to tell him to kiss her ass. Ever since she'd been promoted to detective, not once had he, or any of the others in the small department, made any death notifications. Nope, they left that to her, even for the cases that weren't hers. It might be hard to say no, because she was the newest detective, but it was damn easy to resent.

Mustering as much calm as she could, she answered. "You don't genuinely care what I do, or don't, want to do. I'll do the family a favor, though, and make the call so they don't have to talk to you." She rose so abruptly that the chair flew into him and he took a step back.

She heard him mutter something, but Anika didn't stick around to decipher the words. If she was going to make the call to Mr. Khan and inform him that his son was dead, she was damn well going to do it on her own terms.

Leaving the building, she walked across the street to the park and took a seat on a bench under a flamboyant tree. Unlocking her phone, she logged into the secure system and pulled up the phone number for Hameed Khan's father that Angela's team had helpfully added to the report.

Taking a deep breath of the sweetly scented air, she dialed the number.

"Hello," a man with a slight accent answered.

"Mr. Khan?" Anika asked.

"Yes, this is Ahmed Khan," he responded.

"The father of Hameed Khan?"

He hesitated. "Yes."

"My name is Detective Anika Anderson of the Tildas Island Police, sir. I'm sorry, I have some bad news."

The call was, blessedly, short. In all the calls she'd done, not that there had been many, that was the one thing that had always struck her—how few words it took to tell someone their life would never be the same.

After hanging up with Khan's father, she called the victim's sister. Technically, she didn't have to, but Ahmed Khan had lost a child, and whether it was right or not, Anika thought it was important that his surviving child know. Especially because she lived not far away and could, if the Khans were that kind of family, be at her father's side within thirty minutes.

The call to Maryam Khan took a little longer. The woman was shocked, but slightly more composed than her father. Despite not being able to provide concrete information or answers to many of the questions, Anika did her best to assure Maryam they were doing everything possible to find out what had happened to her younger brother. Then, to Anika's surprise, Maryam ended the call by offering to do anything the department needed to help find answers. It wasn't the offer itself that surprised Anika, family often spoke words to that effect, but it was the sincerity Anika heard in the woman's voice. It was as if she knew her brother's death wasn't going to have straightforward answers and she was prepared to wade into the fray if need be.

When Anika ended the call, she looked up at the view of the sea several blocks away and took a deep breath. She held her phone loosely in her lap, needing some distance from it after what she'd just done. She listened to the birds, to the traffic, to the sounds of the breeze rustling through the trees. The sounds of laughter from the bar around the corner from the station floated in the air, and a child darted into the park on his way up the street with his mother.

Despite the news she'd just delivered, life would—and did—go on.

Leaning against the back of the bench, she inhaled deeply

one more time, drawing strength from the enduring sweet smell of the trees. Then she picked up her phone and called Dominic.

"Your boyfriend meeting us?" Mateo asked as they pulled into the upscale chain hotel where Hameed Khan had stayed.

Anika chose not to rise to the bait and instead, pointed to where Dominic stood, leaning against the back of his jeep, waiting for them. He looked damn good standing there in jeans, a T-shirt just loose enough to cover his weapon, and sunglasses. Even without looking at his face, Dominic had the kind of presence that caused a woman to look more than once. Some men, too.

"Always comes when you crook your finger, doesn't he," Mateo commented, pulling into a spot two down from Dominic.

Again, she said nothing. Mateo had been pissy with her since she'd returned from speaking with Khan's father and sister. She hadn't wanted to make the calls, but as it turned out, it got her out of the office when the chief had stopped by to ream Mateo a new one for not officially closing Taglia's case. Mateo had put him off again but had at some point—presumably after getting his hide torn into by the chief—decided his shitty day was all her fault. What constituted "all" still remained to be defined, but at the very least, she assumed it was her fault they hadn't closed the case and her fault they'd found Khan's hotel room before Mateo had had a chance for a proper breakfast. It was also her fault that Dominic was there. She'd take responsibility for the latter, but as for the rest, well, Mateo was a big boy and she wasn't about to let him put his shit on her.

"Hey, Nik," Dominic said, pushing away from his car and ambling over. It was a nickname he'd started using a few months back. He didn't use it often, but Anika had to admit, if only to herself, she kind of liked it. She'd always corrected people when they tried to shorten her name—but somehow, coming out of Dominic, it made her feel unique, maybe even special. She had no explanation for why hearing him say the name caused the warm fuzzies it did, but it was what it was and she wasn't interested in trying to convince herself otherwise.

"Hey, Dom," she said, adjusting her holster and walking toward him.

"Burel," Mateo said.

"Garza." Dominic did one of those little chin raises that guys do when they greet someone they don't want to acknowledge too much but know they have to at least a little.

"So, what's the story?" Dom asked, falling into stride beside her as they walked toward the lobby of the hotel.

"Hameed Khan, thirty-three years old. He works for an audit firm. He was down here conducting an audit of a tech company that's owned by a private equity company in New York," Anika answered.

"Anything from the lab?"

"I haven't had a chance to check in today. We got the ID, made the call to the family, and by the time I finished that, Rosey had tracked this down," she answered, gesturing toward the lobby as they walked in the front door.

"I'll go talk to the manager," Mateo said, peeling away from the group to approach the reception desk.

"What's up with him?" Dominic asked once Mateo was out of earshot.

Anika shrugged. "I think life crawled up his ass today."

Dominic chuckled. "Yeah, that'd make a guy a little moody."

They stood in silence, contemplating the view until Mateo joined them. "Room 576," he said, holding a card key out. Without a word, the three of them made their way to the elevator where Dominic hit the button for the fifth floor.

"You have an evidence team coming?" he asked.

"Nah," Mateo said. "Nik and I thought we'd handle it, 'cause that's how we do things down here on the island."

"Stop being an asshole," Anika said as the doors slid open. "Whatever the fuck your problem is, pull yourself together, Garza. We have a father who lost his son and a woman who lost her brother today. That's more important than your temper tantrum."

She stepped into the hallway and glanced at the arrows pointing guests either left or right, though she didn't miss the fact that Dominic was very intentionally studying his shoes. She didn't fight the smile that teased her lips. Four months ago, Dominic would have said something more to rile Mateo up. She wasn't sure what had caused the change, but she liked that he held his tongue now and let her have the last say.

She paused in front of room 576, and Mateo placed the card key over the reader. When the light flashed from red to green, he pushed the door open and they entered the room.

To say that Taglia and Khan were different would have been a gross understatement. Where Taglia's room was meticulous, Khan's looked as though a hurricane had torn through it. Clothes were strewn across the chairs and table, two beach towels hung over the back of the two lounge chairs on the balcony, half of the drawers in the dresser were open, a computer sat on the desk, and a computer bag was tipped over on the floor beside it with a stack of files spilling out.

"Did someone go through this room?" Garza asked.

"No," Dominic said, pointing to the nicely made bed. "I dated a woman once who managed the housekeeping staff of a large resort and one of the complaints she often had—and she had a lot of them—was how hard it was to walk the line of picking a room up enough to clean it but not so much as to potentially disturb whatever state the occupant might like it in. I'd say this room was cleaned yesterday."

"The bathroom's a little better," Anika said from where she

stood in the doorway between the bedroom and the bathroom. "Not much, but it's not disgusting."

Dominic came to stand beside her and they both looked into the room. It was large for a bathroom, but not cavernous. Her eyes swept the space, pausing at the items on the counter.

"No prescription drugs at all," Dominic said.

"Yeah, I noticed that, too," she replied. In fact, other than a toothbrush, a comb, a travel sized toothpaste, and an electric razor, there was nothing on the counter. Randomly, she wondered if he wore deodorant because there was none in sight.

"All right, kids," Mateo said, drawing both her and Dominic's attention. "Where do we want to start?"

"Why don't Burel and I start with the room and you start with the interviews?" Anika suggested. She'd much rather do the interviews, and she was pretty sure Dominic would get more out of anyone who worked here than Mateo would. But if she suggested she and Dom do the interviews and left Mateo to start the room search on his own, he would have pitched another fit that she didn't feel like dealing with.

Mateo grunted as if he understood why she'd made the suggestion, but he didn't say anything before he turned and left.

"He's a ray of sunshine today," Dominic said, donning a pair of gloves and kneeling beside the computer bag.

"Like I said, something crawled up his ass today. I thought it was the chief, and I think that's a part of it, but he's more surly than usual," Anika replied, pulling out her phone and starting to take some pictures. Dominic moved to the side when she photographed the bag and its placement in the room. When she had enough shots, she waved for him to carry-on.

"It's me, you know," Dominic said, reaching in and sliding a file out.

"It's you, what?" Anika asked, only half-paying attention as she continued to photograph the room. She and Dominic would leave everything where they found it for the evidence team, but she wanted pictures of the room before they started going through it.

"He doesn't like that we spend so much time together. I told you, he has a thing for you."

Anika didn't stop taking pictures, but her mind processed Dominic's words. Usually, Dominic just teased her about Mateo and his supposed interest in her. The thread of irritation she'd heard in Dom's voice was new.

Her gaze flitted over to where he still knelt beside the bag, one knee on the ground the other raised with a file resting on top of it. Damn that man looked good in jeans—and pretty much everything else she'd ever seen him wear. From where she stood, with his back to her, she had a good view of the play of muscles as he flipped through a file. She couldn't see his arms but knew their contours well enough to know that if she were standing three feet to her left, she'd have a view of them subtly flexing which each movement.

The burnt orange color of his shirt contrasted with the dark of his skin and when he leaned forward to pick up another file, she had the strongest urge to place her lips on the smooth skin at the back of his neck; to kneel behind him, wrap her arms around him, and feel his body against hers.

"Nik? You okay?" Dominic asked.

She snapped her eyes up to see Dominic watching her in the reflection of the glass sliding door.

She cleared her throat. "Yeah, spaced out there for a minute. I'm going to go take photos of the bathroom."

She didn't need to linger or look to know that Dominic watched her as she fled the room. Because as cowardly as it was, that was what she'd done. That fleeting urge had startled her more than she wanted to admit. Not just that she'd *had* it, but the strength of it.

It had been months since she'd even considered entertaining

anything more than friendship with Dominic. In fact, after that first night they'd met, when he'd flashed her a smile that told her he knew he could give her a good time, she'd shut that shit down. Dominic was not the kind of man she wanted in her life in that way. She had no doubt he'd be fun and there wasn't a question in her mind that a night with him would be memorable, but he was too much for her.

Anika didn't begrudge him his player ways at all, and it wasn't like he was without morals. He tended to hook up with women who were on vacation and looking for a good time. She had nothing against two consenting adults doing whatever they wanted, and it wasn't like she was one for commitment either. She'd been known to do the same with men who traveled to the island for a week of fun and sun. Those kinds of hook-ups were uncomplicated, usually fun, and if she picked the right man, they definitely scratched an itch.

She continued taking pictures of the items around the sink but frowned as a truth flitted into her mind and settled there. She *used* to do the same with men who visited the island. But how long had it been since she'd been with a man? Three months? Four?

Then again, when she really thought about it, when was the last time she'd seen Dominic head home with a woman? Not since he'd returned from visiting his family in Louisiana around the holidays.

"I did a cursory look at the files, and I assume Gamba Technologies was the company Khan was auditing?" Dominic asked, interrupting her train of thought. Something she was definitely okay with since her mind seemed to be going down a path she was pretty sure she didn't want it to.

She shook her head. "I don't know. Rosey's doing the background work now since we only ID'd him this morning. If those are the files you're finding, then I'd bet it's likely."

"You familiar with the company?"

Anika nodded. "They provide some sort of WiFi boosting technology. Was started by a local woman a few years behind me in school. She went off to MIT and no one expected her to come back, but after selling off one successful start-up, she moved back about four years ago and founded Gamba."

She moved out of the bathroom and tucked her phone into her pocket. She had enough pictures for now. The evidence team would take more, but she felt comfortable enough to start going through Khan's clothing.

"Is it normal for a start-up to have investment from a private equity firm? I thought they all looked for venture capitalists," Dominic said, joining her at the table and picking up a pair of Khan's khakis that had been tossed over a chair.

Anika glanced up and laughed. "That is so far outside my realm of expertise, it's not even funny. I can barely manage my 401K and it's through a fund."

"Not into investing, then?" he asked, pulling out a wadded-up tissue from a pants pocket. He made a face and shoved it back in.

"Not much to invest. You know how expensive this island is. I own my condo and have my retirement fund. Not much left after HOA fees, groceries, and all the other day-to-day expenses. You?"

This was not a conversation she ever thought she'd be having with Dominic. They talked shop, they talked about their favorite movies and restaurants, occasionally they talked families, but they'd never talked about finances.

"I had a friend on my team when I was in the Air Force and his brother was a big investor. He kind of took us under his wing and managed investments for those of us who wanted him to. Most of our expenses were paid and I didn't live big, so I had some cash for him to play with. He played well and I have a little nest egg now."

"You're not blowing through it living here?" she asked, holding one of Khan's button-down shirts in her hand.

Dominic shrugged and picked up another pair of pants. "The Bureau gives us each a stipend to help with expenses. Alexis donates hers, but I know it covers Jake's mooring fees and rent for Damian and Beni. It mostly covers my rent, just a couple hundred a month short, but I have a condo in DC that I've rented out while I'm here, so I'm still ahead. Not making bank or anything, but Shah didn't want any of us to need to consider finances when she was recruiting us to the team."

Anika set the shirt down and moved toward the stack of shoes piled against the wall beside the dresser. There were at least seven pairs...how many pairs of shoes did one man need for a business trip?

"I had no idea the Bureau was so generous," she said, kneeling to pick up a pair of leather loafers. She wasn't entirely sure what she was looking for, but maybe something would stick out.

Dominic snorted. "They aren't. I mean, I'm sure we make a little more than the police, but I think their generosity in this particular instance has more to do with Shah than anything else."

Anika had met the team's director on more than one occasion and had a lot of respect for her. Shah, like Anika, was a petite woman who was making her way in a world dominated not just by men, but generally by large, physical men. Well, more to the point, Shah had already *made* her way in the world of law enforcement and Anika was a little in awe of her.

She wasn't the only one though. On more than one occasion, members of the task force had alluded to how well-respected their director was—so much so that Shah had garnered an almost mythical-like reputation.

"Yeah, I can see that," she said, flashing a quick smile at

Dominic before picking up another pair of shoes. "It's a nice gig you all have. Not that you aren't working hard, but it's a nice gig." If she hadn't happened to have been looking up at that moment, she would have missed the tiny drop of Dominic's brow, as if her comment had reminded him of something that he'd forgotten.

But then in a flash it was gone, and he smiled back. "Yeah, it's not bad. I like to think we've done some good in prepping both the island and the resort for the upcoming Summit."

She heard a "but" in there, but it never followed as Mateo walked back into the room.

"All CCTV is digitized, so the manager is emailing it over along with all of Khan's charges in the few days he was here. He arrived last Thursday and was scheduled to leave the day after tomorrow. The cleaning staff I talked to said he was messy, but polite and left a tip every day. The waitstaff said the same, minus the messy part—polite and tipped well. Based on my quick perusal of his records, it looked like he ate breakfast and dinner here every day until yesterday when he didn't come back for dinner. You all find anything?"

"Just that he was a minimalist with personal hygiene and a maximalist—is that even a word—with everything else," Anika said, gesturing to the array of clothing and shoes.

"And he's a bit of a slob," Dominic added as his phone rang. Excusing himself, he stepped out onto the balcony to take the call.

"How far out is the evidence team?" Mateo asked.

Anika all but rolled her eyes. He could text them as well as she could, but rather than point that out, she turned her back and shot off a quick text to the lead. His response came just as Dominic returned to the room.

"They're pulling in now," Anika said.

"The evidence team?" Dominic asked and she nodded. "Good, Alexis called, and I need to head out to Hemmeleigh for something," he continued, slipping his phone into his pocket. "Catch up with you later?"

Mateo's head came up, but Anika ignored him and nodded to Dominic. "Say hi to Alexis for me," she added. Her eyes followed him when he walked past her and out the door. She'd like to think her attention was just friendly, but the truth was, the sight of Dominic's backside as he left was going to be the best thing she saw for many, many hours.

CHAPTER SEVEN

Dominic backed his jeep out of the spot and started toward Hemmeleigh. A glitch had shown up in the security cameras around one of the blocks of rooms and Alexis had asked him to come take a look. Passing the rows of parked cars, a white SUV caught his attention. It wasn't the same white car he'd seen before at Taglia's hotel or up at The Shack, but it did remind him that he hadn't checked out the license plate yet.

Hitting the Bluetooth setting on his phone, he called Jake.

"Yo, my brother, what can I do you for today?" Jake asked when he answered. Always a happy-go-lucky guy, Jake had grown almost annoyingly chipper since he and Nia had begun dating. But hell, Jake was one of his closest friends and he wouldn't begrudge the guy.

"Can you run a check on this license?" Dominic asked without preamble then rattled off the number. "I'm sure it's a rental, but I'd like to know who it was rented to."

"You got it," Jake responded without any hesitation. "Anything else?"

Dominic hesitated as he turned onto the main road that

would take him to the north side of the island where the resort was located.

"Tell Uncle Jakey everything. You know there are no secrets between us."

Dominic laughed at that. "Right, you mean like the time you told me you were in love with Nia or that time you told me about the spider the size of Godzilla in the bathroom or that time when you and Nia were unusually close-lipped about whatever it was that happened on your boat that one night a couple of weeks ago?"

"Some things aren't secrets; they are just best left unsaid. Or, in the case of the boat, never mentioned again."

Dominic laughed again. "Right. I'm sure whatever happened on the boat *isn't* something I want to know about. But the spider? Really, you could have told me about that before I walked in and squealed loud enough that the whole office came running in."

Jake snickered. "I could have, but where would the fun be in that? I know how much you like spiders."

"You are such an asshole," Dominic shot back.

"Ah, and there's my love for the day. Now that you've buttered me up, are you going to tell me what's on your mind that had you hesitating a few seconds ago?"

Dominic hesitated again. He didn't want to step on Anika's toes—god knew she had enough of that from her own department—but she wasn't getting the support she needed. Support he could give.

He let out a long breath. "Can you run deep background on Joseph Taglia of Los Angeles and Hameed Khan of New York?"

"The two dead guys Anika is investigating?" Jake asked.

"Yeah. I know, it's not my business—it's not *our* business—but she's got good instincts, and right now her chief is handcuffing her."

"And so you want to ride in and save the day. Very interesting…"

Jake was trying to get a rise out of him, and it almost worked, but instead, Dominic laughed. "I'm not a knight on a white horse and Anika doesn't need saving, but if she needs some ammo to fire off her shots, I don't mind being the one handing it to her."

Jake let out a huff of a laugh. "Yeah, that's definitely a better analogy," he said, then, more seriously, he added. "I'll start it in a few minutes. Come by the office when you're done out at Hemmeleigh and we can go over anything I find."

"Thanks, Jake," Dominic said.

"Anytime. See you this afternoon," he said, then ended the call.

Having Jake do an additional background into the two DBs wasn't that big a deal. It might not be protocol, but Dominic was hard pressed to care too much. Because the more he thought about it, the more he acknowledged that he just didn't like how the chief was treating this investigation.

Sure, Dominic also didn't like the way Anika was treated in the department, in general, but it went against everything he had ever learned, both as a pararescuer and as an agent, to ignore a good officer's instinct. If Anika's instincts were telling her that the two deaths were more than they seemed, then he wanted to both help her *and* the investigation. She might be wrong, but if she was, then at least she'd know that no stone was left unturned. If she was right, though…well, she'd need all the help she could get to sway her chief. The trick would be in not letting him know she had a little help from the FBI.

The chief had taken the presence of the task force on the island as an insult to his department—a sign that officials didn't think he and his team could handle security for The Summit—and he'd been pissed off since the day the team had landed. That he was right—there was no way the Tildas Island Police Force was equipped to manage everything needed for the event—didn't seem to matter, because Chief Maddox didn't care about being right so long as no one questioned his position.

Pushing aside thoughts of Anika and her department, he pulled into the parking lot at Hemmeleigh where he spent the next two hours with Alexis figuring out that it wasn't really a glitch in the camera, but that an iguana had decided to try and take a bite out of one. The real problem was that, like an old string of Christmas lights, when one camera went off, so did the other six on the same system. It wasn't a documented failure of the system, and the company had no idea why or how it had happened, but the good news was, Alexis had put the fear of god into them and they were sending someone down to upgrade the entire set.

It was close to four when he and Alexis walked into the FBI offices. Jake would still be there—no way would he have left before briefing Dominic on anything he'd found—but he was surprised to also see Beni, Damian, and Director Shah huddled around Jake's desk.

All four of them looked up at the sound of the door shutting behind him and Alexis, and for a moment, he and his teammate froze.

"What happened?" Alexis asked.

Dominic felt a moment of triumph because he *knew* that Jake had found something. Anika had been right after all, and the chief could suck it. That wasn't quite how it worked, though, and the implications of Jake finding something came crashing down on that moment of glee. If Anika was right, then something cagey was going on. Which also meant that it was likely either the serial killer or the hitman theory they'd discussed at The Shack.

"Well," Jake drew the word out as he stood. "It might be good for us to all convene in the conference room. Director, what do you think?"

Shah motioned everyone toward the largest of their three conference rooms. Once they were all seated, she nodded to Jake to start.

"Well, it looks like it's possible your woman was onto something," Jake said. Shah cleared her throat and cast Jake a repressive look. He grinned. "It looks like Detective Anderson might be onto something," he restated.

"And what might that be?" Dominic asked.

"Joseph Taglia and Hameed Khan both worked at The Bank of DC—Taglia in their tax department and Khan in their audit department—before moving to the companies they were with at the time they died." As Jake spoke, Damian had typed some commands into a laptop and the images of the two men came up on the large screen at the front of the room.

"The bank that was investigated four years ago for funneling funds to terrorists?" Alexis asked.

Jake nodded. "The very same."

"It was also the bank that handled—maybe still handles—the bulk of Calvin Matthews' investments," Beni said. That drew Dominic up short. He'd known that, of course he had. When the front running candidate for Vice President was investigated just before the election for being associated with an institution that funneled funds to terrorists, that tended to stick in your mind. Still, it wasn't at all what he'd expected when he'd asked Jake to look into the two deaths.

"Okay, so this might be bigger than we think," he conceded. "But other than the fact that they both worked there, what else do we have?"

"Not a lot more than that," Damian answered. "Both men were deposed at the time of the initial investigation, and we were just discussing getting those transcripts, but there was one more odd thing that caught our attention."

"Both men left their positions within three months of Matthews and Cunningham winning the election," Beni said. Calvin Matthews and Anne-Marie Cunningham had done the unthinkable a little over three years earlier—the Republican presidential candidate had picked a Democrat for her running mate and the two had swept the election. Their platform had been radical in its simplicity and the fact that it was relatively sane. After the years of ugly partisan politics that had preceded their win, they were the salve the country had craved. Now well into their first term, their approval ratings were among the highest of any administration in the history of the United States.

"So, are you saying you think there might have been something to the investigation that got swept under the rug, and moving those two out of the way," Dominic said, gesturing to the images still displayed on the large screen, "was part of the clean-up?"

"And then having them killed now, eight months before the next election is what? Additional security that the issue won't arise again?" Alexis asked.

"We're not sure what it means, if anything," Shah stepped in. "There are lots of powerful people who bank with that business, Matthews just happens to be one that has also shown up on our radar before."

Dominic glanced at Damian. The last time Matthews name had been bantered around the office was during the case that brought Charlotte back into his life. It had to do with potential mismanagement of funds at a World Bank site on a nearby island. Charlotte's friend had discovered that the Vice President's ex-wife—a woman with whom Mathews was still close—had been asked to submit a bid to replace an existing contractor. It wouldn't have been so unusual—after all, her construction firm was very well regarded in the public works field—except that Duncan Calloway, an old fraternity brother of Matthews, had been the project lead. Well, that and the fact that Matthews' wife's firm had never done any work in the Caribbean before. They'd never found any proof that Matthews had asked his old fraternity brother to invite the bid, but they hadn't found any proof he hadn't either.

And then there was Duncan Calloway himself. *He'd* been on their radar for over a year. They might have first learned about him in the World Bank case, but that hadn't been the last time his name had cropped up in one of their investigations. In fact, if he was involved in The Bank of DC, too, this would make it the fourth time his name was associated with something nefarious going on in their region.

"What about Calloway?" Dominic asked. "Does he bank there, too?"

"Like I said, there are a lot of powerful people who use that institution. The reason we know about Mathews, specifically, is because it was so public during the investigation," Shah answered.

"Any way we can get the client list?" Dominic asked with a pointed look at Damian. Before the two of them had joined the task force, Dominic had helped Damian with a case he'd been working on with some of his friends who were, to put an inadequate title on them, super hackers. The same super hackers who'd helped the team close down a designer drug ring five months ago.

"We're not there yet, Dominic," Shah interjected. "First, we need to find out what precipitated each man's departure from the bank and if there's any connection as to why they are both on Tildas Island at the same time. Then we need to work with Detective Anderson on the cause of death. My understanding is that, as of twenty minutes ago, the department still hadn't called cause of death for either case."

"Yeah, well, that's not going to last long. Chief Maddox has been pushing her and her partner to declare Taglia's an accident and Khan's a suicide. I'm not sure how much longer they'll be able to hold him off, although I'm confident Anika will give us access to the documents if we need them. Especially since I've already been helping out in an unofficial capacity," Dominic said.

Shah seemed to consider his words, then she nodded as if coming to some decision. "Let's keep our investigation to ourselves for now and leave Detective Anderson out of it. If it looks like something we need to take over, we'll try to do it without tanking her career."

Dominic couldn't argue with that. Anika would gladly give them any documentation the team might ask for, but she would definitely pay the price for it. She'd view it as worth it, if it led to closing the case based on evidence rather than the chief's whims. But Shah was right, there were ways to gain control of the investigation, if they needed to, without implicating Anika.

"Damian," Shah said, rising from her seat. "You have night shift at Hemmeleigh tonight and Jake, you've been in all day after taking it last night. You two head out, and Alexis, Beni, and Dominic will stay here to follow up on Taglia and Khan. I want you three to dig into the public lives of both victims and see what you can find online. I also want to start gathering some data on The Bank of DC investigation, but don't pull the official files yet. For now, let's stick to what we can find in the various news sources."

There were murmurs of assent all around, but as soon as Shah entered her own office and closed the door behind her, Dominic swung his gaze around to his teammates to find the same expression of curiosity on their faces that was probably on his.

"Anyone want to take any guesses as to why she doesn't want us to pull the official files?" Beni said. It was a rhetorical question. They all knew that if they pulled the files there'd be a record of it, and if someone was paying attention, they'd know the team was getting curious. The real question was why Shah didn't want anyone to know they were looking into it.

"You think this might be why she's also controlled the investigation into Calloway?" Damian suggested. When they'd first confirmed eight months ago that Calloway wasn't the stand-up guy he pretended to be, Shah hadn't let them pursue an investigation into him. She'd given them some leash back in October when his name had cropped up again, but to date, she still hadn't authorized a full-scale investigation.

"Like she doesn't want us to tip our hand too soon?" Dominic suggested.

"Yeah, but tip it for what?" Beni asked.

"Is it possible Calloway is the errand boy for Matthews, and she's worried about an investigation getting noticed—and shut down—before we can find the evidence we need?" Alexis suggested.

"But evidence of what?" Jake asked. "Do we really think the Vice President could be involved in everything from human trafficking to drug distribution to funneling money to terrorist organizations?"

"Matthews is a choir boy," Beni said. "The only errand boy he'd have is someone to pick up his pressed jeans at the dry cleaner."

"Isn't it always the mighty that fall?" Damian posited. "Think of all those anti-gay male legislators who were later caught hiring male prostitutes. Maybe Matthews isn't as clean as we think, and Shah thinks there's evidence of that somewhere."

"Somewhere we haven't come across yet, so she wants us to proceed with caution," Alexis said, finishing Damian's thought.

"I don't like the idea of Matthews being anything other than what he seems to be because he seems like a stand-up guy, but that reasoning sounds like it *could* be true," Jake said. "Not that it *is* true," he added when Beni narrowed her eyes at him.

"Look," Dominic said. "I think it's too soon to be linking

Calloway and Matthews together in any other way than what we know, which is pretty limited. We don't need to be jumping to any conclusions when we have a bunch of real work in front of us. Damian and Jake, why don't you both head out? Alexis and Beni, why don't I start with Hameed Khan?"

Alexis nodded. "I'll take The Bank of DC if you want to take Taglia, Beni?"

Beni nodded and the team filed out of the conference room. Rather than get started right away, Dominic lingered with Damian and Jake as they packed up, then he followed them outside.

"You going to call your woman?" Jake asked as the three men entered the elevator.

"She's not my woman, as you well know, but yes, I'm going to call her," Dominic snapped back, making both Damian and Jake snicker. Dominic thought about trying to set them straight but then held his tongue knowing it would make things worse.

"You do realize that we're all trained investigators and on top of that, we're a pretty observant bunch?" Damian asked.

"Yeah, sitting out on the ocean for hours every day watching and waiting for the perfect wave made *me* pretty observant," Jake interjected. He'd been a pro surfer before joining the FBI. It was kind of a weird career shift, and one that only Jake could pull off.

"I agree, and since I was a sniper back in my Ranger days, I notice shit you wouldn't believe," Damian said.

Dominic sighed as they reached the ground floor. "And your point is?"

"He doesn't get our point, Jake," Damian said.

"Maybe he's not as observant as the rest of us," Jake replied.

"Just get to the fucking point so you can both go home to your women and leave me alone," Dominic said, knowing full well that until they'd said what they wanted to say, they'd keep sucking up more of his time.

"Someone's losing his sense of humor," Jake said.

"But I'll take pity on you," Damian said, stepping forward and clapping Dominic on the shoulder. "You're in love with Anika. We all know it. You weren't at first. You always liked her, but then something happened when you were visiting your folks during the holiday. Ever since you got back from that trip, you've been different. It took us a little while to notice—"

"Maybe three weeks," Jake interjected.

Damian frowned in thought then nodded. "I think it was a little less for Alexis, because, well, she's Alexis, but yeah, three weeks sounds about right."

Dominic stared at Damian, keeping his expression very carefully blank. They wanted a reaction from him, but they weren't going to get it. Yeah, he *thought* he was in love with Anika, too, but he also *knew* several other things. First, he'd never been in love before so wasn't sure if what he felt for Anika really was love or some weird manifestation of him *wanting* to be in love after spending time with his family. Second, it seemed to him that you couldn't really love someone unless they loved you back—he wasn't sure about this, but it seemed like it would be really hard to love someone unless you trusted them, but if they didn't love you back then could you really trust them with your heart? He didn't think so, and he didn't know how Anika felt about *him*. And third, there was no way in hell he was going to have this conversation with either Damian or Jake before he had it—or something like it—with Anika.

"Oh, he's playing the silent card," Jake stage whispered. "Should we let him get away with it?"

Damian fixed him with a hard stare, then slowly, he nodded. Letting his hand fall from Dominic's shoulder, Damian stepped back. "Yeah, we'll let him get away with it for now. Love is some heavy shit, and Charlotte just got home today so I'd rather go spend a few hours with her before my night shift begins than hang out and walk him through it."

"Hm, good point. I think Nia and I have dinner reservations in her bed tonight," Jake said. "Take out, of course. She likes those hush puppies from that Cajun place. She always says she doesn't want them, but then she eats all of mine. I've been on to her little MO for months, though, so I load my plate with two orders."

Damian turned and looked at Jake while Dominic shook his head and grinned at his friend's train of thought. Jake might be a pain in the ass sometimes, but most of the time, the way his train of thought went straight from his brain and out his mouth was pretty damn amusing.

"Get the shrimp," Dominic said. "She won't ever order them because the ingredients sound weird, but I guarantee you, she'll love them."

Jake's eyes lit up. "Nice, thanks for the recommendation. Have fun tonight, and I'll see you both tomorrow." He turned and, whistling, made his way to his car.

"What do you think he was like to parent?" Damian asked as they watched Jake leave.

"I have no idea, but I really, truly hope that when he has a kid, it's just like him because he'd like nothing better than to have a 24/7 companion as crazy as himself. Nia's pretty damn close, but not quite there."

Damian chuckled then slung his bag over his shoulder. "Good luck tonight. Let me know if you find anything interesting. You know I'll be up."

Dominic nodded then, once Damian was in his car and pulling out of the garage, he pulled out his phone and dialed a familiar number.

"Now isn't a great time, Dom," Anika answered by way of greeting.

"What's going on?" He could hear her walking and though she wouldn't have answered the phone if there'd been any physical danger, she did sound agitated.

"On my way to Maddox's office. He's going to push to close the cases. It doesn't help that we found out Khan's wife died about nine months ago in a car accident, courtesy of a drunk driver." He heard her push through some doors, but then she seemed to come to a stop.

"So textbook suicide? The guy's bereft by the death of his wife and decides to kill himself?"

"That's what the chief is pushing for." The reluctance was clear in her voice.

"Push him off one more day if you can," Dominic said.

"Might be easier said than done, but you sound like you might know something I don't. If you do, I could sure use the ammunition."

Dominic let out a frustrated breath as a clap of thunder filled the air. Looked like the daily rainstorm was starting. "I don't know anything specific yet," he said, then proceeded to tell her about the connection of the two victims to The Bank of DC. He didn't mention Matthews or Calloway since Shah had made it clear that she wanted that aspect of their investigation kept quiet.

"It might not change his mind," Anika said when Dominic finished.

"It might not, but it's worth a try," Dominic said as a gentle rain began to fall. He was standing in the open-air parking garage and his eyes were drawn to the greenery that ringed the building and was visible from where he stood. Having grown up in Louisiana, he'd experienced lots of thunderstorms, but there was something about the rain failing on the tropical greenery, giving life to the vibrant red, orange, and yellow flowers, that he found soothing.

"Anything is worth a try at this point," Anika muttered, then she took a deep breath. "Look, I have to go. If the chief gives us a reprieve, I'm going to need to be here all night trying to find a reason to keep the cases open."

Which meant he wouldn't see her. He was disappointed, but he had work to do as well so it was probably for the better.

"Good luck and keep me posted if you can. We can touch base tomorrow morning, and I can fill you in on anything we might find," he said.

She murmured something that he thought was agreement mixed in with a thanks, but then he heard Garza urging her to finish her call and she spoke more clearly. "Sounds good, talk to you tomorrow," she said, then ended the call.

Dominic slid his phone into his pocket and stood watching the rain, which had increased in intensity and was now creating a cacophony of percussion as the drops pelted the leaves and trees of the surrounding foliage.

He didn't know how Anika did it. He didn't know how she kept her professionalism, how she kept her commitment to being the best detective she could be when working in the environment that she did. Sure, he'd been in some obnoxious situations, especially when he'd first joined the Air Force. But once he'd made it onto the pararescue team, any hard time his teammates might have given him wasn't because of any inherent trait—like being Black. No, by then, every one of them had proven their value and worked as team, and it was just good plain ribbing.

He couldn't imagine what it would be like to be Anika and to know that every day, despite having proven herself over and over, she walked into the office where almost no one had her back for the simple reason that she was a woman. Sure, some of the techs and non-law enforcement personnel would support her, and Garza might go to bat for her, but taking their cue from the chief, almost no one else would. At least not publicly.

After pulling his phone from his pocket, he brought up the texting app and quickly typed in a message. *"You don't need me to tell you, but in case you* do *need to hear it, you're doing the right thing. No good comes from rushing an investigation. I hope those around you are as smart as you are."*

Presumably, she was still meeting with her boss and wouldn't be able to respond, so he slipped the phone back into his pocket and turned toward the office. If Anika needed ammo, he was going to get her ammo.

CHAPTER EIGHT

THE NEXT MORNING Dominic jogged across the street, dodging several safari taxis carrying tourists along the way. He'd tried to reach Anika earlier, but she hadn't been answering her phone. Instead of continuing to call, he'd decided to pop by the police station and see if he could catch her in person. He had news to share that he thought might make her happy, even if it made her life a little more complicated.

"Whoa," Dominic said as Anika came flying out the front door of the police station. He put his hands on her upper arms to steady her, then stilled. "Why are you in uniform?"

Anika's eyes narrowed at him and she spun away, muttering something about the "damn uniform," as she twisted and tried to adjust the fit.

He wasn't sure what was going on—other than Anika being pissed—so he did what came naturally, he tried to cheer her up. "You wear it well, though, Nik," he said with a grin.

She spun back and leveled a glare on him. He'd seen her use that glare a time or two, but not for a few months. She raised her hand and pointed at him, then dropped it, and turned away. Two seconds later she was back up in his face.

"You think I don't like this uniform because it makes my butt look big? I got news for you, Burel. I'm not on the catwalk and I don't give a rat's ass about how this uniform looks. But whoever designed it, whoever decided that it would be a good idea to make a uniform out of polyester for a police department in the tropics, deserves a special place in hell. You're from Louisiana, you should be familiar with the term 'swamp ass'." And with that, she swung back around and started down the steps to the street.

Dominic watched her long enough for her to hit the bottom step, then, with a note to himself not to try to joke around when Anika was well and truly pissed, he jogged down and joined her.

They walked for a couple of blocks before Dominic decided it was safe to speak again. "Want to tell me what happened?"

Anika was silent for another block, then, when they reached the edge of a park, she paused, took a deep breath, and focused her sapphire blue eyes on him. "I wouldn't go along with closing the cases, so Maddox put me back on the beat."

"That fucker." The words were out of Dominic's mouth before he'd even had a chance to think them. She didn't need to deal with his anger on top of trying to sort through hers. Thankfully, he had something that might cheer her up.

"Come with me," he said, taking her arm and turning her in the direction of the FBI office.

"Dominic, I can't. If I fuck this up, it's not going to be good." She'd taken a couple of steps, but then dug her heels in.

He turned to face her. She was biting her lip and her shoulders were so tense they were practically around her ears. Her body was stiff as a board. His tough, intrepid detective was barely holding it together.

He slid his sunglasses up and ducked his head a little bit to be sure she could see everything in his expression when he spoke his next words. "You were right, Detective Anderson," he said, emphasizing her title. "There's more to those deaths than an accident and a suicide. If you come with me, we can show you."

She pursed her lips and studied him. "Who's 'we'?"

"Me and the team. Including Director Shah."

She turned and focused on the park for a moment before she turned back. "I was right all along?"

He nodded.

"And you guys believed me?"

He nodded again. "Believed you and found some new evidence to back you up."

She took a shuddering breath and let it out slowly. He'd never seen Anika even close to tears, but he thought she might be now. Whether they were tears of frustration, anger, or relief, he didn't know, but as far as he was concerned, she was entitled to all three.

After a beat, she nodded. "Lead the way, then."

He fought the urge to take her hand. Her boss had already taken so much from her that he didn't want the gesture to be interpreted as him thinking she needed his support. She might, but she might not, and if she did need his support, he had other ways of showing her.

They walked in silence the remaining three blocks to the FBI office. When they stepped into the lobby, Steven, their receptionist stood.

"Detective Anderson, nice to see you again," he said.

Anika nodded in response, but Dominic spoke before she said anything. "We have a meeting with Director Shah. Anika, you'll need to hand your service weapon over to Steven. He'll lock it up until we're done."

Anika's eyes jumped to his. "I can't give you my weapon."

Again, he held her gaze. "Do you trust me?" He didn't like her slight hesitation, but she'd had a shit day so far, and it was only nine in the morning, so he'd overlook it. Finally, she nodded. "We don't allow anyone to carry weapons in the office except the team. It's protocol and policy. It will be here in the safe when we're done."

She hesitated again, then unsnapped the holster and slid her weapon out. After checking to make sure the safety was still on, she handed it over to Steven. Without a word, he used his palm and a complex code to open the safe below his desk then he slid the weapon inside and locked it back up.

"I'll buzz you in now," the receptionist said.

Dominic gestured for Anika to precede him and she pushed through the first door as soon as Steven released the lock. They walked down a short hallway and when they reached the end, he placed his hand on a scanner—they'd recently upgraded their security from key cards to biometrics—and the door to the office opened.

The door clicked shut behind them as Director Shah emerged from her office. She was holding a file in her hand, and her head came up at the sound of the door. Her eyes quickly took in the sight of the two of them, and Dominic knew it didn't take her long to figure out what had happened. Her gaze narrowed, then she gestured to Jake, who was standing by a conference room. In fact, all of his teammates were in the office and every one of them had their eyes on Anika and him.

"Agent McMullen, please follow up on that," she said, handing him the file. "Detective Anderson, Burel, in my office please."

She didn't wait to see if they'd follow and Anika threw him a quick, questioning glance before starting toward the door Shah had left open.

"Please close the door behind you," Shah said, taking a seat behind her desk when they joined her.

Dominic did as asked, then once Anika took a seat, he sat in the chair beside her.

"Maddox bumped you down to the beat because you pushed back, didn't he?" Shah said.

Anika nodded.

Dominic could only imagine what went through his director's head in the five seconds that followed—five seconds in which she neither moved nor spoke. No, scratch that, he couldn't imagine…there was a lot about Sunita Shah that was a mystery and he sometimes thought it was better that way.

"My team will officially be taking both cases over, Detective," Shah began. "As I'm sure Agent Burel told you, you were right to question the obvious. Here, take a look at this." Shah picked a file up and held it out.

Anika took, then opened, it. Dominic leaned over to read, there were a few things Shah could have given her, and he was curious which one she'd chosen.

"This is the autopsy of Hameed Khan. I only had preliminaries yesterday afternoon, how did you get this?" Anika asked.

Shah smiled. "Dr. Rasmussen and I play poker together. He did me a favor. Now what do you see?"

Anika's attention dropped back down to the file and she thumbed through a few pages before pausing. Several seconds ticked by before she raised her gaze. "There were no traces of the pills in his stomach contents."

Shah shook her head.

"Which means the ketamine got into his system in some other way."

It was a statement, not a question, but Shah nodded.

Shah held her hand out and Anika handed the file back over. "The most obvious way would be an injection," Shah said.

"But there weren't any injection…ah, there weren't any *obvious* injection sites," Anika said. "I can think of a few non-obvious ones, including pretty much anywhere there was significant body hair."

"And that's what I've asked Dr. Rasmussen to look into. I suspect he'll find it in the young man's armpit. The report said he was found with a water bottle in his hand."

"So, if he'd stopped to take a drink of water, it would have been easy to slip behind him, force his arm up more, and give a quick injection," Anika said.

Shah inclined her head. "That's what we're thinking but Dr. Rasmussen will confirm."

"I assume you have something on Taglia as well, but even so, two deaths doesn't really make it FBI jurisdiction," Anika pointed out.

"If that were all we had, it would be a stretch, but there's more. Both Taglia and Khan worked at the same bank prior to their current jobs. This morning, we received a list of accounts that both men worked on and there were more than a few names on that list that we're familiar with."

Despite Damian not committing to ask for help from his super hacker friends, he'd been bored in the middle of the night and had decided to reach out. Turned out two of them were night owls and by the time the team had walked into the office that morning, the duo had sent an encrypted list of sixty-two accounts that both Taglia and Khan had touched. They still didn't know how deeply either man had been involved in any of the accounts, but the fact that both Matthews and Calloway were on the list was enough for Shah.

Anika took a deep breath, everything in her body relaxing as she let it out slowly. "Good. I mean, not good in that it means those two men were murdered, but I'm glad you all are going to investigate and find out what happened."

"And you, if you agree," Shah said.

Anika blinked. "I beg your pardon."

"I'm under no illusions that what I'm about to offer you is anything other than a double-edged sword. We'd like to name you as the liaison between our team and the police department. It would mean that you are embedded with us for the duration of the investigation, but also have responsibilities to report back to your own department. It's a unique opportunity, but I think we both know it's not without its cost given who your chief currently is."

"I'm in," Anika said before Shah had even finished her sentence. "I know it will make my life hell once I go back, but honestly, it's not that great right now so I'd rather gain the experience you all are offering me and help close these cases the right way."

Again, a small smile flashed across Shah's face. "Then why don't you go home and change while I make the call and inform Chief Maddox."

Anika nodded. Her eyes met Dominic's when she rose from her seat. She looked a little nervous about the opportunity she'd just agreed to, but it was the excited kind of nervous and it brought a smile to his face.

Moving to the side so she could walk by, he reached for the door. They were almost through, when Shah called them back.

"And honestly, since I'm going to be on the phone already, who can I call about your uniforms? No one should have to wear synthetic fiber in the tropics when walking the beat."

CHAPTER NINE

After her meeting with Director Shah, Anika drove straight home, stripped out of her uniform, then took a quick shower before spending way too much time in front of her closet trying to decide what to wear. It wasn't every day that she had an opportunity to work with the FBI, and though she'd known all the agents for several months, having them as friends and working with them as colleagues were two different things.

She finally decided on a pair of light blue slacks, a white button-down shirt, and simple flats. She'd just slid her shoes on and was pulling her hair into a low ponytail, when a not-unexpected call came in.

"I heard a rumor, baby bird," her brother, Brody, said.

His voice made her smile. Her brothers, Brody, Colin, Adolphus, and West, might not be her brothers by birth, but they were ever the protective older brothers. "What rumor might that be? Because we've already talked about the ones about me and that BDSM club over on the other side of town."

Brody chuckled at that. "Nice, Anika. Is it true you're working with the FBI?"

Deciding to take the call on the road, she grabbed her keys and headed out. "Garza call you?"

"Yeah. Though why I'm hearing it from him and not you is another question."

"You're hearing it from him and not me because he's a gossip to the nth degree and rather than come talk to me, he has to go complain to you. But to answer your question, I am."

"You sure that's a good idea?" Brody was well aware of the struggles she faced at the department and the additional challenges taking this role would present.

She let out a long breath before answering. She'd never hidden anything from Brody before, and she didn't intend to start. "No, I'm not. This is an opportunity I can't pass up, though, Brod. The caliber of agent that Sunita Shah has on her team is a level of competence I may never have the opportunity to learn from, and work with, again. I have no doubt that Maddox will make my life miserable when this case is over, but as I told Director Shah this morning, it's already pretty bad. I may as well take the opportunities where I can. Maybe I'll move into private security at some point—I don't want to, but I have to be realistic—and this experience might help."

"And your decision doesn't have anything to do with Dominic Burel?"

The question took her aback for a split second. Then she barked out a laugh. "Dominic is the only one who trusted my gut enough to go to bat for me. No one in my own department did that. So yeah, my decision has a lot to do with Dominic Burel and the other agents who seem to respect me way more than the team I actually work with. But if you're asking if there's a personal reason? No, there's not. There isn't anything going on between the two of us and you know it. We enjoy each other's company, we're friends, now we're going to work together."

It wasn't quite as simple as that and they both knew it, but what she'd said hadn't been a lie.

"He wants to be more than friends, Anika, and you know it."

Anika rolled her eyes at that, not that he could see. Brody sounded just like Dominic when Dominic was talking to her about Mateo. Only she didn't feel the need to disabuse Brody of the idea in the same way she did Dominic, so instead, she changed the subject.

"Is Garza pissed? Not that I care too much, but it would be nice to know if I can expect him to shoot daggers at me the next time I see him."

"Yeah, he's mad, but I'm pretty sure it's because it means you'll be spending more time with Burel than with him."

"Right, it doesn't matter that I'm a good detective or that I deserve this because it was me who stood up to Maddox and took the hit for that. All that matters to him is that the woman he wants to fuck is now gone and he doesn't have access to me anymore." The words came out of her mouth before she could stop them, surprising herself and, no doubt, Brody. But in her heart, she knew she was right. If she tore off her blinders, it wasn't hard to see that Mateo treated her as if she was just playing at being a detective until she decided to settle down. She was good at her job, and he credited her with that, but it was always with the equivalent of a pat on the head, rather than the recognition she truly deserved.

It had been easier to deny Mateo's interest in her and defend her partner when Dominic brought it up than to admit the depth of frustration she felt in her job. Her instant reaction to Brody's words made it impossible to hide from the truth anymore. With the Band-Aid torn off and the confidence boost that Shah's invitation had given her, she was done playing the game. She was done defending men who weren't worth her defense.

Brody didn't bother to contradict her, but his loud sigh

before he spoke again conveyed his opinion of her judgment. "You'll be safe?"

And like it always had, her brother's concern wrapped around her like a warm blanket. "Yeah, I'll be safe," she promised. "Your birthday is next month, and you know I've been working on that epic glitter bomb with West."

"You better fucking not," her brother shot back. "I'm still finding confetti in my house from last year."

They ended the call as she pulled into the parking garage used by the team, and her brother's laughter had soothed her nerves before she exited her car and headed into the building. Now, at just past noon, she was back at the reception desk and Steve was going over some paperwork with her.

"Once you have these filled out," he said, handing her three forms. "We'll be able to get you access to the office so you don't have to be retrieved by one of the agents every time you arrive. It will also allow you to bring your own weapon inside so we don't have to go through the whole lock-it-up-in-a-safe every time you come in."

Anika nodded and took the papers and pen he offered. "I'm assuming you have everything you need in terms of running a background check and all?" She really didn't know if the team would need to run a check on her, but if she were in Shah's position, she would have.

"Already done," Steven said. "Director Shah ordered it this morning when she came into the office. Of course, she wasn't sure you would agree, but if you did, she wanted to be ready."

Anika snorted a laugh at that. "I think we both know she knew I'd agree, Steven."

Steven didn't say anything, but he did smile. A few minutes later, she handed back the completed forms and, after filing them away, the receptionist beckoned her to a small room situated to the right of the desk.

After getting her picture taken and her fingerprints and

palm prints scanned, she was officially considered a part of the team—temporarily, of course, but a part of the team, nonetheless. And she'd be lying if she said she didn't get a little thrill when Steven buzzed her into the first door and the scan of her own palm opened the second.

"Oh good, you're here," Dominic said, waving her toward his desk. Alexis, who was on the phone, waved, and Damian stood when she passed and gave her a dramatic welcome-aboard handshake that made her smile.

"Where are Beni and Jake?" she asked, setting her bag down and taking the seat Dominic pointed to at a desk to the left of his.

"They are both at Hemmeleigh for the day. We decided to run some impromptu situational exercises with the employees today," he answered before handing her a little Post-it. "Your login and temporary password to that computer," he said, gesturing to the PC on the desk. "We can't give you a laptop, but you'll have access to everything we have access to while you're here. Why don't you get set up and play around with what's on there now, including the case files we pulled. Once you've done that, we can talk about a game plan for moving forward."

She nodded and turned to the computer. A few minutes later, she was perusing the apps and databases she now had access to, some of which she'd worked with before and some of which were new. When she had a pretty good handle on the purpose and scope of each, she opened the full case files for Taglia and Khan that had been pre-loaded onto her machine and began to read through.

She lingered on the information about Bank of DC and the list of overlapping clients Taglia and Khan had had. Then she pulled up the information about the original investigation into the bank. She remembered reading about it when it had first happened but hadn't paid too much attention. Matthews had been implicated—along with about a dozen others—but since residents of the US Virgin Islands couldn't vote for president, she hadn't paid too much attention. Then, when Cunningham had come forward and said the scandal was nothing but a last-ditch effort to discredit her Democratic running mate, the whole thing seemed to die as quickly as it had arisen. With the bipartisan show of unity between Cunningham and Matthews, the press was left with very little to report.

Anika dug a little deeper into the files, figuring that regardless of what the politicians may or may not have said, if there was actual funneling of money to terrorists, the Department of Justice would have gotten involved, along with the FBI and several other federal agencies. When she opened the third file, she found her answer—three months after the election, the investigation closed with a finding of no wrongdoing.

She sat back in her chair and wondered if the initial investigation had just been a spurious attack on the Cunningham-Matthews ticket or if there had been actual wrongdoing that just hadn't been found. It was also interesting that the investigation closed around about the time both Taglia and Khan left the bank.

She swiveled her chair to ask Dominic about digging into what caused the two men to leave the bank when both their computers dinged with an incoming email message. She glanced at Dominic, then turned to her computer.

"Ah, just what we've been waiting for," Dominic said. "Confirmation that you were right all along."

Anika glanced at the subject and sender of the email then quickly clicked it open. The message was short but to the point, Khan had been injected with ketamine in his left armpit and had not ingested it. Anika had known it all along—not specifically that Khan had been injected, but that his death hadn't been self-induced. Even so, she couldn't help but feel relieved that what she'd suspected was now backed by evidence.

"So, what does this mean now?" she asked Dominic.

As she spoke, another message dinged, this one from Director Shah. It was a response to Rasmussen's email asking the doctor to re-examine Taglia's body and see if he could find anything to support the supposition that his fall had been assisted.

"Well, there's that," Dominic answered, gesturing with his head toward his computer where he'd obviously read the same message. "It might be harder to find something on Taglia, but it will be interesting to see."

"We never got around to tracking the movements of either Taglia or Khan," she said. "We know Taglia had dinner at the restaurant in the hotel before he died, same with Khan, but we don't know much about what they did in the days leading up to their deaths. Maybe it's time to pin that down?"

Dominic agreed and they split the task with her taking Khan and him taking Taglia. Shah and the team had already obtained warrants for credit card and cell phone information, so Anika dove right in and began making a timeline of Khan's activities from the day he arrived to the day he died.

Many of the days were relatively easy to track—he had an early breakfast at the hotel, then took a taxi to Gamba, the company where he was conducting the audit, and at a little past one in the afternoon, there was a lunch charge at some nearby restaurant, then an early dinner charge back at the hotel. She confirmed this schedule by placing a call to Gamba. They'd been shocked to learn of his death but had confirmed what his credit cards implied.

The weekend he'd spent on the island was a bit more difficult, but eventually she tracked down a personal credit card—rather than the business one he'd been using during the week—and found a couple of charges that led her to believe that he'd gone diving both days.

Again, she called the company that had run his card and they confirmed his attendance on the two all-day dives. The excursions had ended at four each day, and on Saturday, there'd been a charge at a bar near where the dive boat docked, though there was a dinner charge back at the hotel not long after. She assumed, then confirmed, that he'd gone for drinks with the rest of the folks who'd been on the dive that day before retiring to his hotel.

She was about to map the probable routes Khan would have taken to and from the hotel when her phone rang. Not recognizing the number, she considered letting it go to voicemail, but then decided she better answer.

"This is Detective Anderson," she said.

"Detective Anderson, this is Maryam Khan, Hameed Khan's sister."

Anika sat up in her chair. "Ms. Khan, how can I help you?"

"I'm not sure. I called the police station and they told me the case had been transferred to the FBI and that you were the person I should contact. I, well, I know it hasn't been very long, but I was hoping for an update. The man I spoke to yesterday said it looked like a suicide, but I can't believe that, so I'm calling again. I'm sorry, I don't mean to be a pest, but I truly just can't believe that."

Anika considered asking why, but the truth was, Maryam was right and why she thought the police were wrong about labeling her brother's death a suicide was no longer really relevant. "I don't know if this will put your mind at ease at all, but you are right, it wasn't a suicide. We just received confirmation that your brother's death was murder and due to resourcing issues, the FBI has taken the case over. I'll be working with them, though, to find out what happened to Hameed and who was responsible." She thought it best not to mention Taglia's death, but that didn't mean she couldn't ask about the bank.

"I'm sure this is a shock, but do you have a few minutes to answer some questions?" Anika asked gently.

Maryam was silent for a moment. "His death was, is, a shock, and while I think it will take some time to accept that someone killed my brother, at least the ridiculous notion that it was suicide is no longer being considered, and for that I am grateful. And if I can answer anything for you, I will."

Anika glanced over at Dominic, who was on his own phone facing toward the window with his back to her. "I saw that your brother joined the audit company he worked at a little over three years ago. Do you know why he took that job?"

"I...I don't actually. He'd been at the bank for almost nine years. I think he was recruited maybe? I know he wasn't actively looking for something new when the job came around. He liked working at the bank."

"Did he like his new job?"

Anika could hear the smile in Maryam's voice when she answered. "Yes, he did. Like I said, he wasn't actively looking for something new, but he was very happy when this role seemed to fall into his lap. He's always loved traveling—both he and Sumaya, before she died. She was a teacher, and when he traveled during the summer, she always went with him. Do you think his job had something to do with it?"

Anika shook her head even though the woman couldn't see. "We're exploring all lines of inquiry at the moment. His job was a big part of his life, so we have to look at that, too. If I give you my email, would you be able to send me a list of any of his close friends or others who might have insight into his life?"

"Of course. If you give it to me now, I can put that together." Anika rattled off her new FBI temporary email and after inquiring how Maryam and Hameed's father was faring with the news, the two ended the call.

"Was that Khan's sister?" Dominic asked, having finished his own call.

She nodded and glanced out the window, surprised to see that the light was already changing. Looking at the clock on her computer, she realized she and Dominic had been at their respective tasks for over four hours and it was now nearing five.

She made a few notes, then, shutting her notebook, she quickly summarized her conversation with Maryam for Dom. When she finished, he asked what she'd found during the day and she walked him through what she'd learned about Khan's movements, so far.

"It's interesting that Khan's sister said that the job sort of fell into her brother's lap," Dominic said. "We were having trouble getting Loose Ends—the production company Taglia worked at—to call us back so Jake called in a favor and had an agent stop by. I just finished the call with him and it seems Taglia was headhunted off of his professional social media page. A recruiter that works for the company hired by the production studio brought him in. While his background was unusual for them, they'd liked him immediately and he was hired within four weeks of when the recruiter first reached out to him."

Anika frowned. She didn't know much about how the corporate world worked on the mainland so wasn't sure if, within a month of each other, having two jobs fall into the laps of the two men who had been murdered was common.

"How many employees does The Bank of DC have?" she asked.

"A little over three thousand," Dominic answered. "And if you're thinking what I think you're thinking, then I agree, it is a little weird to have two mid-level employees essentially have dream jobs offered to them at basically the same time and then to have them both end up murdered here."

"What was the name of the recruiting firm that found Taglia?"

"Here," Dominic handed over the paper where he'd written the name and an address in New York City. Neither looked familiar to her.

"You going to call them?" she asked.

Dominic glanced at the clock on the wall then shook his head. "It's five minutes to five, they'll be closing up soon. I'll give them a call tomorrow. How about a workout then dinner?" he asked.

"I could use a good work out," she mulled over out loud. Tomorrow was one of the usual days she and Dominic met up, but with the stress of the last two days, going a couple rounds with weights and maybe a kickboxing session sounded like a good idea.

"Let's do it. I'd rather go to Grecko's than Fins or Harvest and Honey, though," she said referring to the beach café in their complex rather than either of the restaurants.

"Sounds like a plan," Dominic said, shutting his computer down. "I think I might owe Sandra twenty bucks," he added.

"You forget to pay one night? I can't imagine she'd let you get away with that," Anika said, shutting her own computer down. Sandra was the usual bartender at Grecko's. She was good with the tourists who rented condos at the complex, but only the full-timers ever got to see her true snarkiness.

"Ha, no way would she let me get away that. No, I bet against her in a shots contest after hours one night. She and Roxy decided they'd have a show down. I bet on the wrong woman."

Roxy was Sandra's wife and despite being in their mid-thirties, they still occasionally acted like women in their early twenties—probably not unlike they had been when they'd first met in college. "You seriously bet against Sandra?" Anika asked as they left the office. "Even Roxy never bets against Sandra."

"My only excuse is that I'd had a few myself, and I'm pretty sure Roxy egged me on to do it knowing that she'd get my twenty dollars either way, but that it would also give Sandra something to gloat over with me."

Anika laughed. "Yeah, that sounds like Roxy. Meet at the gym in forty-five minutes?" she asked when they stepped out onto the ground level.

"Sounds good and bring your gloves. I'm in the mood to hit a few things."

Anika lowered herself into a chair facing the ocean at the open-air beach café. She and Dominic had had a good bout at the gym, and she'd be sore tomorrow, but it felt good to use her body and get out of her head for a little while.

"Hey, sorry I'm late," Dominic said, jogging up the path toward her. When he slowed to a walk, she couldn't help but admire the way his shorts and shirt fit, or the grace of his movements when he wound his way through the café to the table she'd grabbed.

"My mom called as I was walking out the door," he said, taking the seat opposite.

"I just got here, though I placed our usual order before I grabbed a seat, so hope you don't mind the executive decision-making."

He shook his head as Sandra brought over a couple of beers. Without a word, Dominic pulled twenty bucks from his wallet and handed it over. "I still think you and Roxy fixed that competition," he muttered.

Sandra grinned. "I'm not admitting to anything, but I wouldn't put it past us either. Your platter will be here shortly," she added before leaving them to return to her bar.

They made casual chit chat as they waited for the mixed platter they usually ordered to arrive. It was filled with everything from fried plantains to mango salad to conch fritters—a little healthy, a little unhealthy, and a whole lot of goodness—and it was perfect for sharing.

They talked about everything and nothing and occasionally lapsed into a comfortable silence when they watched families and couples who'd rented condos for the night or the week walk along the pristine beach. The moon rose overhead, and a gentle breeze came in off the water as a toddler frolicked in the ocean's edge. Anika knew that this night was one of those tiny inconsequential nights that would become a memory of a lifetime—there were no revelations or no big events, but a quiet sort of peace and beauty that filled her senses.

"You want another?" Dominic asked, pointing to her drink. His voice was quiet in the late evening darkness, his face lit by the gentle lights of the bar. She glanced at her nearly empty glass and though she didn't want the night to end, she also didn't want a third beer. Except on rare occasions, she tended to draw the line at two drinks.

She started to shake her head when her attention caught on a young couple stumbling into the café. Her gaze held and she catalogued their behavior. They looked in their early twenties and on closer inspection, were probably brother and sister rather than a couple. Thankfully, their giddiness seemed to have more to do with excitement of being on vacation than being drunk.

She was about to return her attention to Dominic when the young woman looked up and met Anika's gaze. With no explanation as to why, Anika found it hard to look away. Maybe it was the way the woman's eyes widened in surprise or maybe it was the way she almost frantically reached for the young man, but for whatever reason, Anika's attention remained fixed on the pair.

The two leaned toward each other and whispered something, neither taking their eyes off her. Then the woman, reached into her large purse and pulled out a file. Flipping it open, the two appeared to be examining something as they continued to talk. After a beat, they both looked up at the same time, as if a string had pulled their gazes up.

"Nik?" Dominic asked.

Anika heard him, she really did, but so caught up in

watching the pair—the pair that were now walking toward her—she didn't answer.

Slowly but surely, the two made their way through the café. When they stopped a few feet away, Anika realized why they'd caught her attention. She hadn't been able to make it out before—though obviously her subconscious had—but the two had the exact same eyes as she—same shape, same color.

"Excuse me," the woman said, then hesitated. "Are you Detective Anika Anderson?"

Anika hesitated, too, then nodded.

"See, I told you, Brett," the woman said, her face splitting into a huge smile.

"Don't freak her out, Eva," the young man said, taking the folder from his companion. "I'm Brett Riley and this is my twin sister Eva. We, ah…this is a little bit weird—"

"Give her the file," Eva said, tugging her brother's arm.

"The file?" Anika asked.

Brett cleared his throat then, with hands that trembled a little bit, he held out the folder. "This is, well, I'm not really sure how to say this, but—"

"Just read it," Eva interjected. "When you have the time that is. I mean, I don't mean to be weird, or any weirder than this already is. But please—"

"Just have a look inside. There are contact numbers in a couple of different places and for a few different people," Brett cut his sister off. "Please…please contact us. If you don't, we'll respect that. If you do, we'd all really, really like it." And with that, Brett Riley all but dragged his sister away. If they'd been coming to get food, they skipped that part and made a beeline for the exit.

"What was that about?" Dominic asked.

Anika tore her attention from the two departing figures and glanced at her friend. She had an idea, but it was so unbelievable that she couldn't even bring herself to say it. Instead, she opened the file and picked up the first page.

In her job, Anika had seen any number of people pale in surprise at bad news. But never before had *she* felt all the blood drain from her face. She closed her eyes in an effort to stave away the dizziness. Dominic's hand covered her free one. It was warm and steady and filled with concern, but at the moment, she didn't know what to do with that.

"I need to get out of here," she said, opening her eyes and meeting Dominic's worried gaze. His hand tightened on hers.

"Nik, talk to me."

She opened her mouth then froze in uncertainty.

"Nik?"

"I think…" She paused, took a deep breath, and fixed her gaze on Dominic, anchoring herself with his strength. "I think that was my half-brother and sister."

CHAPTER TEN

INVOLUNTARILY, Dominic's hand twitched as it still covered Anika's. He'd always known she was adopted—she looked like a miniature Nordic goddess with her sapphire blue eyes, very fair complexion, and white-blond hair, while her father, Philip Anderson, and Anika's four brothers, were darker than he was. Not to mention she barely topped out at five foot two and her father and brothers were all big men, each clocking in at six-feet-two or more. But he'd never asked her how her family had come to be, and she'd never offered. Now, as he saw the shock on her face, he wondered how much of that story she even knew herself.

"Take the file and go sit at our bench," he said, referring to a little bench that was tucked away in the foliage that only a few of the full-timers, and none of the tourists, knew about. "I'll wrap up with Sandra."

The look in her eyes was slightly wild and he could all but feel the edge of panic creeping into her body. He squeezed her hand and held her gaze. "It will be okay, I promise. Just promise me you will wait for me at the bench?"

She hesitated, then nodded. With jerky movements, she rose

and quickly fled with the file. Grabbing the purse she'd left behind, he approached the bar.

"She okay?" Sandra asked as she dried a glass and set it upside down on the counter.

"Maybe, maybe not," Dominic answered.

"Signing out?"

He nodded, his eyes drifting to the exit. He hoped Anika was where he had asked her to be, but if he were honest with himself, he only half-expected to find her there when he arrived.

"Here you go," Sandra said, sliding the piece of paper over. One of the perks of living in the complex was that all owners could have restaurant charges added to a monthly bill rather than having to pay each time.

Without even glancing at the tab, he added a tip, signed, and handed it back. He was almost to the door when he heard Sandra tell him to let her know if there was anything she could do. He waved in acknowledgement of her offer and walked toward the bench.

He let out a breath of relief when he saw her sitting where she'd said she'd be. Her head was bowed, and the folder Eva and Brett Riley had given her was open on her lap. In one hand she was holding what looked like a piece of paper, maybe a letter, and in the other a photo. Without a word, he took a seat next to her.

The minutes ticked by and she continued to thumb through the contents of the file. Turning her attention back to the letter, she seemed to read it—possibly for the second or third time—then her hands fell to her lap and her eyelids drifted closed.

"I have a father," she said quietly. "He didn't know about me."

Gently, Dominic put the paper back in the file, closed it and took Anika's hand in his. "Talk to me."

She took three measured breaths then opened her eyes and faced him. "I'm sure you've figured out that my dad, Phil, isn't my biological dad. I mean, I always knew I had one," she said gesturing to the folder, "But I never knew anything about him, not even his name. My mother and Phil had been married at one point—I think they got married when I was two then divorced three years later. Six months after that, she abandoned me at a mall in Texas but left a note that told CPS to find him."

There was so much in that statement that both broke his heart and raised so many questions. Questions that would have to wait because it wasn't the time or place to interrupt. Instead of saying anything, he simply wrapped both his hands around hers and let her talk.

"She left me at a mall. She sat me down on a bench, not unlike the one we're sitting on now. She told me to sit like a good girl and soon someone would be along to get me. She'd left me before, dozens of times, so it didn't strike me as odd. She'd left me with a small bag that had some food and water and my favorite books." She paused, her mind back in that time. "I had just learned to read, and she'd packed four of my favorite books.

"I don't know how much time passed—kids aren't the greatest with time—but eventually, a security guard came up to me and asked where my parents were. I remember telling him that my mom had left and said someone would be by to get me. In retrospect, I'm sure she meant the guard, or one of his colleagues."

She paused again and a frown flitted on her lips as her gaze drifted to the small glimpse of the moonlit ocean. "I don't remember the specifics after that, only that the guard brought me to an office and eventually someone from CPS came. I suppose they tried to find my mom during that time, but I don't remember."

"Did they find the note she'd left?" he asked.

Anika nodded. "They did, but they didn't know who Phil was. My mom was married to someone else when I was born, so she was listed with that name. I don't know if CPS just never looked, or if they couldn't find her marriage certificate that would have had her maiden name. And there was no father listed for me." Anika inhaled deeply then let it out slowly. "So, they couldn't track my mother or identify who her kin might be, they had no idea who my paternal family might be, and Phil was a mystery, since there was no record of him being in Texas. I ended up going into foster care."

Dominic didn't think his heart could break any more than it had a few minutes earlier, but the idea of Anika as a confused, abandoned child tore at him. He'd known she had a back story—everyone did—but he hadn't imagined hers to be like this.

"But they found Phil eventually?" he asked.

Again, she nodded. "I was in and out of different foster homes for three years before Phil happened to come back to Texas and when an employer ran a check on him before hiring him to do some work on one of the oil rigs, the CPS flag came up. He told me that once he spoke to the CPS case worker, there'd never been any hesitation. He wasn't my biological father, but he'd always loved me as his own, so he started adoption proceedings that month. Eventually, he was able to bring me to Tildas and make me part of his family."

"That couldn't have been easy."

She cast him a wan smile. "It was easier than you'd think. Phil was familiar to me, and I clung to that familiar-ness once he was back in my life. As for Brody, Collin, Adolphus, and West, well, they got a little sister who, as tiny as I was, not only *looked* like I needed their protection, but actually *did* need them—not their protection, per se, but I needed people on my side and, with Phil as their father, it's in their blood to step into that role."

Surprisingly, Dominic could easily see that. The Anderson brothers were well respected on the island, and the family was tight. He wasn't sure what had led Phil to leaving them in the first place and going to Texas where he must have met Anika's mom, but Phil was, for all intents and purposes, a model parent and the biggest evidence of that was in the five kids he'd raised.

Dominic rubbed her hand with his thumb. "Phil never knew anything about your mom?"

Anika shook her head. "He knew the name she had when they married, but it was the same name as what was on my birth certificate. He also said she never talked about her family, so he'd always assumed she had none. When I was a teenager, we talked about her—about the situation—and he asked if I wanted to try to find her. I declined because, at that point, Phil and my brothers *were* my family. I might occasionally have a passing curiosity about her, but then I always figure it isn't worth my time to dredge up my past. I have family, I have friends, a job I like…I'm not going to lie and say I don't have *any* issues from my early childhood years, but I have a life I like and family I love. There didn't seem to be anything to gain from finding her either then or now. If she was even findable."

Dominic didn't know what to say to that, but then again, maybe there wasn't anything that he *needed* to say. What was most important was that Anika knew he was there for her.

"Tell me about your family, Dom," she said, surprising him.

"My family?"

Her gaze met his again, and she gave him a tentative smile. "We've never talked about our families. You've met mine, or at least the family I know. What about yours?"

For a microsecond, he considered giving her the abbreviated version, the recitation of facts. But that wasn't what she was asking, and, in this moment, he would give her anything.

Flashing her a smile, he told her everything. He told her about his upbringing, about his professor of a father, his mother who'd made a name for herself as one of the most beloved Louisiana chefs, about his successful sisters and their husbands, and most importantly, for the first time, he talked about what had happened during his trip home over the holidays. He talked about the stark fear he'd felt, the relief, and the longing to have someone with whom to share the burden—and the joys.

She asked a few questions along the way and at some point, he pulled out his phone to show her some photos. She smiled when she saw his parents, ooo'd over a picture of Pamela at a gala, dressed in some designer gown, and laughed when she saw the picture of Katherine shoving cake in her husband's mouth at their wedding.

It was long past the time when most families had gone to bed when quiet finally fell over them. The gentle lapping of the waves combined with the rustle of the palm tree leaves was all they could hear in the dark of the night, and in the relative quiet, Dominic slipped an arm around Anika and pulled her against him. She laid her head down on his shoulder and, together, they let the night air, carry away some of the weight of their conversation. Only they weren't done yet.

"Do you want to tell me what's in the folder now?" he asked.

Anika sighed and he could feel her breath whisper across his shirt, her head still tucked against him. Laying a hand on top of the file, she answered. "I don't know the whole story, but it's a letter from my birth father and several family photos. He says he didn't know about me until a few months ago and he's been looking for me ever since. He's married now and has the twins, who we met. As soon as he learned about me, he and his wife hired a PI to track me down. They found me here and all came down to try and meet me. They picked our complex to rent a condo in because the PI knew I lived here."

"And the pictures?"

"Of my mother when she was younger. I look just like her, but I have his eyes. The same eyes the twins have." She opened the file and pulled out a picture. In it, were a young couple, definitely high school aged. The boy had Anika's blue eyes—or she had his—but she was right, there was no denying the resemblance between the young woman and Anika. Dominic flipped the photo over and read the names, Brian Riley and Leanne Bowman, and the caption "Prom, junior year."

"I guess he thought I might need some convincing," she said, taking the photo back and sliding it into the folder.

He rubbed her shoulder, then dropped a kiss on the top of her head. "You don't have to decide anything right now. They've known about you for a few months and have gone to the effort of hiring a PI to find you. Those actions strike me as those of a man—of a family—that would be more than willing to give you the time you need to decide if you are up to meeting them."

She was still for a long moment, then she nodded against his shoulder. "All this time," she said, her voice barely louder than a whisper. "I assumed he'd left me. I'd assumed they'd all left me— my mom, my biological father, any grandparents I might have. I think it might take me a little while to understand, and maybe even longer to accept, that it's possible they didn't leave me at all. After all, you can't choose to leave something you never knew you had."

CHAPTER ELEVEN

It was ten o'clock the next morning when Dominic walked into the office. He'd had to stop by Hemmeleigh before joining his teammates, and as he walked in, he caught a glimpse of Anika in Shah's office. Her back was to him, and she was standing and talking to the Director, who was seated at her desk. The conversation looked serious, but not dire, and though his curiosity spiked, he forced himself to keep walking to his desk because neither woman would appreciate his interference.

"What's up with that?" Dominic gestured with his head toward the office when he passed Jake and Beni's desks.

"No idea," Beni said. "But if we needed to know, we'd know."

Dominic cast Jake a knowing look. For as badass as Beni was, she was also sometimes the biggest buzz kill.

"I disagree," Jake said. Beni's gaze swung up to look at him as Dominic pulled his computer out of his bag and took his seat. "I think if they were plotting to take over the world, or maybe forming a new professional group of women under the height of five-two who could seriously kick your ass, we should know, but they wouldn't tell us."

Dominic's gaze flitted to Beni as he docked his computer and powered it up.

After a beat, she nodded. "Fair point, but I'm pretty sure they're talking about the case."

As soon as Beni had finished her sentence, the door opened, and Anika walked out. "Hey Dom," she said, walking toward him—or more likely toward her desk that sat beside his.

"Hey Nik," he responded.

Jake's head snapped up and he spun in his chair, to face both him and Anika. "You guys have the perfect couple name. Has anyone ever told you that? I mean, think about it, Dom-n-Nik... like Dominic. It's genius."

Anika paused at her desk and cast Dominic a questioning look. She'd spent time with Jake before, but she'd never been blessed with the full Jake-effect of being with him eight-plus hours a day.

"Do you want to do the honors, Dom?" Beni asked, her eyes back on her computer.

"Yeah, I got this," he said, then swung his gaze to his best friend. "You know you're an asshole, right?"

Jake gave a dramatic gasp. "I know you love me, so I'll forgive you, but seriously, Nia and I have been trying to come up with our couple-name for months and as close as we get to something cool is Jaia. But you guys, seriously, it's perfect. Right-out-of-the-box perfect."

"This is what I missed just being on social terms with him, isn't it?" Anika asked, taking a seat and bringing her computer to life.

"He's special," Beni said. "And I don't mean always in a good way, but he's right, we do love him. Mostly because he brings Nia around and she's awesome."

"Hmm," Jake said, "Can't argue with you there. Nia's definitely *way* cooler than me to hang out with."

"So, anyone got anything?" Dominic asked in an effort to bring the conversation back around to something work related.

"I finally got ahold of Taglia's doctor yesterday, thanks to Jake's friend putting a little pressure on him," Anika said. "He swears he never prescribed sleeping pills. He emailed over Taglia's records, and they correspond with what he told me, and he couldn't explain how the label ended up with his name on it."

"Someone else from his office?" Dominic suggested.

Anika wagged her head. "He seemed on the up and up and when I suggested that, he didn't sound happy. Not mad at me, but mad that it was a possibility someone in his office had breached protocol—and broken the law—and he said he'd look into it."

"We should call the pharmacy that prepared the meds and check with them, too," Beni said.

Anika nodded. "Yeah, I did that as soon as I spoke to the doctor. It was too early for the pharmacy to be open, but I left a message."

"Any news on Taglia's autopsy?" Dominic asked.

"Got it here," Jake said, holding up the file, before handing it over. "Unfortunately, unlike Khan, who was pretty easy to spot as a murder once we knew what we were looking for, Taglia is a bit more nuanced."

"Not your strong point," Beni muttered under breath.

"Ha, that's where you're wrong, woman," Jake exclaimed. "Take a look at this." He rotated his computer screen so the three of them could see it, then he typed in a few commands. When he finished, a rough rendering of a man—Taglia—standing on the edge of a building filled the screen.

"What are we looking at?" Beni asked, leaning forward and scooting her chair closer.

"What you are looking at is a simulation of Taglia's fall from the roof into the dumpster," Jake answered. As they watched, he hit a button and the illustration of the man fell forward into the dumpster. Once the body was inert, the program began highlighting where the likely injuries would have been by lighting up parts of the "body" in red. Only about half of which matched Taglia's actual injuries.

"What the fuck?" Dominic murmured.

"Did you do this, Jake?" Anika asked.

Jake nodded. "But it's not over yet." He hit a few more keys and they were back to the original image, or at least close to. This time, there was a simulation of a second person "throwing" Taglia over the edge, though it was more of a tip-and-drop than an actual throw.

When the body landed in the graphical dumpster, it once again began highlighting likely injuries, and this time, more than ninety percent of them matched Taglia's actual injuries.

Silence filled the room, and Dominic, at a loss as to what to say, heard nothing but the clock tick until Beni sat back in her chair and let out a low whistle. "I got to admit, Jakey, when you impress, you really impress. Where did you learn that?"

Jake shrugged. "Nia has to do a lot of modeling and data visualization for her job and we've been playing around with it."

Dominic glanced back at the screen and thought that Jake and Nia were doing a little more than "playing around." Sure, Nia had to do all sorts of ocean modeling for her job at the Research Center, but not quite in the same way as what Jake had produced.

"I sent it to Dr. Rasmussen this morning and he concurred with the modeling," Jake said.

"So most likely, someone dumped Taglia off the roof once he'd taken enough sleeping pills to make him groggy," Anika said.

"It aligns with your theory, Nik," Dominic said.

"Yeah, but how'd he get the sleeping pills in him in the first place?" Beni asked. "Unlike Khan, he had remnants of pills in his stomach, so we know he swallowed them."

They all stared at the computer screen, the graphical image of the body lying in the dumpster face down.

"That, I don't know," Jake said, abruptly closing the program and rotating the screen to its original position. "But I think it's safe to say he was dropped from the roof, rather than jumped. The rest I will leave to you." He punctuated his last statement with a dramatically regal wave.

Dominic snorted and both Beni and Anika rolled their seats back to their desks.

"You are the nosiest person I have ever met, Jake McMullen," Beni said. "I give you twenty minutes, thirty tops, until you start hypothesizing about how Taglia got those pills into his system."

"I say fifteen," Anika interjected.

"Bet?" Beni said.

"You're on," Anika responded. "Dinner at Fins?"

Rather than answer, Beni held her hand out over her shoulder and Anika leaned forward and gave her not-quite-high five to seal the deal.

"So that's one line of inquiry. What about the Bank?" Dominic asked.

"Seriously, Burel," Jake said with yet another dramatic gesture—this time it was an eye roll. "We can't be wasting our time updating you all the time."

"Yeah, speaking of which," Beni said, swiveling her chair around. "What happened at Hemmeleigh this morning?"

Not much had happened and Dominic perused his email while he answered. "As you know, we decided we didn't like that the current company wasn't aware of such a glaring deficiency in their system, so a new company came down today." He paused and turned to Anika to give her a brief update and bring her up to speed about the issue with the cameras. It wasn't part of her investigation, but if she was going to be hanging around the office, she'd inevitably hear updates on the goings on at Hemmeleigh and it would be rude to keep her entirely out of the loop. "We had a glitch with some of the cameras. Rather than ask the company to come fix them, we decided to hire a security firm that Damian's worked with to come in and replace the system. They don't have any brand loyalty, and no sales commissions are at stake, so we thought they'd be more impartial than the other company, and just install the best product."

Anika nodded. "So, they were here this morning?"

"Yeah, four of them," Dominic said, turning his attention back to his inbox. "The system is all set up and functioning the way it should. We ran a couple of tests and stress tests, and it did its job. I don't think we'll have to worry about it."

Anika had been typing while he'd been speaking and when he finished, she turned to say something, but was cut off when her phone rang. Glancing at the number, she frowned and picked up the device.

"Hey, Garza," she answered.

Dominic couldn't help it, but his attention zeroed in on her. If she'd been interested in Garza, she would have acted on it long ago, so Dominic was sure there was nothing but a friendly professionalism between the two, but even so, the guy bugged him.

"What time?" she asked, scribbling something on a piece of paper. Then after a beat when Garza must have answered, she asked, "Is Rasmussen there?"

Well shit, there was only one reason Dr. Rasmussen would be called out. Dominic straightened in his chair as Beni and Jake swiveled to face Anika. By the time she was done with her call, she had three FBI agents waiting with bated breath.

"Another DB," she said. "This time out at Seasons on the West Side," she said without prompting.

"What made Garza call you?" Dominic asked.

"The guy looks like he died while attempting autoerotic asphyxiation, but after I sent over my report outlining the leads we're following with respects to Taglia, as well as Khan's cause and method of death, Garza didn't want to assume that something that looked like one cause of death was, in fact, the cause of death. He decided to err on the side of caution and call."

"For once, he's playing it smart," Dominic said, rising from his seat.

"Or Dr. Rasmussen told him to call us," Anika added a much more likely explanation.

"You guys want company?" Jake asked.

Dominic shook his head. "Nah, we got this. Can you keep looking into the DC Bank connection? As soon as we know the victim's name, I'll text it to you and we can see if he fits in the picture."

"I can do you one better than that, Burel," Anika said, holding up her phone. "Garza texted his driver's license and business card. His name is Jason Grant and he's an account manager at The Bank of DC."

Dominic navigated his car out of the parking garage and toward the road that would take them west to Seasons, a small resort filled with bungalows and no one under the age of twenty-one. Anika had attended a wedding there once, years ago, but hadn't been back since. She'd heard the restaurant was nice, but honestly, despite not having any kids herself, she wasn't a fan of places that didn't allow them. Chalk it up to being raised in a large family where family was everything.

"Is Garza going to stick around?" Dominic asked. She was sitting beside him in the passenger seat, and she shot him a quick look to see if the question was coming from FBI Dominic or Snarky-Friend Dominic. It appeared to be the former, so she let her gaze drift back to the scenery and answered.

"Yes. If we don't think it's part of whatever is going on, and it lands back on his desk, he wanted to be there." Dominic made a few turns, dodged some tourists, and merged onto the road that would take them west. They were leaving the outskirts of town when she spoke again. "What *do* you think is going on?" she asked. Then before he could answer, she clarified. "I mean, we suspect it has something to do with The Bank of DC, and if there was something going on with one or more of the accounts that the victims were involved in, I could see why someone would want to eliminate anyone who might be a loose end. It's the Tildas Island connection that I don't understand, and I think we all know there is a connection. We might not have found it yet, and when there were only *two* bodies it was still possible to consider it a coincidence. But with three?" She shook her head. "No, someone went to a lot of trouble not just to kill the three men, but to kill them *here*."

She was curious about what Dominic thought, but she also understood that he, like she, didn't have any answers, so when he didn't answer right away, she settled into a comfortable silence and watched the scenery.

They were halfway to the resort, which was situated forty minutes from the FBI office, when Dominic answered. "You know, the team has been here for over a year and part of prepping for The Summit is getting to know the lay of the land, so to speak. In fact, that's why they sent us down here in the first place. There's always been a small FBI presence on the island, but when the Organization of World Leaders selected Tildas as the location of the event, the government realized they were lacking in any significant intel on the area and that's how the task force came about.

"Since coming, we've done all the things we need to be doing to secure Hemmeleigh as the host resort, but we've also spent countless hours gathering intel on the island, and more specifically its criminal elements. The weird thing is, sure the island has a fair bit of petty crime and an occasional murder, but for the most part, its crime rate is pretty low compared to other similarly situated cities."

"I hear a 'but' in there," Anika prompted.

"But there have been a few weird cases, like the one Nia was involved in last fall when we met you..." Dominic's voice trailed off, then he shook his head, as if shaking off a memory or a cobweb. "Anyway, first there was the potential misdirection of World Bank funds. Technically, that wasn't on Tildas Island, but it was in the region. Then we had someone selling out CIA asset identities, which, again, didn't really happen on Tildas, but we ended up uncovering, and ending, a human trafficking ring on the island. Then there was the drug manufacturing that Nia's stoned fish led us to." He paused again and waited for a car to pass before turning into the entrance of Seasons Resort. "The cases all had a little something, well, I'm not sure what to call it other than that they didn't seem to fit with the intel we were gathering about the island and surrounding area."

"And now there's been two, maybe three, deaths that, although we're keeping an open mind, are probably being carried out by a hitman for a reason we haven't uncovered yet," Anika said. "And once again, the crime is taking place on Tildas Island, and there's something about it—like the fact that the victims are all here at the same time—that doesn't fit."

Dominic nodded and pulled into a spot. "When put like that, I think the thing that ties all these cases together, is that they don't fit—not together and not with Tildas Island's regular crimes."

"Except that that isn't the only thing that ties them together. Apparently, Duncan Calloway, and maybe Calvin Matthews, might be the common thread," Anika said.

Dominic made a face at her as he locked the car then they walked toward the reception. "I don't want to admit it, because I like Matthews—I want to go on thinking he and Cunningham are the first real statesman and stateswoman we've had in office in decades—but you're right."

"I might be right about Calloway and Matthews, but that still doesn't answer the question of *why Tildas?*"

And it was a question they'd have to set aside because the second they walked into the lobby, the manager of the resort, as evidenced by her name tag, rushed out to greet them. As she walked them to the bungalow, she kept up a constant state of chatter that ranged from trying to sell them on the magnificence of the resort to all but begging them to remove the body of Jason Grant as quickly and as quietly as possible.

"Thank you, Florence," Anika said when they came to a stop in front of Grant's bungalow. "We'll take it from here."

The manager's gaze flitted to the door and she chewed her lower lip. Anika could feel the woman's hesitancy—no doubt she wanted them to do their job as efficiently as possible, but she also wanted to be able to run interference with the other guests, should the activity at the bungalow start to draw attention.

"We will need your guest list before we leave, please," Anika added, fixing the woman with a look that brokered no argument. She didn't want to come across as antagonistic, but she also wasn't about to have this woman hanging around what was, most likely, a crime scene.

"His girlfriend was supposed to arrive today…or I guess she still is?" Florence's statement came out as a question. "I don't know what airline, but he asked for the shuttle to take him there to meet her at two-thirty today."

"Thank you, Florence. That's the kind of information that's helpful. When we're done here, would you mind sitting down with us?" Dominic asked, then flashed her a grin—a sympathetic and entirely appropriate-to-the-situation grin, but Dominic's grins should be studied for mind control purposes as far as Anika was concerned.

And, to absolutely no one's surprise, Florence bobbed her head, then turned on her heel and left them standing at the bottom of the stairs.

"That's a handy trick you have there, big guy," Anika said, rolling her eyes.

He smiled at her, his real smile. "Hey, if you got it, there's no point in not using it."

She shook her head to hide her own smile then proceeded up the three steps to the bungalow's lanai. They'd passed eight similar buildings on their way to the scene, each with a view of the water, a large lanai, and complete privacy. She still wasn't buying into the no-kids policy, but it wasn't hard to see the appeal.

"Garza, Dr. Rasmussen, what have we got here?" she asked, stepping into the room. Garza's attention lingered on Dominic, then came back to her.

"Like I said, looks like auto-erotic asphyxiation gone wrong, but I guess you'll have to tell us," Mateo said.

Dr. Rasmussen glanced at Mateo, before turning his attention to her and Dominic. "It appears that he used a tie from one of the complimentary resort robes and tied it to the bed. There is evidence of recent sexual activity, so it's possible someone else was controlling the tightness."

Anika took in the scene as the doctor spoke. Jason Grant was a thirty-six-year-old man who had, in life, likely been good looking. He had brown hair that fell just so, and his body looked fit in the way that corporate men who go to the gym do. He was lying with his head near the headboard and twisted in an awkward angle as most of his naked body laid sprawled over the edge of the bed, his feet resting on the polished wood floor.

"So, he was having sex with someone, they were playing around with asphyxiation then what? She, or he, took the opportunity to turn something sexual into something deadly?" Dominic asked.

"Mostly that's for you to find out," Dr. Rasmussen said. "But the reason I had Garza call you was because there are no signs of struggle. If someone started to strangle me to death I'd struggle, no matter how pleasurable it might have been to a point. It's a body's natural response to the lack of oxygen."

"What if he was doing it to himself? I assume evidence of a sexual encounter means there's semen somewhere, but could he have been playing around by, and with, himself and maybe misjudged his capacity, blacked out, then fell?"

"It's possible, but unlikely. In that circumstance, the body still jerks and, to a certain extent, spasms."

Anika studied the scene more closely. She could see why Rasmussen was dubious. The bed was still made and other than a small spot in the middle where the comforter looked a little twisted, it basically looked like Grant had been tied up, then draped over the side of the bed. There was no evidence of any kind of struggle, be that with himself or someone else.

"So, assuming someone else was involved, Grant was likely already unconscious when he was strangled," Anika said.

Dr. Rasmussen nodded. "That's my guess, but I won't know until I get him to the lab and can run some tests."

"Is it possible he wasn't strangled at all?" Dominic asked.

From where he knelt beside the body, Dr. Rasmussen loosened the makeshift noose around Grant's neck to reveal heavy bruising. "Again, I won't know until I get to the lab, but he was definitely strangled. Although, to your point, Agent Burel, that might not be the final cause of death."

They moved away from the body as Dr. Rasmussen rose and gestured for his team to begin the retrieval process.

"The evidence team is on stand-by," Mateo said, leaning against the doorframe leading out onto the lanai, staying out of the way of everyone else in the room.

"Good," Anika said, stepping around the bed and examining the floor for any footprints. There were two photographers, dressed in booties, photographing the room and she gestured for one of them to get a particularly good angle of the bedspread. The slight disturbance in the middle wasn't much, but it was easier to see from the end of the bed.

"Dominic, do you want to have a look in the bathroom before we call the evidence team in?" Anika asked. Without a word, Dom slipped past the ME's team and stepped into the bathroom while she continued her perusal of the room.

Twenty minutes later, they were standing outside as Jason Grant's body was loaded into an ambulance for transport to the morgue where the autopsy would take place. Garza had remained, but stayed out of the way, and the evidence team was loitering behind, waiting for the all clear.

"You think he's one of yours?" Mateo asked.

"I'd be surprised if he isn't," Anika responded.

"You going to talk with the manager?" he asked.

Anika turned her attention to Dominic who flashed her the same grin he'd given Florence earlier. She shook her head and chuckled. "Yeah, I think I'll let Burel take the lead on that. You coming?"

Mateo shook his head. "Nah, I'll leave you to it. I assume if it's not one of yours you'll send me the report." It wasn't a question, and not waiting for a response, Mateo turned and walked toward the main parking lot.

When he was out of earshot, Dominic spoke. "He doesn't seem too pissed about everything."

Anika's eyes lingered on Mateo and to her surprise, she agreed with Dominic. Based on her conversation with her brother the day before, she'd expected…well, not quite hostility, but some sort of strong reaction. Or something stronger than what she'd gotten. It was possible Mateo regretted not backing her up more publicly and his attitude was his way of showing that, but she suspected it was more because he'd realized that something he'd taken for granted wouldn't always be the way he wanted it.

She shrugged and turned back in time to see the ambulance door swing shut. "Well, that's that until the evidence team is done. Shall we go talk to Florence? I have to admit, I'm kind of looking forward to watching you dazzle her."

Dominic chuckled. "Like I said, if you got it, use it. At least I'm deploying it for the greater good."

Anika laughed. "Anyone ever tell you how arrogant you are?" she teased as they started toward the main building.

"All the time. But facts are facts, and you can't fight it."

And it was true, but for the first time, Anika realized that she wasn't interested in fighting it. When she'd first met Dominic, his looks and charm had sent her—metaphorically—running for the hills. He deployed his smile too easily, got what—and who— he wanted too easily, and was, in short, everything she wasn't interested in spending any time with.

Slowly he'd worked his way into her life, though, and had shown himself to be a good man who, despite his killer grin, would go to the mat for those he cared about. Which was more than she could say for a lot of people—including her former partner.

So, did the way Florence blushed when she and Dominic walked into her office bother her? Or did the way he flashed his grin and, in seconds, had Florence scrambling to pull up the digital security recordings, bother her? Nope, not one bit. Not anymore. She knew him better now than she knew most people and what had once struck her as the over-the-top attempts of a player, she now saw as a part—a small one—of who he was as a man. His looks didn't define him any more than hers defined who she was.

As Dominic and Florence chatted, the manager emailed them the CCTV video then answered a few questions about Jason

Grant's activities while at the resort. He'd arrived three days before his death and had booked two deep sea fishing excursions through the concierge. Based on the room charges, it appeared he'd spent the first day enjoying the resort amenities and the next two out on the all-day excursions. The trip he'd been on the day before—in the hours before his death—had ended at three, and he'd had a bar charge at the resort at five, then a dinner charge at nine. All in all, there was nothing suspicious about any of his activity. Then again, they still had the video to look forward to studying.

And the girlfriend to pick up.

Florence remembered him referring to her as Laura and, by process of elimination based on flight arrival times, they were able to narrow her flight down to two—one from Miami or one from Atlanta. Laura would be expecting to find Jason waiting for her, she'd be expecting to kick off the week-long vacation they'd booked in the bungalow. Like with Hameed Khan's family, Anika was aware of how quickly the woman's life would change when she and Dominic delivered the news.

CHAPTER TWELVE

As if they both needed the mental space to prepare for what was sure to be a rough moment, the ride to Havensted, and the airport, was mostly completed in silence. When they arrived, Dominic pulled into the nearby hourly lot and found a spot not far from the entrance. Exiting the car, Anika grabbed the placard the resort had given them that simply had "Laura" written on it.

The somber mood followed them inside and side-by-side they stood at the baggage claim, holding the sign, as the passengers from the Miami flight, which landed twenty minutes before the flight from Atlanta, began filtering through the gate.

Anika scanned the crowds, looking for a woman traveling alone. There were a few, but the first four were women who looked to be in their seventies and next two in their late teens. Finally, a woman rounded the corner into the baggage area who looked like she could be a candidate. She appeared to be in her late twenties or early thirties. Her blond hair was pulled into a high ponytail, and she wore a long sundress and sandals. What really gave her away, though, was the color of her skin. She wasn't as pale as many of the snowbirds, but she had the kind of tan that looked like it came out of a bottle—a good bottle, she wasn't orange or anything, but a bottle, nonetheless. In other words, she looked like someone who spent the winter in a cold climate like DC but was ready for her tropical vacation.

Anika nudged Dominic then gestured toward the woman. He nodded and they started walking in her direction.

"Excuse me," Dominic said as they approached. "Are you Laura who's staying at Seasons?"

The woman looked at Dominic, then her gaze dropped to the placard he held with the logo of the resort. When she looked back up, she smiled. "I am. I was expecting my boyfriend, though, so you took me by surprise."

Dominic looked at Anika and she gave a very subtle gesture of her head for him to continue.

"My name is Dominic Burel, I'm with the FBI and this is Detective Anika Anderson. We're wondering if you could come with us for a short while?"

Her eyes bounced between the two. "Why, what's happened?" she demanded almost immediately.

"We think it might be best if you come with us. TSA has set aside a small room where we can have some privacy," Dominic said.

"Where's Jason? Has something happened to Jason?"

"Please," Anika said, gentling her voice. "It would be best if we had some privacy."

The woman's eyes filled with tears, but none fell as she gave a jerky nod. Dominic reached for her arm and led her to the small room Jake had organized with TSA.

"Have a seat," Dominic said, once the door was shut behind them. Laura's carry-on bag slid from her shoulder to the ground and she sank onto the worn, vinyl chair.

Anika was grateful that the room was set up for conversation and not interrogation, and both she and Dominic took seats a few feet away.

"May I ask your full name, please?" Dominic asked.

The woman hesitated, as if delaying her answer might also delay what she'd surely guessed was coming. "Laura Gordon."

"Thank you, Ms. Gordon. You're here, on Tildas, to spend a week with your boyfriend, Jason Grant?" Dominic continued.

Laura gave a shaky nod.

Dominic cast Anika a quick look and she inclined her head, urging him to continue.

"Is this your boyfriend?" Dominic brought up the image of Jason Grant's driver's license on his phone, and again, Laura nodded.

"I'm sorry to have to tell you, but Jason was found deceased this morning in his hotel room," Dominic said. His words were quiet, but no matter how soft they were, nothing would dull the impact they'd have.

Laura froze then and shook her head. The tears came back, but this time they fell freely. "No," she said. "It's not true. I talked to him last night. He caught a fish, I don't remember what it was, but he was excited. He said the hotel would cook it for us to-tonight."

When neither Anika nor Dominic said anything, Laura's head began to shake even more. "No, it's not true," she said. "It's not. I think he was going to propose while were here. We were going to get married, start a family..."

Her voice trailed off and silence weighed heavy in the room. Then she all but whispered, "What happened?"

"We don't know yet," Anika said, leaning forward and resting her forearms on her thighs. "But we're exploring every lead and every avenue of investigation."

Laura blinked furiously and Anika wished they'd thought to bring tissues. As it was, the woman just wiped her eyes with the back of her hand. "You said you're looking at leads. Does that mean his death...wasn't natural? That he was killed? Who would want to do that?"

"Again, we don't know for certain, but we do have reason to believe his death wasn't natural," Anika answered. "As for who might have done it, that's something we'd like to talk to you about, but it can wait a little bit. Is there anyone we can call for you?"

Laura started to shake her head again, then paused. "I don't want to call my parents, but can I call my friend Kristy? I was staying with her in Miami last night."

"Of course you can call her. If she can come down here to be with you, we can help arrange for that," Anika said.

But Laura didn't reach for her phone, instead, she stared vacantly at the opposite wall. "What am I going to do now?" she whispered. "I don't want to stay…I can't stay at that resort."

"We can get you booked into something in town, if you'd prefer that," Dominic said, already pulling out his phone.

"I think…I think that would be best." Laura's voice cracked on the last word and again, the tears fell.

"Would you like me to call Kristy?" Anika asked.

Listlessly, Laura nodded, then reached down and pulled her phone from a side pocket of her bag. After unlocking it, she hit a couple of buttons, then handed the phone over. Not wanting Laura to have to hear the news a second time, Anika took the phone and left the room before she hit the call button.

Thirty minutes later, they delivered Laura to a sister hotel of Seasons in downtown Havensted. It wasn't as nice as Seasons, but none of that seemed to matter to Laura. When Anika and Dominic ushered Laura into the room, she went straight to the bed and curled up on top of the bed covers. Her friend, Kristy, was going to try to catch the last flight out of Miami for Tildas and she'd be there by nine that evening. Anika was pretty certain Laura wouldn't move before then.

As Dominic shut the door behind them, Anika reflected on the reality that it was one of the world's worst ironies than when something like this happened, the person you wanted most by your side was the one person who'd never be by your side again.

"Do you want to take the CCTV from Seasons, and I'll start the background on Grant then dive back into Taglia and Khan, or the other way around?" Dominic asked Anika once they were back at the office and in the elevator.

"I'll take the CCTV," she answered. "It's kind of grunt work, but I have to admit, between the three murders and the family I never knew existed showing up, I wouldn't mind a couple of hours staring at a screen."

Dominic held the door and as Anika passed by, he took a good look at her. She wasn't going to shirk her job or wallow in the weirdness of her family appearing on her doorstep, but the circles under her eyes told him she wasn't getting much sleep.

"Sounds good," he agreed as Steven acknowledged them with a nod, then buzzed them in.

"Is it one of yours?" Jake asked the second they set foot in the office.

"No," Anika said. "It's one of yours. Remember this is an FBI case now."

Jake narrowed his eyes at her. "You're getting cheeky, Detective."

"Getting?" Dominic teased, sliding onto his seat.

"You do both remember that I have four older brothers and I can make glitter bombs in my sleep," Anika said.

Jake started to say something, but Dominic cut him off. There was no way he was going to fuck with a glitter bomb. "Don't, my friend. If you do, you will be finding glitter in places on your body you don't even know the name of for weeks."

Jake stilled. "Really?"

Dominic nodded.

"Even…" he slowly tilted his head down. Dominic wasn't entirely sure what part of his anatomy Jake was referring to, but regardless the answer was the same.

"Yep."

"How do you know?"

Dominic smiled. "There might have been a glitter bomb war during one of our training exercises when I was a PJ," he said, referring to his time as a member of the pararescue team.

At her desk beside his, Anika chuckled and powered her computer up. "How'd your superiors take to that?"

Dominic laughed. "About as well as you can imagine. They tripled our training regime after they made us clean up the course. It took thirty-eight hours straight to get it off everything, but we were still finding it in cracks and crevices weeks later."

"Your cracks and crevices or the courses?" Jake asked.

Dominic hit the power button of his computer. "Yes."

Jake let out a dramatic sigh. "Fine, no more teasing—what'd you find?"

Dominic took a few minutes to fill him in and about halfway through, the rest of the team arrived and he ended up repeating the first part so everyone could get up to speed. Shah's office was empty, but he figured they could send her an email before leaving.

"It's definitely a hitman," Alexis said.

Anika nodded from behind her computer screen, she was half-listening, half-watching the CCTV Florence had sent over. "Not that either is good, but in some ways, I'm glad it's not a serial killer for the simple reason that I assume the hitman has a specific group of people he's going after and it's not some group of indeterminate size. And Jesus, I can't believe I just said that," she added.

"So now the big question is, why these victims?" Beni asked. "Were they all involved in something shady together at the bank, or did they happen to be in the wrong place at the wrong time and were inadvertently caught up in something shady?"

"I read some of the reports while I was at Hemmeleigh," Damian said. "I'm not going to stake my life on it, but I'm leaning toward the latter. Both Taglia and Khan seemed to be regular guys living the life regular professionals live."

"What about today's vic?" Alexis asked.

"Nothing popped on the preliminary background check," Damian said. "Owns a condo in Alexandria, has one speeding ticket, has worked for Bank of DC for five years. Before that, he worked for several years at a non-profit in Guatemala before returning stateside and completing his MBA. He's not a boy scout, judging by his credit card statements, but he doesn't appear to be doing anything sketchy."

"What about his girlfriend?" Anika asked.

Damian shook his head. "We didn't have her name when we submitted the warrant request so we can't get anything on her other than what's in our databases or publicly available—although I doubt the judge would have extended it to include her anyway. From what I did get, though, she works as a buyer for a bespoke boutique, buying the fabrics the designers use to make their custom creations. Based on her social media profile, she travels a fair bit, but nothing stood out as being a red flag."

"Whoa," Anika said, straightening in her chair and clicking her mouse. All eyes turned toward her. She frowned, then leaned closer to her monitor.

"What?" Dominic asked, rising and joining her. In seconds, the rest of his team surrounded them.

"Ah, that's not Laura," Anika said, her head tilted as she examined the image on her screen. She stopped the CCTV and the still image on her monitor showed Jason Grant, with his shorts down around his ankles, buried balls deep in a woman who was pressed up against a palm tree. His face was visible, but hers wasn't. Though from what they could see, the woman, with her long, black hair, was most definitely not Laura.

"You're watching CCTV, and *this* is the spot you chose to freeze the frame?" Jake asked. Everyone turned to look at him. He threw up his hands. "What? You have to admit, it's weird she picked *that* moment to freeze the video," he said pointing to the monitor. "I mean, there must be video of them walking together or talking or, well, anything less graphic."

Dominic studied his friend, then turned to Anika. On a sigh, she backed the video up thirty seconds. A couple, not Jason and his mystery woman, walked by, then, fifteen seconds in, a man wearing shorts came onto the screen. He was carrying a woman with her legs wrapped around his waist and her large sun hat, covered his face. Had they not seen that first image, the one with Jason Grant's head thrown back in obvious pleasure, they wouldn't have recognized him either, which explained why Anika hadn't stopped the video earlier. In fact, as they watched Jason back the woman against the tree and drop his shorts, it wasn't until that exact frame that Anika had previously stopped the video, that they could see Grant's face.

"Okay, fair enough. Although I have to admit, I was kind of hoping you had some pervy voyeuristic tendencies," Jake said.

"Murder investigation, McMullen," Beni said, smacking him on the shoulder.

"Right," Dominic said, cutting off anything more Jake might have said. "So it looks like our vic's sexual activity wasn't self-induced."

"Or at least not then," Anika said. "Who knows what happened once they got back to the privacy of the bungalow."

"Did they go to the room together?" Alexis asked.

Anika hit the play button and, as awkward as it was, the team watched Grant and the mystery woman complete their hasty coupling against the palm. When they finished, Grant pulled up his shorts, the woman let the hem of her dress fall back to her ankles, and the two walked off, hand-in-hand.

"Any other cameras?" Beni asked.

Anika shook her head. "This was taken about thirty feet from the bungalow where Grant was staying, and his was the last bungalow at that edge of the property."

"See if you can catch her leaving," Dominic said.

Anika fast-forwarded the video and they all watched as several couples came in and out of view. Then, at a few minutes past midnight, the woman hurried past the camera, her head down, wearing the sun hat in such a way as to obscure any view of her face.

"Think she knows the cameras are there?" Damian asked, the sarcasm in his voice making the question a rhetorical one.

"If he'd just picked her up in the bar or somewhere nearby, it would be an odd thing for her to be thinking about, let alone know," Alexis said.

"And not to mention the hat," Jake chimed in. "Who wears a sun hat at midnight?"

"So, we're thinking an experienced sex worker?" Anika asked.

All the evidence leaned toward the woman being a professional, but Dominic wasn't convinced.

"What are you thinking my friend?" Jake asked.

Dominic frowned. "If we're assuming she's a professional sex worker, I guess he seemed awfully *comfortable* with her. I mean, holding hands, smiling, carrying her? If he has a lot of experience with this sort of thing, maybe acting like a happy boyfriend with a prostitute is his thing, but it seems weird to me."

Everyone on the team stared at the image on the monitor once again. This time, it was stopped on the image of the woman's back as she walked away.

"Yeah, maybe," Anika said, almost to herself.

"Maybe tomorrow we can go interview some staff?" Damian suggested.

Alexis was the first to break rank and she stepped away from the group. "I think that's a good idea and, in the meantime, you aren't going to get an answer to that," she pointed at the screen, "tonight, so why don't we all call it a day and pick everything back up tomorrow?"

There was a chorus of agreements and twenty minutes later, the office was empty except for Dom and Anika. He had his computer bag slung over his shoulder and he was leaning against the edge of his desk, waiting for her to gather her things. Only she kept glancing at her phone.

"You're thinking about calling them, aren't you? Your biological family," he asked, his voice soft in the still of the office.

She exhaled and lifted her eyes from her phone to his. "Do you think that's a bad idea?"

"More to the point, do *you* think it's a bad idea?"

Anika didn't jump to an answer, but after a beat, she shook her head. "I don't know. Part of me thinks that it's a bad idea. I like the family I have, and god knows what kind of chaos a whole new family I know nothing about might bring into my life. What if they are all crazy?"

"That's not what's holding you back." The words were out of his mouth before he'd even thought them through, but the moment they hung between them, he knew they were the truth.

"How would you know?"

Her question sounded a bit petulant, but he ignored that. "Because if they are crazy, you'll kick them to the curb without the slightest hesitation. You know I'm right about that."

She reached down and toyed with her phone, spinning it slowly on the desk. "The fact that I'm going to say what I'm about to say is one of the reasons that makes me hesitate because I hate feeling insecure…but what if they don't like me?

It was one thing to think they'd rejected me without knowing me, but if they *know* me and *then* they reject me…"

He studied her for a good long moment, wanting desperately to ease the vulnerability he saw in her eyes but knowing the only thing he could really do for her was let her feel—and experience—everything she was feeling.

"You won't know how any of you feel about each other if you don't meet them," he said. "I'm not advocating either way, but I would ask you one question, if you *don't* meet them, will that be something you will regret?"

If her family didn't like her—which he couldn't imagine—or she didn't like them, she was strong enough to work through that. But just because *he* knew that, didn't mean she did.

Hesitantly, she nodded. "I keep thinking about the people like Taglia and Khan and wonder if, in their final moments, they had any big regrets. And as nervous as it makes me to meet them, I know that if I don't, in my final moments, it would be a decision I regretted."

"You may not know how it will turn out, but you do know that you have family—and friends—who will be there for you either way," he said.

She nodded and her gaze drifted back down to her phone. She picked it up and held it before raising her eyes to meet his. "If I meet with them, will you come with me?"

Dominic's heart started beating in a heavy rhythm, the veins pulsing under his skin. His eyes searched hers, and she stared back at him. It was a small moment, but he didn't underestimate how important it was to whatever he and Anika might become in the future.

"Of course," he said. "Whatever you want, I'll be there."

CHAPTER THIRTEEN

THERE WAS no two ways about it, Anika was more nervous than she'd ever been in her entire life. Her first day of school after moving to Tildas, her first day at the police academy, taking the detective's exam…well, they all paled in comparison to how she felt walking through the condo complex with her dad and Dominic to meet her biological family.

She'd thought about not telling her dad, but only for about ten seconds. Sure, there were things that, as a daughter, she'd kept from Phil Anderson, but never any of the big important stuff and this was definitely big important stuff. She'd called him while she and Dominic had had a glass of wine on her balcony and filled him in on what little she'd learned from the file Eva had given her. She hadn't thought to ask him to come—she hadn't wanted to put him in an awkward spot—but when he'd offered, it had felt so right to have the man who'd stood by her nearly her entire life be beside her for this, and she'd accepted immediately.

Now the three of them were making their way to the large, penthouse condo in the ocean front building next to Dominic's. Other than what Eva and Brett looked like and what she'd gleaned from the letter and photos in the file, Anika didn't know anything about her biological family, but she figured they must be pretty comfortable financially if they'd been able to rent the penthouse. Then again, she didn't really know how many people she'd be meeting—maybe there were a lot and they needed the space?

"I should have asked who we'll be meeting tonight," she managed to say through the nausea roiling in her stomach. Once she and Eva had decided a time, and Eva had texted the condo number, there hadn't been any further conversation.

"Whoever and however many it is, they'll be lucky to know you," her dad said.

"As my dad, you have to say that, but thanks for saying it anyway."

"I don't have to say it, and I agree," Dominic said. "You don't know anything about these people, but you do know yourself and what's important to you. Stop thinking about whether or not they are going to like you and start thinking about whether or not you'll like *them*."

"He's right, baby girl," her dad said, making her groan.

"You know I hate it when you call me that, Dad," Anika said, stepping into the elevator. Thankfully, their card keys got them into the building so they didn't have to stand around outside waiting to be buzzed in.

"Well, 'baby woman' doesn't sound right and 'baby lady' makes it sounds like you deliver babies to people."

"How about nothing 'baby'," she said.

"You are my youngest child, therefore you are my baby. You're thirty-two years old, you should know this by now."

Beside her, Dominic chuckled. "He has a point you know. My mama still calls me 'baby' all the time."

Anika didn't have any time to retort as the doors slid open and right across the hall were Eva and Brett standing in an open door. Eva wore a gleeful, excited smile that was hard not to react to and her brother, though a little more reserved, was also smiling.

Both twins took in the two, tall Black men who flanked her, and while they'd seen Dominic before, it was obvious Phil Anderson came as a surprise. Not one that threw them off for more than a split second, though.

"Come in, come in, come in." Eva all but bounced on the balls of her feet.

"Gee, Eva, you think they should come in?" Brett said, moving to the side and gesturing them in.

"Oh, shut up, Brett. It's not every day we get to meet a long-lost sister. *And* one who's a detective in the Caribbean. Seriously, how cool is that?" Eva said, pushing her brother to the side and stepping in front of Anika. "Can I hug you?"

Anika blinked. "Uh, sure."

Eva squealed, a charming squeal, but a squeal nonetheless, and threw her arms around Anika. After a second, Anika remembered she should hug the young woman back, so she awkwardly raised her arms.

"Now," Eva said, stepping back. "Why don't you come in and you can introduce these two handsome men to everyone so we can all meet at once."

Eva took her hand and, without pausing for an answer, tugged her into the living room. She heard Brett issue a quiet apology to both Dominic and her dad for Eva's boisterousness, and she wasn't surprised when she heard the smile in both their voices when they told him he had nothing to apologize for.

But all that was forgotten the second she walked into the room and was faced with not just her biological father, but four women—one of whom looked nearly identical to her mother—and two other men. She felt, more than saw, Dominic and her dad come to stand behind her.

Three of the women gasped as Anika came to a stop, and the

man, her biological father, let out a low sound that reminded Anika of an animal in pain.

"Oh my god, she looks just like Christine," one of the older women said.

"But she has James' eyes," the other older woman said.

"Oh god," the man who must be her father said. "Oh god, I didn't know. I swear to you I didn't know." Two tears fell from his eyes, and the woman who was perhaps his wife, put a hand on his shoulder. He turned at the touch. "I have another daughter. We have another daughter."

The woman blinked away her own tears and offered her husband a watery smile. "We do, we definitely do."

A flash of panic lanced through Anika. She didn't know any of these people and while the emotions she was feeling were more curiosity and nerves, clearly the emotion she'd elicited from them was something much stronger. Her breathing quickened, and her heart rate increased. She wasn't going to run. No, she'd come this far and she was going to see this through, but somehow, she had to work through the panic that seemed to want to take over her body.

"You're okay, baby girl," her dad said quietly, placing a hand on her shoulder.

"You got this," Dominic said, taking her hand in his and giving her something to anchor herself to.

She forced herself to take a slow deep breath and when she let it out, she saw something else in the eyes of the people who had been waiting to meet her. In them, she recognized the same fear she had—there were terrified she'd reject them. That, more than anything else gave her strength.

"Please will you tell me who you all are?" she asked.

Her biological father cleared his throat and stepped forward. "I'm James Riley, your father," he said. Then his eyes darted to Phil, and Anika had to give the man credit, he was struggling, in much the same way she was, but yet he recognized the bond he saw before him and corrected himself. "Your biological father."

He held out his hand and Anika stared at it. Then raising her eyes to James', she reached out with her own. He let out a shuddering breath when his hand wrapped around hers and Anika had no doubt he wanted to pull her into a giant hug, but was restraining himself for her sake. A little of the tension in her body released at seeing his control—he was struggling with his own demons, but it was clear he was putting her first.

When he released her hand, he moved back a few steps. "You've met—well, sort of met—Brett and Eva already, and this is my wife, Helen." As he spoke, he gestured to the woman who had comforted him earlier.

"We are so very glad to meet you, Anika," she said, stepping forward and shaking her hand. After those first introductions, the floodgates opened. Inez and Michael Riley, her paternal grandparents had joined the family on the trip, as had Rick and Lorraine Bowman, her maternal grandparents. And last but not least, was Evelyn, her mother's twin sister.

An awkward moment passed once Anika had met everyone, but then James' gaze strayed to the two men standing behind her, and Anika all but jolted at the reminder that she wasn't alone.

"This is my father, Philip Anderson," she said, pulling her dad forward and wrapping her hand around his forearm. It tended to surprise people when she introduced the six foot three, barrel built, Black man as her father, but the Riley-Bowman clan didn't appear surprised in the least, which made her wonder if perhaps, in their search for her, they'd already learned who had adopted her.

She let go of her dad when he stepped forward to shake hands with everyone, ending with James. James grasped her father's hand, but he also placed a hand on Phil's arm. "I have no right to say this," he said. "But I can't thank you enough. I don't know the whole story, and maybe it will all come out tonight or over the next few days. But it's obvious Anika is loved and that you two are close and while I wish to hell things had been different all those years ago, you will never know how grateful I am that she has you."

In a surprise move, her dad released James' hand and pulled the man into a hug. They were about the same height, but Phil dwarfed James in size. "The pleasure and the honor are all mine," her dad said.

It wasn't until Dominic handed her a tissue that she even realized she was crying, but once she did, it seemed like she couldn't turn the waterworks off. She gave a tearful introduction of Dominic, who she simply said was one of her good friends, then sat quietly as James, Lorraine, and Inez told her the story of her mother.

It wasn't a complicated story, but one that, in the minutiae, had impacted so many people. James and Christine had been high school sweethearts and had, against their parent's wishes, run off together right after graduation. But while James had tried to stay focused on school, while still filling the role of an eighteen-year-old fiancé, Christine had taken a different path. She'd hoped moving out of her parents' house—moving out of Louisiana—would give her more freedom, but she'd struggled with the restraints that the lack of finances had put on them and started getting more and more wild. A year after they'd run off, it had been clear to James that the relationship wasn't healthy, so he left Christine, moved home, and dove into school in an effort to make up for the credits he hadn't been able to take while living with his fiancée.

He'd never heard from Christine again and the one time she'd returned to their hometown in Louisiana, he was living in Atlanta and in medical school so hadn't seen her. The same couldn't be said for the Bowmans, as Christine had made the trip for the sole purpose of asking her parents for money.

They'd declined to give her any and Christine vowed to never set foot in her hometown again. She'd never mentioned a child, so Lorraine and Rick had grieved for the—emotional—loss of their daughter but hadn't ever considered that they'd lost even more than they knew.

"So how did you find out about me?" Anika asked. They were all seated in a large, haphazard circle in the living room, and her father was to her right while Dominic sat on her left.

James looked to Lorraine, and Rick handed her a tissue.

"Six months ago, we got a call that your mother had died. The cause of death was unknown, so they'd done an autopsy. In the report, it made mention of the fact that she'd given birth," Lorraine said.

"Honestly," Rick said, with a sad shake of his head, "We assumed the child had died since she'd never said a word to us. Still, we needed to know. We needed to know if we had a grandchild out there, buried in some cemetery without any family."

"And so, we started looking," Lorraine said, picking the story back up. "We found your birth certificate first and when we saw your date of birth, we knew we needed to tell James and his family."

"When they told me, I hired a private investigator to track you down. That was two months ago," James said, finishing the tale.

"So, Christine is dead, then?" Phil asked.

Anika reached over and grabbed hold of her dad's hand. He and Christine hadn't been together that long, but Phil was a man who loved completely and though he hadn't loved what Christine had done to him, and he really hadn't liked what she'd done to Anika, Anika had never doubted that he'd loved her mother.

"We're sorry, but yes," Lorraine said.

"How did she die?" Anika asked.

"Cirrhosis of the liver," James answered.

Anika wasn't sure what to do with that answer, she'd asked more out of habit than anything. She didn't have any particular familial feelings for the woman who'd given birth to her. She was sorry Christine was dead, but she didn't feel anything more than a vague sorrow for the life wasted.

A heavy silence fell over the room. Anika didn't know what was going through everyone else's head, but she wouldn't have been surprised if they were thinking some variation of what she was thinking—how one woman's decisions had affected so many people.

"Well," Eva said, jumping up from her seat beside her mother. "I don't know about the rest of you, but I could use a drink."

Everyone turned to look at her standing at the entrance to the kitchen. After a beat she rolled her eyes. "Come on guys. If ever there was a time for a drink it's when you find your long-lost daughter, granddaughter, niece, sister, father, brother, etcetera. Now, don't be shy, tell me what you want."

A beat went by, then Phil spoke. "If you have a beer, I could definitely take one."

Dominic was leaning his forearms on the railing of the balcony, listening to the waves lap up onto the beach eight floors below them. He held a beer bottle in hand and though his gaze was on the water, his ears were attuned to Anika. Right now, she was sitting with her half-sister and her grandmothers talking about her life on Tildas Island. Phil's laugh filtered through, too. He was talking to Rick and Michael about refurbishing some old car. Phil was the best mechanic on the island and could work on anything, but his passion was definitely old cars. He didn't get the opportunity often, not on the island, but it seemed the three men had found a common ground.

"Mind if I join you?"

Dominic looked over to see James standing in the open doorway. He gestured to the spot beside him and James stepped out. For a minute or so, the two men remained side-by-side looking out at the vast Caribbean.

"Is it wrong that there are some days in the past two months that I really hate Christine?" James asked.

Dominic glanced over. He wasn't sure why the man was choosing to speak to him, but he seemed to be genuinely struggling with the question.

"I know she gave us all Anika, so I couldn't ever really hate her. But what she did to her own daughter, and to us, her family, is almost incomprehensible," he continued. After everyone had had their first round of drinks in hand, Anika had told them all the same story she'd told him the night before about her early years with her mother, being left at the mall, the series of foster homes, and then finally reuniting with Phil and being adopted into her Tildas Island family. There hadn't been a dry eye in the house, and more than once James had looked like he would have happily killed Christine if she weren't already dead.

"Anika told me the story last night," Dominic said. "I've known her five months, and known her well for three, and it was the first time she'd ever talked about it. I knew she was adopted, but she held the story close to the vest. I've been deployed countless times then I joined the FBI, so I *know* how shitty people can be. But yeah, what Christine did to you all is something that's hard to forgive."

They lapsed back into silence, each sipping their drinks. Then James asked, "How close are you to Anika?"

Dominic arched an eyebrow and slanted James a look.

James shifted to face Dominic and lifted his hands in a gesture of denial. Then with a shake of his head and a smile, he clarified, "I'm not asking if you're her boyfriend or questioning your intentions or any of that," he said with a chuckle. "I know I don't have that right and even if I did, if Anika is anything like Eva, she'd have my head if I tried. The reason I'm asking is because this," he gestured with his beer bottle to the room where everyone stood chatting, "is a lot to take in. Me, my parents, the Bowmans…we're all staying here together, we'll all have each other as we process everything over the next few days. It's obvious Anika and Phil are close, but I asked you because she could probably use a good friend, especially in the next few days."

Dominic eyed the man but saw nothing but sincerity in his expression. James might have just met Anika, but it was obvious he cared for her and wanted the best for her.

"I live in that building there," Dominic said, pointing to the one other building in the complex that sat on the water. "We're also temporarily working together on a case. So aside from being her friend, these days, we're pretty much together more time than we're not. Anything she needs, she knows I'm there."

James' eyes searched his, then he nodded. "Thank you," he said. His eyes lingered for a second, then he frowned. "Did I hear a hint of Louisiana in your voice?"

Dominic smiled. "Yes, you did, sir. My family is from there. I grew up outside Baton Rouge."

"You an LSU man?" James asked with a smile.

"Me and my two sisters. My father was a professor there."

"You close to your family?"

Dominic nodded. "Very. Being in the service made it hard to see them sometimes, but we're still close."

"What about your mama? You said your dad was a professor, does your mama work, too? Though with three kids, maybe someone needed to stay home?"

A burst of joy flowed through him, he loved what he knew would happen next. "My mama is Korryn Burel."

James stared, then blinked at him. "Did you say Korryn Burel? The chef?"

Dominic grinned. "The very same."

"Holy shit," he said, in awe. "Hey, Helen, guess who Dominic's mama is?"

Helen glanced up from where she stood behind her mother-in-law's shoulder. The group had obviously been looking at pictures, and the others looked up, too.

"I have no idea," Helen said.

"Korryn Burel," James answered.

Helen's eyes weren't the only ones that went wide, and in seconds, the room was filled with "I *love* her," "That thing she does with her biscuits," "Have you tried her muffuletta?" and several more compliments.

Anika may have had her misgivings, but by the smile on her face as she listened to her biological family sing his mama's praises, he'd wager those misgivings had vanished.

And in their place, was something infinitely more precious. Hope.

CHAPTER FOURTEEN

"Want to come in for a drink?" Anika asked Dominic as they walked toward her apartment. After making plans to introduce the Riley and Bowman families to her brothers, they'd said goodbye to her family then walked Phil to his car, and now it was just the two of them. He wasn't sure he needed another drink, but he did want to spend some time with her and see how she was doing. He also sensed that she could use a little time to decompress with a friend.

"Maybe some Pellegrino instead? We do have a murder or three to solve and a hitman on the loose," he added with a smile.

She grinned back at him and, pushing her door open, she walked into her apartment. "You know, for a few minutes, I was able to forget about the case. Not all together, but it wasn't occupying all my brain space."

He shut the door behind him and followed her into the living room, though she turned right and detoured to the kitchen. "You had a few other things on your mind," he said.

He sank onto one of her upholstered chairs, and in the few minutes that Anika was in the kitchen, he realized that she wasn't the only one who might need to decompress from the evening. His emotions hadn't been as powerful as Anika's, but now, in the quiet of her apartment, he admitted to himself how anxious he'd been on Anika's behalf. It would have killed him to watch her get hurt had her biological family turned out to be crazy or awful or any number of other things that were less than the loving people she deserved.

"Here," she said, handing him a tall glass of sparkling water as she passed by.

"Thanks," he said.

She kicked off her shoes and took a seat on her sofa, curling a leg under her. For several minutes, neither of them spoke, they just sipped their drinks and let the still of the night, and each other's company, smooth out the intense emotions of the last several hours.

"It wasn't what I'd expected," Anika said. He hadn't turned the light on, so the room was lit only by the ambient light of the kitchen, but he could still see enough details of her face to know she wasn't looking at him but was rather somewhere inside her own mind.

"My dad's parents died two years after I came to live here on Tildas. I never imagined I'd have grandparents. Let alone two sets who, by all appearances, look healthy…and so happy to have me in their lives now."

He smiled. "They were definitely beyond thrilled that you were willing to meet them. Everyone was. I think Eva was about to explode. She reminds me a little of Jake and Nia."

Anika laughed. "Yeah, she does. I'd hate to see the three of them together. Or well, maybe I'd love it. I bet they'd have a blast despite the age difference."

"No doubt," he agreed. They sat for a few more minutes, then Anika got up to open the sliding door to her balcony. Her apartment looked out onto a vibrant tropical forest, rather than the beach, and though it wasn't visible in the dark of the night, they could hear the nighttime birds and creatures calling out to each other.

"Everyone felt so guilty," Anika said when she'd returned to her seat. "It wasn't their fault, and we all know that, but I guess it's the classic example of the heart leading rather than logic."

"I think it will take a while for that feeling to go away, especially for James," Dominic said. "He's devoted to Helen and the twins. I think he's struggling with the idea that Christine basically led you to believe he'd abandoned you."

Anika set her empty glass down on the coffee table then curled back up on the couch. "You know, that's one of the reasons I never let you cross that line," she said.

He stilled. "What line?" It wasn't the most astute question, but her leap from talking about her family to talking about them had taken him by surprise.

She smiled at him in the dark. "You know I love my dad and brothers, and I've basically accepted everything my mother did and moved on, but that didn't mean I didn't—that I don't—still have scars. In my mind, pretty much everyone except my dad and brothers, abandoned me. And it took me years to really believe that they wouldn't do the same at some point."

"You thought I'd abandon you if we ever got together?" he asked.

Her quiet laugh filled the space between them. "Oh, I know you would have, it's more complicated than that, though. You see, I'm not all that different from you, or, I suppose I should say I'm not all that different from how you *were*. My reasons were different, of course. You picked women to have fun with, never made any promises, so you never had to be the bad guy. Me? I picked men who were easy to leave, men who were fun and who I liked, but none of whom it would bother me to leave."

"So that you could leave first," Dominic said, now understanding what she was telling him. "But what does that have to do with us?" He hadn't intended to have this conversation tonight. Hell, it was a terrible idea to have it after everything that had already happened. But he didn't think he had it in him to stop it—Anika asked so little of him that if she wanted to talk about this tonight, then he'd talk about it tonight.

"If we'd ever gotten together in those first months, I think it would have been a race to the door the morning after, with both of us wanting to be the first one out," she said. He sensed a "but" so he remained quiet. After a long pause, she looked up and met his gaze. "The problem was, you were the only man I'd ever met that I worried I wouldn't be fast enough. That I wouldn't have it in me to leave you before you could leave me. So, I never let us, let *me*, go down that path. I'd been left, or forgotten, by so many —or so I thought—that I wasn't willing to put myself in that position voluntarily."

Dominic's heart started to thud at the direction this conversation was taking. He still wasn't sure it was the best time to be having it, but that horse had left the barn as soon as he'd set foot in her apartment twenty minutes ago.

"And now?" he managed to ask. He knew the answer he wanted to hear, even if he might not be ready to hear it.

Anika lifted a shoulder. "Now it seems like there was only ever one person who'd abandoned me and that was my mother. That's not insignificant, I know. But the people I always assumed never cared, were never given the chance. They never left me, they never abandoned me. Maybe it's time that I stop assuming everyone will, because when I think about it, I've had way more examples of people who care, of people who stick, than people who leave."

As she spoke those last words, Anika rose and held her hand out to him. He hesitated. Not because he didn't want to take it, but because there was so much possibility between them that it was overwhelming. Almost.

He stood and took her hand. They didn't have to decide everything right now, but he very much wanted her to know that *that* path was one he wanted to take with her. Pulling her to him, she wrapped her arms around his waist, and he wrapped his around her shoulders, placing a kiss on her head.

She pulled back enough to see him, then slid a hand from his waist to his neck and pulled his lips to hers. The kiss was gentle as they tentatively explored this foray into something new. Then her hand slid under his shirt and pressed against his bare back, and there was nothing he could do to stop his body reacting.

He took control of the kiss, deepening it, as one hand tangled in her hair and the other dropped to the hem of her sundress. She hissed a "yes," when his fingertips made contact with her thigh then inched up.

"Dominic," she said, wrapping a leg around his hip and pulling herself closer. His body was on board with this new development, even if, in the back of his mind, he still questioned whether now was the time and place.

But when Anika's phone rang, the decision was taken away from both of them. "You need to get that Nik," Dominic said, feathering kisses down her neck and releasing her leg.

"I don't," Anika countered, trying to pull him closer.

"It could be one of your brothers, and they'll be wanting to check in with you. If you don't answer, you know they'll drive over." He placed his hands on her shoulders and held her still as he took a step back. As if to prove his point, the phone stopped ringing, but not three seconds later started again.

With a frustrated exhale that had Dominic smiling, Anika took a reluctant step away from him and swiped her phone up off the coffee table. Just before she answered, she flashed the screen at him letting him know that it was, indeed, one of her brothers.

"Hey Brody," she answered.

Dominic picked up their empty glasses and took them to the kitchen. After placing them in the dishwasher, he leaned against the counter, giving Anika some privacy to fill her brother in on the events of the evening. Several minutes later, she appeared in the doorway looking more beautiful than he'd ever seen her before.

"Can we pretend that call didn't happen and pick up where we left off?" she asked with a hopeful smile. Though by the tilt of her head, she looked to be anticipating the answer he didn't really want to give but would.

"A lot has happened tonight, Nik. I don't think there's any doubt where we both want this thing between us to go, but maybe we should slow it down and start with something a little less intense, like a dinner date or something."

The face she made brought a smile to his lips. "I knew you were going to say that, spoil sport. For the record, *I* don't need to take it slow and *I* don't need to slow things down. This day *has* been intense, but among the many things I've been feeling, the certainty of what I want with you is one of those. But if you need to slow it down, I can respect that. I may be a little disgruntled about it, but the last thing I want is for you to feel pushed into anything."

He wasn't feeling pushed into anything but knew that if he spoke those words out loud, he'd be weakening his own argument. So instead, he reached for her hand, and when she placed it in his, he tugged her into a hug.

"Dinner at my place tomorrow. I'll cook," he said.

She hummed something that sounded like "yum" against his chest. His mother may be the chef in the family, but she'd taught all her babies a thing or two in the kitchen.

"Okay, you need to go now," Anika said on an exhale as she moved out of his embrace. "If you don't, I won't be responsible for my actions."

He chuckled at that then scooted around her and walked toward the door. "See you at the office tomorrow?"

"As you so succinctly put it, we do have three murders to

solve and a hitman to find. So, yes, you'll see me at the office tomorrow."

He opened her door and stepped out into the hallway, where he hesitated. He turned to look back at Anika who was leaning against the wall of her entry hall watching him. Pulling up some inner strength he didn't know he had, he took one more step away. "Sleep tight, Nik."

A ghost of a smile graced her face. "I think I might have slept better, but I'll get by." And with that, she gently closed the door.

Dominic stood in the hallway, contemplating the closed door, then, with a shake of his head, he walked toward the elevators. In his mind, he was doing the right thing, but if it was the right thing, why did it feel so wrong? Why did it feel like there was an invisible string pulling him back to Anika?

He stared at the doors, waiting for them to open and once they did, he stared at the empty car. The doors began to slide shut, and yet his feet hadn't moved. He held his hand out to keep them open, but still couldn't bring himself to step inside. To leave Anika.

What the fuck was he thinking? On the surface, it might seem like a good idea to slow things down, but both he and Anika knew their own minds. Why was he suddenly throwing up roadblocks that didn't need to be there? Why was he wasting one more night without her?

He spun on his heels and took the twenty strides back down the hallway to her door. With the blood pounding through his veins, he knocked. His hand hadn't even dropped before Anika opened the door.

For a heartbeat, they stared at each other. Then in the next, they were wrapped in each other's arms. Dominic was distantly aware of the door closing behind them as he backed Anika against the wall. Their lips fused, their tongues tangled, and only for a moment—just long enough to pull his shirt over his head and her dress off—did they separate.

He pressed her against the wall, lifting her as he did. She shoved her underwear down and, kicking them to the side, Dominic experienced a little bit of heaven when her legs came around his waist. In the cool, whitewashed hallway, they explored each other in a way they never had before—in a way he'd fantasized about more times than he cared to remember. Unhooking her bra, he kissed his way down her neck while her hands made fast work of the button and zipper of his shorts.

But before they fell, he had the presence of mind to issue one order. "My wallet, Nik. Get my wallet."

With a fucking sexy chuckle, she reached into the back pocket of his shorts and grabbed it before shoving them down. He kicked them off and as soon as the barrier was gone, she pressed against him, with just his boxer briefs separating them. He heard his wallet hit the floor then suddenly Anika's hands were back on him, pushing away the last barrier between them.

"Hold on," he demanded. She instantly wrapped her arms around his neck and he released his hold on her long enough to pull his boxer briefs down. The heat of her body scorched him, and he sucked in a breath.

"Fuck, Anika," he said, dipping to drop a line of kisses along her shoulder as she rolled the condom on him. It took every ounce of control he possessed to wait until she had it on before sinking into her, and the second they were both protected, he did just that. With one long thrust, he buried himself in her heat.

From somewhere deep inside him, a strangled groan worked its way out as he tried to catch his breath. He inhaled once, then once again. Anika's little moans and the way her body gripped his wasn't helping his control.

Resting his forehead against the wall above her shoulder, he pulled almost all the way out, then pushed back in again.

"Dominic," Anika huffed and squirmed against him.

He drew back enough to look her in the eye, then stroked

into her again, then again. Her blue eyes went hazy with their movements, but then he paused, buried deep inside her, and she raised her eyes to meet his gaze.

"This is what we're supposed to be, isn't it?" he asked. Whatever it was that flowed between them, whatever it was that was more than just the physical pleasure, she felt it, too. Because it wasn't something he could be feeling on his own.

Slowly, but without hesitation, she nodded. "Yes," she whispered. "This is what we're supposed to be."

CHAPTER FIFTEEN

"Any news on Grant's autopsy?" Beni asked as she dropped her computer bag onto her desk. Dominic and Anika had been in the office reviewing records and files for about an hour. Beni had just finished a night shift at Hemmeleigh, and Alexis, Damian, and Jake were each in one of the small conference rooms having their weekly phone meetings with the security teams of the various attendees of The Summit. Dominic was scheduled to do his today as well, but as most of the attendees' teams he liaised with were in earlier time zones, he'd start his that afternoon.

Dominic looked over to Anika to answer. "Yeah," she said with a nod. "There was enough ketamine in his system to knock him out, but not kill him. The doc thinks he was drugged then placed in such a way that as he slowly went under, his body would slip farther and farther off the bed."

"Thus, strangling him slowly," Beni finished then made a face. "That's some weird, sneaky shit."

Anika shook her head. "I know. What I can't figure out is why he isn't just killing them. Why go through these semi-elaborate scenarios? Why throw Taglia off the roof when he could have just drugged him, and why leave bottles of ketamine in Khan's backpack when he'd been injected?"

"And why, if you have access to ketamine, give someone just enough to make strangling them easy?" Beni said.

Again, Anika nodded.

"It's like whoever he is wants to be sure we know it's a hit," Dominic said, sitting back in his chair, thinking that statement over. That was more the MO of a serial killer who was taunting law enforcement than that of a professional hitman. As far as Dominic knew, hitmen, like assassins, preferred to be in and out with as little fanfare as possible.

"Is it possible it's a serial killer?" he asked, then ran through his thought process with Anika and Beni. While he spoke, Alexis joined them, leaning against her desk as she listened.

When he finished, they all looked to Alexis for her input. As the only trained psychologist of the group, she often had a different take on things. She didn't answer right away and seemed to be considering the options.

"You're right in that there seems to be some sort of game going on which *is* more like a serial killer," she said. "But given that all three victims worked for The Bank of DC, I'm still leaning toward the deaths being a hit."

Everyone lapsed into silence after Alexis' observation. Even though they knew she was likely right, that still meant they had a hitman playing some weird-ass games. But was it the hitman playing games with law enforcement? Or were the hits being carried out exactly the way whoever was paying for them intended, and it was the employer playing games?

"Guys," Damian said entering the room. Everyone's attention swung to him as he joined their group. "I was doing a little research while I was on my last call—that particular security team likes to talk among themselves *a lot* when we have our calls," he said as an aside to Anika. "And I looked up the name of the recruiting firm that Loose Ends Studio said they used and there's no record of the name of the recruiter they said recommended Taglia."

"I'm assuming you've already considered that maybe they've moved on and are no longer with the company?" Beni asked.

Damian slid her an unimpressed look. "Of course I've considered that. The thing is, there is no record of that person at all. When I couldn't find her, I asked my friends to have a look, and no one by that name, or any similar name, was ever on the payroll, or a consultant, with that firm."

"So, either Loose Ends was lying to us or the recruiter they worked with gave them a fake name," Anika said.

"And based on how this case seems to be shaping up, I'm gonna go with door number two," Dominic said. "Hiring a hitman to kill three people and being able to orchestrate their presence on the island at the same time makes me think that someone with money—"

"Or a lot of power," Alexis interjected.

Dominic nodded. "Or a lot of power is involved. The kind of person who can infiltrate a recruiting firm then vanish into the wind."

"But someone at Loose Ends must be involved," Anika said. "Taglia changed gears from working at a bank to a movie studio…not your usual kind of career move. Someone at Loose Ends must have advocated for hiring him."

That made sense, too, but the question now was who. As to *why*, well, it was becoming clearer by the day that Taglia, Khan, and Grant had been involved in something while at the bank—whether knowingly or not—and someone wanted to do a little housekeeping.

"And then there's the whole branding competition, you know the one Taglia won that got him this trip in the first place. Are we suggesting that was rigged?" Damian asked.

Dominic's head swam with the possibilities. But all of those possibilities were edging closer and closer to conspiracy theories, something he was innately reluctant to consider.

Anika leaned back and stretched, her chair creaking with the movement. He couldn't help it if his eyes were drawn to the way her back arched. She wore a black pencil skirt, white button-down blouse, and low black heels today. He'd be lying if he said he hadn't thought about bending her over something and having his way with her.

She threw him a look that told him she knew what he was thinking, then she lowered her arms and picked up her phone. "I don't know. It seems like too much, but if someone has the money to somehow get three people to Tildas Island for the sole purpose of killing them and then hiring someone to do that, then maybe pulling all those strings—like orchestrating Taglia's branding contest—isn't such a big deal."

Dominic's phone lit up on his desk and he picked it up. His attention darted to Anika when her name appeared on his screen. He unlocked the phone and opened the message.

"I'm not wearing any underwear," it said.

He about swallowed his tongue at the thought.

"I'll look into Khan," Beni said. "If there was something hinky about how Taglia was hired, maybe there was something weird about Khan's move, too, and if so, the more data we have the better."

"Really," he wrote back.

"What about Grant and the woman from the video? Have you been able to ID her yet?" Alexis asked.

"No, I'm kidding, now get back to work," she responded, drawing a laugh from him. Until he noticed everyone was looking at him.

"What?" he asked.

"Something funny?" Damian asked. His head was cocked to

the side and he was studying Dominic closely. In fact, so were Alexis and Beni.

He cleared his throat. "No ID and we won't get one. I talked to the manager this morning, and it appears the woman was dropped off at the resort and the first sighting of her on their cameras is when she walks across the parking area to a path that runs alongside the main building. There's a blind spot in the coverage for about fifty feet, and the next time we see her, she's with Grant."

"We haven't talked to the girlfriend about it though," Anika said. "Maybe that should be our next stop?" she asked, looking at him. Great, just what he needed, time alone with Anika while contemplating other people's sex lives.

"Sure," he said, locking his computer and rising from his seat. "Why don't we head over now since I have calls I need to make this afternoon." At least those hours he spent discussing security protocols would give him a little breather from the temptation that was Anika Anderson.

"While Beni looks into Khan, I'll look into the overlapping accounts. Maybe now that we have a third case, we can narrow the list even further?" As Alexis asked, she shot a pleading look at Damian. It had been his computer experts that had been able to get them the initial list.

Damian sighed dramatically. "I still have a few more calls to make, but come with me to the conference room and I'll call Brian and Naomi first. Wouldn't hurt to introduce you to them, anyway."

"Oh, is that the Naomi that's married to Jason Greene, the soon to be Hall of Fame pitcher?" Beni asked.

Dominic chuckled as he and Anika gathered their things. Beni was a diehard Boston Rebels fan and had been jonesing to meet Naomi DeMarco since she'd first found out that Damian's good friend was married to the now-retired pitcher.

. . .

"You already know it's the same Naomi, and given that she and Jay just had twins, I'm thinking that the little fantasy you've built up about talking all-baseball-all-the-time with him, isn't going to come to pass," Damian said, though he didn't object when Beni joined him and Alexis as they headed toward the conference room Damian had been using earlier.

"I get it, I do, but maybe I could say hi?" Beni asked. Whatever Damian said in response was lost when he shut the door.

"My dad is a big Rebels fan," Anika said as they walked toward the exit. "Is Damian really friends with him? Have you ever met him?"

Dominic shook his head and chuckled. "God save me from rabid baseball fans."

"No, he never would have done anything like that," Laura managed to say through her sobs. Her friend Kristy had arrived the night before and now sat beside Laura, comforting her. "Jason's dad left his mom for an endless string of women when Jason was about twelve, or maybe thirteen. He saw what that did to his mom, and he always vowed he wouldn't become his father," Laura added.

Most of the time, Anika liked her job, but pulling back the veil, and revealing who someone really was to those who'd thought they'd known them, was one thing she didn't care for. And there was no mistaking what Grant had been doing with their mystery woman the night before he'd died, despite what Laura believed.

"There must be some other explanation," Kristy said, running a hand down Laura's back.

There wasn't, but Anika didn't need to drill that fact home.

"When was the last time you talked to him?" Anika asked, changing the direction of the interview.

"Two nights ago, the night before I arrived," she answered. "He called me. Or maybe I called him. I don't remember."

Anika glanced at Kristy. Based on what they'd already been told, Laura had flown down to Miami from DC the day before her flight to Tildas in order to catch up with her friend before joining Grant at Seasons. Maybe Kristy remembered?

Kristy shook her head. "I was on a twenty-four-hour shift and didn't get home until seven in the morning. I'm a resident at the city hospital," she added.

Anika paused. "You were on shift the night your friend came down to visit you?"

Kristy made a face. "When you're a resident, you go where they tell you to when they tell you to. It wasn't ideal, but the few hours we got to spend together in the morning were better than nothing. It's been a few years since we've had a chance to see each other in person."

Anika wanted to ask if Laura had stayed in a hotel but wasn't quite sure how to do it without it sounding like she suspected Laura. She didn't. After all, she and Dominic had been there when Laura had gotten off the flight the afternoon *after* Grant's death, but she felt like she was missing part of the story.

She glanced at Dominic again, who gave a slight nod of his head, then he spoke. "Yeah, I get it. My sister is a doctor and they worked her to the bone during residency. I'd sometimes crash at her place when I was on leave, and she'd come straggling in at odd hours of the day or night. It was so rare that I had leave when she had any time off, though, so we took what we could."

Kristy nodded. "Yeah, I definitely wasn't my best when I got home. But Laura had a pot of coffee going, reservations for brunch, and an appointment for a mani-pedi. I crashed pretty hard after she left, but we took advantage of the time we had together."

"Can you tell me if there is anyone in Jason's family we should notify? We talked to his office yesterday and you're listed as his emergency contact, and we know his mother passed away, but is there anyone else?"

Laura sniffed then dabbed her eyes with a tissue. "He's estranged from his dad, for obvious reasons. I'm not even sure if the man is alive. He has a grandmother and an aunt, but I can call them today. I think it might be better coming from me."

"If you think that's best," Anika replied gently, then both she and Dominic rose. "If there's anything you need, you know how to reach us."

"Do you have any leads? Any idea who might have done this?" Laura asked. "And when can I arrange for a service for him?"

"We're pursuing several leads, and we'll keep you updated. As for when we can release the body, we'll check with the Medical Examiner today and let you know," Dominic said.

Laura gave them a watery smile but didn't rise from her seat.

"We'll be in touch," Anika reiterated, then she and Dominic left the two women. Without a word, they made their way down to the lobby and back onto the street.

"Walk to the cab stand?" Dominic asked when they paused outside the door of the hotel to don their sunglasses. The hotel where Laura was staying was close to the heart of Havensted and the main beach. The area was notorious for its lack of parking, so they'd taken a cab down rather than drive.

"It's a little far, but I wouldn't mind walking back to the office."

Dominic's eyebrows went up. Very rarely did anyone who lived on Tildas suggest walking anywhere in Havensted. Aside from the heat that seemed to get trapped in the asphalt and buildings, there were tourists everywhere—walking, trying to drive, in the plethora of cabs. Overall, it wasn't a great experience if you were simply trying to get from one place to another, but Anika felt the need to stretch her legs and let her mind sift through all the information they'd collected over the past few days.

Dominic gestured her forward and she took the lead, pulling her hair up and into a bun as she walked. They dodged a few cars that didn't heed a stop sign, crossed the street to avoid a gaggle of tourists on a tour, and were slowly making their way to the FBI office, when she had a sudden craving.

"You ever been to Pete's food truck?" she asked.

"Never heard of it," Dominic said, grabbing her arm and pulling her out of the way of a tourist more focused on the camera in his hand than where he was going.

"Not surprised, he gets most of his business from the government buildings during the day and usually parks in an alley by the courthouse, then he heads out to Ruby Beach for the afternoon."

"Yeah, two places I don't usually go," Dominic said with a chuckle. Ruby Beach was a prime tourist beach. It was far enough away from the cruise ships that it looked quintessentially Caribbean, but close enough that it was easy for the visitors to get back and forth.

Anika grinned. "Follow me and let me introduce you to one of the island's best kept secrets," she said, turning a corner and heading toward the courthouse.

Fifteen minutes later they were standing beside Pete's Pate Truck eating little fried pockets of goodness.

"So it's spelled like pate, but pronounced like 'paty'?" he asked.

She nodded as she swallowed. "Only the 'ee' sound at the end isn't a hard sound."

"Why have I not heard about these before?" Dominic asked, taking a bite and obviously relishing the traditional street food that was shaped a little like a large pirogi, but made with dough, stuffed with a variety of fillings, then fried. She was having the chicken and sweet potato while Dominic was having pork.

"Because no one does them like Pete, and for those of us in the know, we like to keep it quiet, so his truck doesn't get inundated at lunch. Then he goes to the tourist spot and you're not there, nor are you likely to talk to tourists who might sing his praises."

Dominic rolled his eyes at her pedantic answer. "I'm just a little annoyed you didn't introduce me to it earlier."

"You didn't earn that privilege until last night," she retorted with a grin.

His head snapped up, and even from behind his aviator sunglasses, she could feel the heat in his gaze. "You have no idea the things I want to do to you right now."

Her grin turned into a smile. "Yeah, I kinda do. But since we're in the middle of a workday, let's grab some lunch for your colleagues and head back to the office."

He grumbled something but dutifully stepped back into line and ordered a dozen pates for the office. She and Pete chatted while he prepared them and once all the goodies were bagged, she and Dominic walked toward the main street that would take them to the FBI offices. They crossed at a light and were about to turn north when a voice called from behind them.

"Anika!"

Both she and Dominic turned to see Mateo jogging up the block on the other side of the street. Beside her, Dominic muttered something under his breath.

"I'll be just a minute," she said.

He shot her a disgruntled look.

"Once this temporary assignment is over, I'll still have to work with him, so yeah, I have to play nice."

Dominic let out a deep breath. "You're right, I'm sorry. I'll wait here for you."

She had the urge to lean up and kiss his cheek and though

they'd done that hundreds of times when they'd been just friends, doing it in the middle of the workday seemed like it could be announcing something they might not intend to announce quite yet, so she forced herself to turn and walk back the across the street.

"Hey Mateo, how's it going?" she asked, joining him on the sidewalk.

"I see you introduced Burel to Pete's?"

The comment didn't warrant an answer, so she remained silent.

Mateo sighed. "Look, I'm sorry I didn't stand up for you. I know how Maddox is, and I knew you were right. Even if it hadn't turned out to be murder, those two deaths warranted a better investigation than Maddox or I would have given them."

It was all well and good to have Mateo apologizing to her now, but the truth would be in the pudding, so to speak, when she returned to her job. Would he finally start to respect her intelligence and abilities as a partner, or would he continue to treat her like she was just passing time as a detective and keep kowtowing to Maddox?

"Apology accepted," she said truthfully and without reservation. That didn't mean she was going to trust him again, though. He'd have to earn that back.

"That's it?" Mateo asked, drawing back in surprise.

"I'm not interested in holding grudges, Mateo," she said. "It takes too much effort."

"So, we're good then? When you come back, I mean?"

She shrugged. "We'll see. Depends on you, really. An apology only goes so far if there isn't a change of behavior."

Mateo studied her and, in that moment, she saw a flash of anger. Or perhaps she was attributing too much to him and it was just frustration that while she was willing to forgive, she wasn't willing to forget.

"I see," he said.

She inclined her head in acknowledgment that he did, in fact, see. They stood there for a beat, the limbo of their relationship hovering between them.

"Well, I guess you better get back to it then," Mateo said with a nod to Dominic. Anika looked over and almost laughed. Dominic stood staring at them, his feet apart, his arms crossed, and the bag of pates hanging from his fingers.

"Yeah, I guess I better. I'll send my update to Maddox tonight," she said. Mateo nodded, then she turned and walked to the traffic light. She heard Mateo walk away, but her attention was focused on Dominic who'd moved from his spot and was currently standing on the opposite corner waiting for her.

When the light turned green, she started across the street, her eyes on the man in front of her and her mind on everything she wanted to do with him that night. That distraction was probably the only reason she didn't see the sneaky little pothole that was the perfect size for the heel of her shoe to sink right into.

She stumbled and lurched to the side when her right heel jammed in the small hole. Holding her arms out she focused on regaining her balance and once she was sure she wasn't going to take a header in the street, she repositioned her left foot to give her leverage and tried to tug her right one out.

But the little bugger was stuck tight.

Glancing at the walk sign and seeing it still green, she slipped her foot from her shoe and knelt to try and pull it out.

"You okay?" Dominic called out as he started crossing the street to help her.

"Got my stupid heel stuck. I hardly ever wear heels, and this is the reason—"

But the rest of the words she'd been about to say died in her throat when she heard the rev of an engine. Her head jerked up and her heart stuttered as her eyes zeroed in on the front grill of a white jeep barreling toward her.

"Anika!" Dominic shouted.

She wouldn't have time to rise and jump out of the way, so she did the next best thing, she pushed off her feet, launching herself backwards. She was prepared to hit the ground and roll, but just as the asphalt brushed her hands, Dominic's arms came around her from behind, lifting and spinning her away.

The motion, coupled with the fear and adrenaline, made her momentarily dizzy, but by the time she processed what had happened, she was already safe. Dominic's body was flush against hers, with her back pressed up against a streetlamp.

"Are you okay?" he asked, breathing hard. She nodded and in the next instant, his hands were all over her, searching for any injuries.

"I'm fine, Dom," she said, wrapping a hand around his bicep. He took a step back and eyed her. "Really, I'm fine. A little surprised. A little hyped on adrenaline, but not injured."

They stared at each other, then slowly, their breathing leveled out. When her heart was no longer trying to escape from her chest, she glanced toward the street to see her shoe, still jammed in the pothole, but now broken and crushed under the weight of the car that had run over it. Dominic's gaze followed hers and he shuddered.

"You're really okay?" he asked softly, then, as if unable to stop himself, he pulled her into his arms and rested his cheek on her head. She nodded against him.

"Not even a scratch, thanks to you."

She felt him smile. "You had already hurled yourself out of harm's way, but I didn't like the idea of you getting all banged up on asphalt."

"And I thank you for that. Now," she said, taking a deep breath and reluctantly stepping away. "If those pates are still in decent shape, I think it's time to head to the office. I could use a drink, but barring that, I know Alexis leaves some of her juice in the fridge in the kitchen and that's almost as good."

Dominic smiled down at her and brushed back a piece of her hair that had come loose in the melee. "Yeah, she does. First things first, though." He nodded to a store three doors down. "I think we need to get you a new pair of shoes."

CHAPTER SIXTEEN

"Guess what I found, Dom-n-Nik" Jake sing-songed when they walked into the office.

"You won't get the opportunity to tell us if you use that name again," Dominic replied. Yeah, he was feeling a little testy. And freaked out. Funny how having someone gun their car at someone you love would do that to you. Wait, love?

He glanced over at Anika who was walking toward her desk, trying not to limp. In the scheme of things, she hadn't hurt herself—thank-fucking-god—but she had twisted her ankle when she'd stepped into the pothole and it was a little tender— something that hadn't been immediately obvious but had revealed itself as they'd walked to the office, after getting her new shoes.

He let out a deep breath, set the bag of pates on his desk, and took a seat. At her desk, Anika did the same, wincing a little when she leaned on her shoulder. He'd tried to be gentle when he'd grabbed her, but adrenaline might have had him responding a little more fiercely than he'd intended. She shot him a look that was meant to reassure him that she was fine, but instead it pissed him off. Yeah, he loved her. Jake and Damian hadn't been wrong. And someone had just tried to run her over. He had a lot to be pissed about.

"Why are you wearing different shoes, Anika?" Jake asked.

Both Dominic and Anika drew back in surprise at the question.

Jake gave a dramatic eye roll and let out a long-suffering sigh. "I *told* you I notice things. Now why are you wearing a different pair of shoes? And favoring your right foot if I'm not mistaken?"

"It's nothing," Anika said.

"Or it's that someone tried to run you over," Dominic countered. If Anika was in danger, he wanted his teammates to know.

"It might not have been on purpose," she said, though her tone said she didn't believe that any more than he did.

Dominic shot her a look then handed Jake the bag of pates to pass around. "It was a crime of opportunity," he said, then he proceeded to tell his teammates exactly what had happened.

When he was done, Alexis turned to him, her brow furrowed. "Didn't you say you saw a white jeep at the hotel where Taglia was found and then again at The Shack the night we were all there? You said you got the plates, but did you ever run them?"

"Uh, that would be my bad," Jake said, shooting Dom an apologetic look. "Dom gave me the plate, but that was the same day we found the connection between Taglia, Khan, and the Bank, and I got a little distracted." He paused and cast a troubled look at Anika before turning to Dom. "Dude, I am *so* sorry."

"There's been a lot going on," Anika said in an obvious attempt to assuage Jake's self-loathing. "Between the additional murders, my screwed-up department, and the arrival of my heretofore unknown biological family—"

"Whoa, wait. Did you say your biological family is here?" Surprisingly, the question came from Alexis and not Jake.

Anika made a face and nodded. "It turns out I have a whole family that I knew nothing about until two days ago and who didn't know that I existed until two months ago," she said.

Dominic looked at all his teammates. To a one, they were all gawking at Anika, each of them with a pate in hand.

"There's got to be more to the story than that," Beni said.

"Oh, there is," Anika said with a wan smile. "But for now, can we focus on the case?"

Damian cleared his throat. "Of course. You going to run those plates now, Dom?" he asked.

Dominic nodded. "And maybe while I'm doing that, Jake can tell us what he was so eager to tell us when we walked in?"

"Well, a little bit of my thunder has been stolen, but if you're still interested, guess who was at a fundraiser in Miami last night?"

Dominic didn't look up from the program that would allow him to look up license plates, but if he was a betting man, he'd place good money on Beni having speared Jake with one of her *looks* because Jake didn't wait for an answer.

"Check out this picture of Calvin Matthews with our very favorite bad guy, Duncan Calloway." At that, Dominic did look up. Jake flipped his screen around and sure enough, there were the two men in question. Calloway stood a few feet behind Matthews, but both men held drinks and were smiling.

"Who's the woman in the photo?" Damian asked.

"Georgina Grace," Jake said.

Dominic leaned closer. "Calloway's half-sister? The one who's on the board of Wainwright Holdings, the company that owns the island we were almost blown up on?"

Jake nodded. Dominic and Damian had been tracking a man who was involved in the sale of a CIA asset when the deal went south. The two of them had almost been caught in the blast intended to take him out.

"Wow, Matthews hangs out with some interesting people," Damian said.

Beni started to say something, but whatever it was, Dominic stopped paying attention when his computer dinged. Sure enough, just as he'd thought, the car was registered to a local car rental company. As his teammates and Anika talked, he did a little more digging and found that the car had been rented ten days ago by someone named Patrick Dearil. Dominic was sure it would be an alias, but even so, he pulled up the databases they used for background checks and plugged in the name and the address on the driver's license Dearil had provided to the rental agency.

When he looked up from his computer, he realized that Anika and the team were making plans for everyone to meet up at The Shack that night. And by everyone, they were talking about everyone in Anika's inner circle. Her two families had wanted to meet so apparently, they, and everyone on the team and their significant others, were going to get together at The Shack for dinner. With that many people, it was bound to be a rowdy night, but whoever had the idea, it was a good one. The Shack was a place Anika knew, and throwing her two families together in the presence of a supportive group of friends, and at a location she was comfortable, was probably the best way to ensure she'd be as at ease as possible.

"You look like you have something," Damian said, reaching for his second, or maybe third, pate.

"Yeah, the car is rented to Patrick Dearil. I suspect that if he's involved in any of this that it's not his real name, but I'm running the usual checks," Dominic answered. If he hadn't been looking at Jake, who'd also reached for another pate, he would have missed the slight hesitation in his friend's movement. Dominic's eyes narrowed. "Anyone know him?" he asked, thinking Jake might say something if prompted.

There was a chorus of nos, but Jake strategically took a huge bite of a pate rather than answer. Dominic turned away but kept watch on his friend from the corner of his eye. If there was something Jake didn't want to say in front of the team, Dom didn't want to draw attention to his behavior.

"I came up blank on Khan's hiring," Beni said. "I'll keep looking, but I talked to the HR department at his company and they said he applied through their website. It's possible he was recruited, like his sister said, then told to go through the system, but there's no record of that and without Khan to talk to, we may never know."

"Who assigned him to the account that brought him down to Tildas Island?" Anika asked.

"One of the partners put him on it. They knew he liked to travel, and he was one of the few lead auditors with no family so he traveled a lot. There could be more to the story, but I want to be more prepared if we're going to push the partner on it," Beni answered.

"Well, while all this is well and good," Dominic said. "I'm going to get back to Patrick Dearil and tapping into traffic cams to see if he was the one who tried to hit Anika. Then I have to make all my security calls. What all are you guys doing?"

His teammates were doing the same thing he was, balancing their duties around The Summit with the investigation, while Anika announced she was going to head over to the morgue and talk to Dr. Rasmussen. Dominic didn't love the idea of her out on her own, but it wasn't like he could keep her wrapped in bubble wrap. Not only did he not *want* to do that, she'd unman him if he even tried.

The sun was starting to drop behind the mountain ridge that ran the length of the island when Jake knocked on the door to the small conference room where Dominic was sitting while making his calls. He was wrapping up his second to last one, so he waved Jake in.

With the rest of the team gone for the day, or at

Hemmeleigh, and Anika on her way home before meeting everyone at The Shack, he and Jake were the last people in the office.

"What's up?" Dom asked as soon as he ended the call.

Jake took a seat, shifted his gaze out the window, and drummed the fingers of his left hand on his thigh.

"Does this have to do with Patrick Dearil?" Not surprising, the background check into Patrick Dearil had drawn a blank, although Dom had been able to confirm the car that had almost hit Anika was the same car rented to the man.

Jake's eyes snapped to his. After a beat, he nodded. "You done for the night?" he asked.

"I have one more call, then I'm done. We need to be up at The Shack in a couple of hours, though."

"Yeah, mind if we grab a beer beforehand at The Queens?" Jake asked.

The Queens was one of their favorite bars in Havensted, one of the few they visited in town, since most of the team, with the exception of Beni, preferred to spend as little free time in Havensted as possible. It was a great city, but it teemed with tourists more often than not.

"Sure," Dominic said. "This last call won't take long. Meet up in thirty minutes?"

Jake gave a sharp nod, then rose and left without another word. He was being so un-Jake-like that Dominic was a little worried. Figuring the fastest way to find out what was going on with his friend was to get the call done, he picked up the phone and dialed the last number for the night.

Forty-five minutes later, Dominic took a sip of his beer as he and Jake grabbed a small table near a large open window. The Queens was the oldest bar on the island and its rock and mortar construction, coupled with heavy beams and shutters of dark wood, gave it a bit of the feel of the days of the pirates. In fact, it wasn't hard to picture Blackbeard sidled up in the back corner drinking his rum.

"So, what's going on?" Dominic asked.

Jake took a drink then met Dom's gaze. "Well, as it turns out, I sort of know Patrick Dearil, and I might know how to track him down and you might—no, you definitely—need to come to Miami with me tomorrow on Shah's orders."

Dominic heard the words. They even made sense, logically. But... "When you say you 'sort of know' Dearil, do you mean you know him personally?" It was hard to imagine Jake knowing a hitman personally, but he had said he "knew" him, not that he "knew of" him.

Jake took another sip of his drink and let his gaze wander to the few tourists out at this hour—too late for afternoon shopping and too early for dinner. "Yeah," he said on an exhale, "There's something you should know about me. Well, not me, but my family. It's a doozy, so you might want to take another sip of that drink."

And Jake—who was the king of hyperbole—wasn't lying. Over the next few minutes, he told Dominic the story of his father and brothers, all of whom were part of an organized crime syndicate that spread across the United States. Jake told Dominic about his mother's suspicious death, about his father's belief that Jake was in the FBI solely for the purpose of helping the family, and about his younger brother's rise to power. Most surprising of all was when Jake told Dom about the deal he'd made with the FBI that had allowed him to even be considered for the Bureau, let alone accepted. Yeah, in a million years Dominic wouldn't ever have guessed that his best friend was essentially a double agent for the FBI, feeding information back to them and misinformation—sprinkled with enough legit intel —to his family.

"Um, okay. Wow," Dominic said, wholly unprepared for what he'd just been told. He wasn't quite sure what to do with the information, so he reverted to what he knew. "How does this relate to Patrick Dearil?"

"The noble angel of death," Jake said. "That's what his name means in Gaelic. Or maybe it's Celtic," he added when Dom raised his brow at him.

"He's a hitman for a family out of New York."

"The family your dad and brothers are associated with?" Dominic couldn't bring himself to refer to them as Jake's family. Jake, despite his somewhat fickle and devil-may-care attitude, was one of the most genuine, caring people Dominic had the privilege of calling a friend. That he was related to the people he was related to made him even more remarkable.

Jake shook his head in response. "No, but I remember hearing my dad talking about him one day. I was maybe twenty and home between surfing competitions. I happened to walk by my dad's office and the phone was on speaker—I guess he'd forgotten I was there, which was a blessing in many ways—but I heard the conversation between him and a family friend, Oscar Olde."

"When you say 'family friend' which family are you referring to?"

Jake gave him a ghost of a smile. "I thought a friend of my biological family, but that trip home was the first time I really caught wind of what my dad was involved in. I've known Oscar my whole life. He visited us many times in Hawaii, and we made a couple of trips to see him in Miami. At one point, I think he and my father were trying to set me up with his daughter, but then Lydia ran off with a guy she met on the train and now raises sheep in New Zealand. She's very happy," Jake added, in a very Jake way.

"But he was the other kind of family friend, too, wasn't he?"

"Oh, most definitely," Jake said, then he took a sip of beer. After he set the bottle down, he continued. "Anyway, he's kind of like a godfather—not the Robert Di Nero kind of godfather, but the traditional kind. He's way high up in the leadership of the family, though. He's the reason my younger brother has been so successful so far."

"And so what's with the trip to Miami?"

"That's where Oscar lives. Like I said, Dearil doesn't work for Oscar's family so Oscar might help us out. Shah also gave me some intel to barter with, and we're booked on a flight tomorrow, if you agree to come. If Dearil is the one behind the killings, every weird, quirky thing he's done, from throwing Taglia off the roof to leaving nearly empty pill bottles of medication Khan never took in Khan's backpack, is for a reason. Oscar won't know the reason, but he might be able to help us track Dearil down."

"And Shah wants me to go with you?"

Jake wagged his head. "She doesn't want me to go alone, and I'm man enough to acknowledge that I don't want to go alone either. She told me to pick a teammate, and I'm picking you if you'll take the job."

"Of course," Dominic answered with no hesitation. "What time do we leave?"

Jake's shoulders lowered a good three inches at Dom's acceptance, and it was then that Dominic saw how genuinely stressed Jake was about the situation.

"There's a nine o'clock flight tomorrow. We can fly in and out on the same day. It will be a long day, but unless we get detained, we should be back by midnight tomorrow."

Dominic nodded. "Sounds good. Want me to pick you up?"

"That would be great," Jake said. He set his empty beer bottle down, then looked up. "I know I don't need to say this, but thanks. Thanks for not freaking out on me. Thanks for not hesitating to have my back. It means more to me than you know, and I'm grateful I get to call you a friend even if you haven't bothered to tell me that you and Anika are a thing now."

For the second time that night, Dominic was caught by

surprise. It wasn't that he and Anika were hiding what was happening between them, but he was surprised Jake noticed given that neither had said a thing. Then again, as Jake was always telling everyone, he noticed things. Maybe Dominic shouldn't have been surprised, after all.

"Okay, my bad. Since we just crossed that line last night and with everything going on with *her* families and the case, I think you can cut us a little slack."

Jake shot him a flat look. "Right, that's what they all say."

Dominic rolled his eyes and rose from his seat. "I don't know who all 'they' is. Or who you're hanging out with that 'they' all say the same thing. But we've got more important things to do, like meet Anika's family tonight, then hop on a plane to meet some aging mafia dude in Miami tomorrow."

"He may be aging, Dom, but don't let him fool you," Jake said, following him as they wound their way past other drinkers toward the door. "You may be fish food before you know it if you piss him off."

"What about you?" Dominic asked as they stepped out onto the sidewalk.

Jake grinned. "I'm his godson. It's against the family code to do anything to me."

CHAPTER SEVENTEEN

DOMINIC SLID his sunglasses on as they exited the airport and stepped out into the Miami sunshine. The flight had been uneventful, and though he wouldn't have chosen to be anywhere else, between the early departure and the extra time needed to clear their weapons through TSA, he hadn't had as much time with Anika as he would have liked that morning.

Thankfully, the gathering the night before of Clan Anika—as Jake and Nia had dubbed it—had gone well and by the end of the evening, the Riley-Bowman families had a boating excursion planned with Brody, Anika's brother, and a tour of the Marine Center with Nia on the schedule. Phil was even bringing James to his shop to show him the classic car he was working on. Hopefully, somewhere in the remaining ten days that her biological family had left on the island, Anika would have some quiet time to spend with each of them. Which meant they really needed to solve this case.

"Cab or car service?" Dominic asked.

Jake arched a brow at him as a large Escalade with tinted windows pulled up. "You don't seriously think my godfather would let me take a cab anywhere, do you?"

Dominic eyed the monster SUV. "You sure it's a good idea to not have our own transportation?"

"You have so much to learn, Cricket," Jake said, reaching for the door handle. "If Oscar wanted us dead, he has people who would make it happen regardless of whether or not we had our own transportation. At least this way, neither of us has to navigate the morning commuter traffic."

Jake didn't wait for an answer but slid into the back seat and scooted over to sit behind the driver. Jake's dubious reassurance didn't do much to quell Dom's doubts. There was no way he was going to leave Jake on his own, though, so he followed his friend into the car.

The driver didn't say a word as they maneuvered out of the airport maze and turned north. About twenty minutes of silence passed before Dominic couldn't take it anymore. "Where are we going?" he asked.

"Golden Beach," Jake answered without hesitation.

"You couldn't have told me that before?" Fine, Dominic was feeling a little testy about having to pull answers from his usually chatty-as-a-canary friend when they were headed into the lair of a powerful mob boss.

"You didn't ask, and does it really matter?" Jake countered.

Dominic glared at his friend, then turned and glared out at the traffic. "Doesn't seem like something I'd need to ask," he muttered.

"So, you and the lovely detective?"

Dom whipped his head around. At least Jake hadn't mentioned her name in the presence of a mob stooge, but still, he didn't like the fact Jake had mentioned her at all. "Seriously? Now?"

Jake shrugged. "It's as good a time as any. Actually, you don't need to say anything. I had all the confirmation I needed last night. Took you a little while, but all good things are worth the wait. Or so Nia tells me when I start complaining about the months we wasted before getting together."

Dominic wasn't sure what to say to that. Or if Jake even needed a response, because half the time he said stuff, he didn't. It was like he had this valve in his head that he sometimes needed to open and say whatever came out and then he'd shut it again.

Dominic sighed. "So how much farther?"

"About another fifteen minutes, right Saul?" Jake asked and their driver nodded.

Dominic was beyond being surprised anymore, so the fact that Jake knew their driver didn't even warrant an arched eyebrow. The truth was, this was just going to be a weird-ass morning and he needed to let it be whatever it was going to be. After all, his only real job was to be Jake's backup, something he could do without having to know every piece of intel. Especially when he was pretty sure that those backup duties included more than physical protection. Jake might look relaxed, but Dominic knew better. This visit—this foray into his father's *family*—wasn't easy on him.

Right on schedule, they pulled up to an impressive set of gates that swung open to reveal a wide sweeping lawn with a pale pink Venetian style mansion at the end of the drive. Oddly, though clearly meant to convey a message of wealth and power, the house made Dominic smile. It was so cliché for an aging mob boss that he half-expected the man in question to greet them wearing a silk robe over a pair of swim trunks while carrying a glass of champagne and a cigar.

Five minutes later, Dominic was eating his own words—or thoughts, to be more specific. Oscar Olde did not look like a man he wanted to mess with. He wasn't particularly physically intimidating—coming in around five foot ten and with a trim build—but the vibes coming off the man were cool enough to freeze a Hot Pocket fresh out of the microwave. Oscar Olde's custom tailored suit probably cost more than a car, and it fit him so well it was almost impossible to see the outline of the gun he carried at his side. The only thing that even slightly resembled the man Dominic had imagined was the cigar tucked into the front pocket of his jacket.

"Jacob," Oscar said as he descended a massive, curved staircase, trailed by four men Dominic would describe as henchmen.

"Oscar," Jake replied. Oscar's gaze flitted to Dominic when he came to a stop in front of them, the four men fanning out behind him, but Jake didn't introduce him. Dominic wasn't sure if that was because Oscar already knew who he was or if it was some strange sort of power play by Jake. Either way, Dom wasn't about to introduce himself.

"Shall we meet in my office?" Oscar asked.

Neither Jake nor Dominic were fooled—it wasn't a question.

A few minutes later, they took their seats on one side of a wide desk while Oscar moved around to the other side and sat in the pride of place. The room, like the house, was clearly designed to make a statement and could rival Versailles with the amount of gilt in it.

Oscar took the cigar from his pocket and rolled it between his fingers. "Unlike your father, Jake, I know why you joined the FBI, and it wasn't to help the family. The reason I agreed to see you was because the information you've shared over the past several years has helped us avoid a few minor annoyances—nothing to give you any special standing, but enough to give you five minutes of my day."

"That and you're my godfather, whether you like it or not," Jake said, his voice conveying an easy—but not glib—statement of fact.

Oscar's eyes narrowed, but he didn't refute the statement. "Your mother was like a daughter to me."

At that, Jake chuckled. There was a story there Dominic didn't know and wasn't sure he wanted to.

"And having me come to you rather than my father will give you one more way to knock him down. Not that I mind. You can knock that piece of shit down as much as you want, and I'll be cheering you on, but that's not why we're here today. Now, since you've limited my friendly visit to five minutes, I'd rather get down to business."

Oscar eyed him, then held a handout. "I assume you have something for me?"

Jake pulled an envelope from his pocket and handed it over. Oscar reached across the desk, took the envelope then opened it. Pulling a piece of paper out, he unfolded it and read. His eyes flickered once to Jake, then returned to the paper. After a few seconds, he folded it back up and slipped it into his desk.

"What can I help you with?" Oscar asked.

"Patrick Dearil," Jake answered. "Though I suspect you already know that."

One of Oscar's manicured eyebrows went up.

"You keep tabs on everything and the man probably came through Miami on his way to Tildas. He's not one of yours, so we'd appreciate anything you're willing to share, as it could be mutually beneficial."

"I'm well aware of how much taking Dearil out of the picture would be a benefit," Oscar said. "There are larger things at play that you wouldn't understand, though."

"You mean like a conspiracy that involves not just our Vice President, but also several very wealthy and powerful people?" Jake countered.

Dominic kept his expression neutral, but inside his head, he was anything but. He'd been heading down the conspiracy theory, too, but had been trying to reason his way out of it for the past several weeks. With the realization that Jake had obviously been thinking something similar, he wondered how many of the rest of the team had also started pondering the possibility.

"I've been hearing things," Oscar said carefully. "But I'm not going to get into that now. You want Patrick Dearil?"

Jake nodded. "He's on our island, and we believe he's already carried out three hits. We know the link between the victims, and we will figure out why, but our priority is stopping him before anyone else dies."

"How do you know he has more than three people on his list?"

"We don't," Jake said. "But he was on the island yesterday and as soon as we ID'd him, we put flags at all the ports, and he hasn't left yet. Unless he's taking a vacation—which I suppose everyone is entitled to every now and then—the only reason for him to stay is if he still has names on his list."

Oscar eyed him, then glanced at one of his henchmen and gave a sharp gesture with his head toward Jake. Confirming Jake's prior assertion that Oscar had already known the purpose of their visit, the man withdrew a piece of paper from his pocket and handed it over to Jake. Jake read it then handed it to Dominic. On it was the name of a hotel and an address that looked like it was on the west side of the island. Dom folded it and tucked it into his pocket.

In sync, he and Jake rose. Oscar did not.

"Thank you," Jake said. "I'd say I'm surprised you had that information so handy, but I'm not."

For the first time since they'd arrived, Oscar's expression softened. "Like you said, you're my godson. You may have taken a path that conflicts with my life, but that doesn't mean I don't consider you family. Even if you'd rather I didn't."

Jake's jaw ticked, as if restraining himself from maybe saying something he didn't think should be said out loud. After a beat, he gave a curt nod. "Thanks."

"Stay safe, Jake," Oscar said. "Saul will take you to the airport now. If you're lucky, you can catch an earlier flight. I know you have things and people to get back to."

Jake hesitated at that not so subtle reference to Nia, but Oscar waved him on. "She's yours, Jake. You have my word no one will touch her. Or anyone that's yours," he added, flicking a glance at Dominic.

Jake held the man's gaze, then just when Dominic thought Jake's restraint might be waning—never one of his strong points—his friend turned his back and walked toward the door.

"There's a three o'clock flight, Dom. We can call on the way and see if they can change our tickets."

Without a word, Dominic followed his friend. He wasn't sure which of the two of them was more glad to be leaving behind this part of Jake's life.

By the time Dominic and Jake landed on Tildas, Anika and Damian had scoped out the hotel Oscar had identified. The information provided was just a name and no context, so they'd done a deep background on it and discovered that it was owned by the same holding company, Imperium Holding, that owned the island where they'd recently conducted a large drug bust. A company that included Duncan Calloway as well as a senator, a high-ranking FBI agent, and several other wealthy individuals, as shareholders.

What they didn't know was if Patrick Dearil was staying at the hotel or if Oscar had provided the information for another reason. The guest list, which Damian had gotten ahold of, didn't have Dearil's name on it, but he could have used an alias. Although why he'd rented the car under his own name raised more questions than they had answers for. Other than the killings themselves, there was a message Dearil had been sent to convey—it was in the way he killed and in the way he was out in the open, but still not—but that message was illusive, and it was making Dominic more irritated by the minute.

"I'm going to relieve Damian," Dominic said when they emerged from the Tildas Island airport terminal. Because they didn't know if Patrick was staying at the hotel, Damian and Anika had taken watch duty. Dominic didn't much like surveillance work, but it gave him something to do, and if he could do it with Anika, he figured it would be better than heading to the office, or worse, home.

"I'll grab a cab to Nia's," Jake said, already turning toward the cab stand. Two steps away, he turned back. "Thanks for going with me today, Dom. I know it's creepy as fuck and I'm really not proud of all the shit in my family's closet. Maybe some night, after a few too many, I'll tell you all about it, but it was good to have you there today."

There wasn't much to say to that, so Dominic nodded. He'd be there to listen if Jake ever needed him to and they both knew it. With a ghost of a smile, Jake turned again and walked away. Dominic watched him, glad he was heading to Nia's for the night, then walked toward his car.

Thirty minutes later, Anika slid into the passenger seat beside him. Once Damian's car was out of sight, Dominic pulled Anika in for a deep kiss.

"Miss me?" she teased when he released her.

"You have no idea."

"Bad day?"

He paused. "Weird. Not really bad, but weird. You?"

"Well, other than this hotel and the address on the west side of the island, which happens to be a shipping warehouse on the commercial docks, we didn't get very far."

"So, frustrating?"

"As hell," she concurred. "Alexis and Beni are researching the members of Imperium Holding, though. Judging by the way everyone in the office was reacting to that piece of intel, including Shah, I know it's important, but since it isn't directly related to Dearil and the three homicides, I figured I'd better focus on this," she said, gesturing to the hotel.

"Did you talk to James or anyone else from the family today?" he asked, grabbing a bag of goodies he'd picked up on the way and reaching into it.

"Yeah, they understand I need to work so they're trying to spend time with each other and my dad and brothers when they can. It's a little weird, but I figure we're all adults and we'll each need to figure out how to negotiate our own relationships in whatever way works."

"Speaking of negotiating changes," Dominic said, handing over a napkin-wrapped pate he'd picked up from Pete's on his way over. "So you know, you seriously changed my life with these." He emphasized his statement by taking a large bite. The taste of slow cooked pork exploded in his mouth. He moaned, he couldn't help it. He hadn't eaten all day—hadn't had much of an appetite. Now that he was back on Tildas with Anika, though, everything felt right again. They still had some shit to take care of, but he was where he was supposed to be.

Anika laughed. "And here I thought it was the sex that changed your life."

"Honey," he said, flashing her his grin. "That didn't change my life. That redefined it."

CHAPTER EIGHTEEN

"I THINK we need to check the warehouse out," Anika said to Dominic as she poured a cup of coffee from the pot.

"What?" he called over his shoulder from where he sat on his balcony. They'd been relieved of duty at five in the morning by Beni and Alexis and had returned to Dominic's apartment to crash for a few hours. Now they were taking a few minutes to enjoy some coffee and breakfast before heading back into the office.

"I think we need to check the warehouse out," she repeated, joining him outside. "I don't know what we'll find, but it was an odd piece of intel for Jake's contact to give us. It has to mean something."

Dominic set his newspaper down—yes, he was one of the few people their age who still received the print version of the paper—and stared out at the vibrant blue Caribbean. "Yeah, you're right," he said. "The hotel makes sense, since presumably Dearil has to stay somewhere while on the island. But the warehouse is odd. Do we know who owns it?"

Anika took a sip of her coffee then shook her head. "Beni was looking into it, but I don't know if she found anything."

Dominic picked up his phone from the side table and hit a few buttons. While he talked, Anika closed her eyes and enjoyed the morning sun and gentle breeze on her skin. She loved her apartment and the view of the tropical forest, but at Dominic's apartment, there was nothing quite like the trade winds that brought with them the smell of the ocean and the unique scents of a tropical island—something that was a mix of humidity, salt, and dense, floral greenery.

She half-listened to Dominic's call and when he hung up less than two minutes later, she looked over.

"It's owned by what appears to be a Chinese company," he said.

"Appears to be?"

He frowned. "Yeah, that was the initial intel Beni uncovered, but she isn't certain that's the end of the trail. She said she'll look into it more today, and she agrees we should go check it out."

Before Dominic finished speaking, Anika was already making plans. Tildas wasn't a huge island—bigger than most people thought, but still not large—and with less-than-stellar roads, it would take them a little over an hour and a half to make it from their complex to the warehouse. If they wanted to make it to the office to do any work that afternoon, they needed to get their day started.

With a disgruntled sound, she rose from her seat. "How long will it take you to get ready? I'll walk home, grab a quick shower and change, then meet you at the car?"

Dominic looked up at her, his green eyes lit with mischief. "Or I could grab a go bag, we could walk to your apartment, grab a shower together, and *then* head out."

She stared at him. They needed to get going, they really did. Not to mention, it wasn't the most professional decision to delay their departure for something so personal—as fun and as gratifying as it would be. The look in Dominic's eyes changed to something all the more intense.

"Ten minutes, maybe fifteen, that's all the time it will add," he all but growled.

Something low in her belly hummed at the promise. Letting out a shaky—and maybe needy—breath, she stepped away. "You have three minutes to grab your bag. Let's see what you can do, PJ."

Thirty minutes later, they were pulling out of their complex and heading west. Dominic wore a huge—well-deserved—grin, while she tried to concentrate on what her half-sister Eva was saying. Admittedly, what Eva was saying wasn't that complex—something about meeting for dinner then a sunset cruise—but to give credit where credit was due, the fifteen minutes in the shower might have scrambled her brains a little bit.

"I'll try to make it Eva," she said. "It depends on how things go today."

"Totally get it," Eva said, sounding every inch a twenty-two-year-old. "What you do is important and saves lives and all that. So, don't worry about us. If you can make it, you know where we'll be. If not, we'll try again another day."

Anika agreed, then ended the call with a promise to call toward the end of the day and, at Eva's insistence, also a promise to stay safe. Her biological family was being so accommodating that Anika had to wonder if the shine would eventually wear off or if they really were as reasonable—and as interested in getting to know her—as they seemed. She liked to think it was the latter, and while she was slowly accepting the fact that a key foundation of her development—her belief she'd been abandoned—had turned out to not be true, she wasn't quite prepared to jump in all the way. The novelty could wear off, they could decide they didn't like each other, all sorts of things could happen that might drive a wedge between her and this new family. She couldn't help but acknowledge that while it may be true that *this* family hadn't abandoned her, her mother *had*, and that had clearly left some scars.

"You okay over there?" Dominic asked.

"Beni's doing more research on the warehouse this morning, right?" She didn't really feel like getting into a deep discussion about her family, so she redirected the conversation.

Dominic glanced her way, his gaze lingering, then he turned his attention back to the road and shook his head. "Beni had something come up about The Summit. Jake's going to pick up the research and he said he'd send over anything he finds."

"What do you think we'll find?"

"Hard to say. Those warehouses store everything from construction supplies to cheap tourist tchotchkes. If it's truly owned by a Chinese company, it's probably one of those two things, but who knows."

There wasn't much use in hypothesizing what may or may not be in the warehouse, and they lapsed into silence. She watched the passing scenery as the miles ticked by. She didn't come to the west side of the island very often. Not many people did. There were two high-end eco-resorts, but other than that, it was mostly farm country. Beautiful, of course, with fields filled with crops of all sorts, from potatoes to mangoes, but not the sort of place someone traveling to the iconic beaches and beach bars of the Caribbean would seek out.

They made idle chit chat as they drove and an hour later, they hit the outskirts of Olmsberg, the port town on the western edge of the southern coast of Tildas. It was a working town with two deep sea harbors—one on the north side and the other on the south side—and an endless sea of warehouses and shipping storage in between the two. It was also the location of the island's primary electrical plant. All in all, an important part of the island's economy, but not a particularly pretty one.

Dominic had plugged the address of the warehouse into his GPS and he followed the directions to the gate of a nondescript yard filled with ten buildings. There was a guard at the gate and, not wanting to call any attention to themselves, Dominic drove by then pulled into a parking spot a block away.

"So, question of the day, do we walk up to the gate, flash our badges, and alert whoever owns the warehouse that we're looking into the area? Or do we find a way in that's less obvious, but risks having anything we find thrown out in court because we didn't follow procedures?"

Dominic's tone might have been light, but it was a serious question. If they were trespassing and found something, it's unlikely it would ever be usable either in court or to get a warrant.

With a disgruntled sigh, Anika stared at her side mirror and ran through the options. A group of four men, all wearing hardhats, crossed the street from one yard and entered the one she and Dominic were interested in. When they disappeared from sight, an idea came to her.

"Hold on," she said, reaching for her phone. She dialed a familiar number and Mateo answered on the second ring.

"Anderson, I heard about your family, your biological family, from Brody. You doing okay?"

Anika suppressed an annoyed retort. Brody had no business sharing that information with Mateo but getting into that now wouldn't be helpful. "I'm fine. Can you tell me if we have any parolees working in the yards at Olmsberg?"

Mateo hesitated. "Why would you want to know that and what are you doing out in Olmsberg?"

She sighed. It was a simple yes or no question. In just three days she'd forgotten what it was like to have someone question her every move. "Never mind, I'll call Rosey," she said.

"No, no, don't do that. Geez, I'll look. Give me a second and I'll send you what I find."

Anika muttered a "Thank you" and hung up before Mateo

could engage her in any more conversation. She turned to find Dominic smiling at her.

"What?" she asked.

"That was a great idea. I suspect more than a few parolees work here. You're just doing your job checking in on them."

To be fair, Mateo hadn't known why she was asking, but she was pretty sure that had it been Dominic she'd called, he would have said "Yeah, I'll send you what we've got," and *then* he would have asked what was going on and if she needed any help. It was a subtle—but significant—difference from questioning why and then grumbling about helping when he didn't get his way.

A heavy weight settled in her stomach. It was going to be tough to go back.

A few minutes later, her phone dinged with a message that included the names of four men and one woman who worked at the yards. Anika held the screen so Dominic could see and in response, he grinned.

"Ready to go check on some parolees?" he asked, sliding out the driver's side door. "You've got the police badge, so I'll follow your lead."

Yeah, it was definitely going to be tough to go back.

Pushing that thought aside, she too slid from the car and together they made their way to the guard gate. The man staffing the entrance was reading a magazine when they approached, and she had her badge out and open for his inspection before he even looked up.

"There a problem, Officer?" he asked. She didn't correct the incorrect use of her title.

"Nope, just a routine check on some folks working here," she answered.

His eyes darted to Dominic then back to her before dropping back down to his magazine as he waved them through. She turned and flashed Dom a grin then headed toward the warehouse Oscar Olde had pointed them to.

There wasn't much of a way to approach by stealth since the entire yard was a cement space dotted with the large, metal buildings, but still, they walked past it then circled around the building and came back along the other side. Once they had a rough lay of the land, they walked away and stopped in the shade of a building three buildings down.

"One roll-up door, one side door, and one rear door," Dominic said. "You ever been inside one of these?"

Anika shook her head. "No, but Vice raided a couple about two years ago. With pallets of stuff everywhere and a couple of lofts in each building, it was a mess. They got the job done, but it wasn't easy. Too many places to hide."

"Lofts?"

"Yeah, they both had office lofts, but they each had…a small apartment," she said, making the same connection Dominic had probably made. "You think it's possible Dearil is here?"

Dominic shrugged. "Hard to say, but Oscar gave this address for a reason. A hotel makes more sense, but it's not outside the realm of possibility that he's staying in a loft here."

Anika looked around the yard—well the parts of it she could see. She didn't spot the white jeep, but it might be parked somewhere else, including inside the building. It was also possible he was out.

"How about we take a little walk around?" she asked, jerking her head in the direction of a row of cars. Dominic's lips thinned and he nodded. Without another word, they started to make a lap of the large yard.

A few of the warehouses had their doors up and they could see people inside, moving goods around and loading them onto trucks backed up to the open doors. Occasionally, the sounds of shouting, laughter, and the beep-beep-beep of a piece of equipment backing up filtered through the mostly quiet afternoon.

When they stopped again at their original spot in the shade, Anika pulled her hair into a ponytail and tied it up with a hair band she pulled from her pocket. They hadn't done much more than stroll, but the tropical heat could be relentless, especially when surrounded by a couple acres of cement.

"I didn't see his car, but that doesn't really tell us anything definitively," she said.

Dominic wagged his head in agreement. "How do you feel about maybe, accidentally, stumbling into the wrong warehouse as we look for parolees?"

She chuckled. "I'm sure the doors are locked."

"I might stumble into it with a lock picking kit."

At that, she laughed. It didn't feel right to have a look without a warrant—if they found anything, they wouldn't ever be able to use it as evidence unless they managed to come back with a warrant. But it didn't feel right to not at least *try* to see what was in the warehouse.

"I'm not committing to anything, but let's go at least check the doors," she said. Dominic wiggled his eyebrows at her, then turned and led the way back to the building in question. When they got close, Anika casually looked up toward one of the upper windows—there weren't many, and they seemed to be clustered in groups of three which she assumed must be the loft spaces.

She was about to motion Dominic toward the back door when she saw a shadow move across a window. It wasn't a person she'd seen, but more like someone had walked through the light that filtered in through the window and reflected it back in a shadowy darkness. Grabbing Dominic's arm, she pulled him past the door they'd been heading to and around the corner of the next building.

"There's someone in what I think is the middle loft. I saw a shadow," she said.

Dominic's brow furrowed. "I wish we knew more about that building."

"Any chance Jake might have gotten anything yet?"

Rather than answer, he pulled his phone out and sent a text to his team. Almost as soon as he sent it, the phone vibrated in his hand with an incoming call.

"McMullen," Dom answered.

Anika wished he could put the call on speaker, but as much as she wanted to know what Jake was saying, she wasn't so anxious as to risk someone else hearing. There didn't appear to be anyone else around, but there were a lot of small windows and corners that could easily conceal someone.

Dom made some non-committal sounds and a couple that let her know he was definitely receiving some interesting information, and then he hung up. "Turns out it isn't owned by a Chinese conglomerate, but rather by Wainwright Holdings, a company Duncan Calloway is connected to through his half-sister."

"When did Wainwright buy it?"

"About two and half years ago. Around the same time the *other* holding company—Imperium Holdings—bought the island where the drug bust went down and the hotel Oscar pointed us to."

"What about the other island Wainwright owns in the BVI? You've mentioned it before, the one you were headed to when that boathouse blew up?"

"They've had that one for a while, closer to eight years."

Anika didn't have time to try and sort through all the threads of what those connections might mean to Dominic and his team. Yeah, they had two shady holding companies engaged in shady activity, but she and Dom needed to focus on the task at hand. "Does that get us anywhere with this warehouse?" she asked, gesturing to the building in question.

Just then, Dominic's phone vibrated and he pulled up a text. He looked at it, smiled, then held it out to her. "Looks like Jake got us the schematic for the building. Won't tell us what's inside, but it does confirm that there is an apartment right where you saw the movement in the window."

She studied the image and tried to come up with a plan that didn't involve them breaking into the building. Especially not when someone was in it and that someone might be a hitman.

"Did you see any cameras?" she asked.

Dominic shook his head. "Not on the buildings. They are all over the perimeter fencing though."

"So, if the shadow I saw *is* Dearil, and he's tapped into the security system, he probably already knows we're here."

Dominic nodded.

"So, assuming he *has* tapped into the system, the element of surprise really isn't on our side. Picking the locks might have worked if the place was empty, but not if there's someone in there who is waiting to see what we'll do next." Her deduction was an obvious one and she almost cringed when she'd finished. Then she remembered who she was with. Mateo wasn't a bad guy, but the more time she spent with Dominic and the team, the more she realized how often her police partner tried to undermine both her capabilities and her confidence. She preferred to think he wasn't intentionally doing it, but she wasn't sure doing it unintentionally was any better.

"So, we should wait for a warrant?" Dominic asked.

"Are there any benefits to knocking on the door of a building that might contain a hitman who is now wanted for questioning in the murders of three people?"

"And for your attempted murder," Dominic added. They both gazed in the direction of the building. After a beat, Dominic spoke again. "Probably not. Might be better to camp out—"

But whatever he'd been about to say, she'd never know, as a deafening explosion threw them both to the ground.

CHAPTER NINETEEN

Dominic yanked Anika toward him and rolled them both away from the direction of the explosion. Pressing her against the wall of the building by where they stood, he shielded her petite body with his.

"Dearil is a hitman, why didn't we know he has explosive experience?" she asked, her voice muffled against his chest.

When no secondary blast came, Dominic eased away. "Because I bet he fucking doesn't and someone is trying to take him out." It was like Philip Mariston all over again. Mariston had worked with Calloway to broker the deal to sell the identity of a CIA asset. In thanks for his assistance, he'd been blown to pieces just before Dominic and Damian were able to bring him into custody.

"Call Jake and the team and let them know what's going on. If Dearil is in there, we need to get him out." They both rose and, once Anika was on her feet with her phone in hand, he moved away. Anika protested him going off on his own, but her objection was cut short when her call connected. The sound of her voice filling Jake in faded as Dominic moved closer to the warehouse now engulfed in flames. Well, half of it was engulfed in flames. Surprisingly, the other half looked nearly untouched.

Crowds had started to gather, and he could hear people calling back and forth to each other. Ignoring them, he jogged closer. The heat from the fire seemed more intense as it bounced off the surrounding cement and metal. Sweat had his shirt sticking to his back, but still he kept going. There was one door on the part of the building still standing. If Dearil had survived the explosion, it was the only way out.

Or in.

"You can't go in, Dom," Anika said, joining him.

"You fill the team in?"

She nodded. "They are on their way as is the fire department. Not sure anyone could have survived that, but just in case, Jake was going to call the paramedics, too."

"I'm going in. Or at least, I'm going to look," Dom said. Anika's words echoed in his head, but they were knee jerk words…neither of them would be able to stay away.

Giving credence to his thoughts, Anika turned to the crowd. "We need gloves," she shouted.

A hard hat would be nice, too but he wasn't sure of the fire rating of the hats the men and women wore and the last thing they needed was melting plastic on their heads.

Two men walked forward and handed them two pairs of leather gloves.

"You going in there?" one asked.

Anika nodded and handed Dominic the bigger of the two pair. "Police and FBI, we need to see if anyone is still inside."

"That roof won't be stable," the other man said. "It will hold for a while, but if the fire burns back toward the part of the building that isn't on fire now, the roof will collapse first and will bring the walls down with it."

Dominic and Anika both nodded at the advice.

"We called the fire department, they're on their way," one added.

"I did, too. Can you let them know we're in there when they arrive?" Anika asked. They both nodded then moved back to join the growing crowd.

"You ready?" Dominic asked.

"As I'll ever be to walk into a burning building with no protective gear," she answered.

Dominic chuckled and held up a hand. "We have gloves. Now if we had duct tape, we'd have everything we need."

She shook her head but didn't fight the smile. What they were doing was crazy, no ifs, ands, or buts about it, but it needed to be done. Anika needed Dearil for her homicides and Dom and the team needed him for something far bigger. He didn't think Dearil would have all the answers to what Duncan Calloway was involved in, but the hitman was definitely a piece of the puzzle.

She stood to the side of the door as Dominic wrapped a gloved hand around the handle and turned. Not surprising, it was locked. Taking two steps away, he turned and kicked out. His foot connected, and though the door bowed under the force, it didn't open. Grounding himself again, he kicked out once more. Once more, the door moved, but didn't give.

"Here man."

Dominic turned to see one of the men who'd given him and Anika their gloves, jogging toward them. His footsteps had been muted by the sounds of the fire and for a split second, the sight of him coming toward them with a huge axe, caused Dominic to swiftly evaluate his options. It didn't take more than two seconds, though, before he recognized the man's intent.

"Thanks," Dominic said, stepping forward to take the axe. Then, without a word, he turned back to the door, calculated where to strike it, and swung. The door cracked on impact, but not enough to break all the way through. On his third swing, the door flew open.

Heat poured from inside the building, and both he and Anika jerked back. When the first wave settled into a steady stream, they peered inside. It was dark and smoky, but they could easily make out the shapes of pallets and shelving as most of the smoke was flooding upward through where the roof had collapsed.

They stepped inside, pausing a moment to get their bearings and let their eyes adjust.

"That's where the loft used to be," Anika said, pointing to their left. Several pieces of lumber hanging haphazardly from the wall was all that remained of the area. Fire licked the beams, although the flames weren't as robust as those currently consuming the contents of the warehouse floor.

"We need to check the area underneath. If someone was in there when the explosion happened, they would have fallen through." As he spoke, Dominic led them over to the wall and, using it as a guide, he started making his way down toward the space below the loft with Anika on his heels. On the far side of the warehouse, something caught fire and a dull roar filled the air as a new plume of black smoke poured upward. Behind him, Anika coughed, making him wish they had masks, or at the very least, some cloth to tie around their nose and mouth.

Inching along the wall, they came to the area that Dearil—or whoever Anika had seen—would have landed as the loft collapsed. What was left was a pile of smoldering timber strewn haphazardly over the floor and nearby pallets. The explosion had most definitely blown the loft apart, but interestingly, it hadn't incinerated it. Nor had the burning timber caught the nearby pallets on fire—they were smoldering, and the wrapping around them was melting, but they hadn't caught fire.

"We need to move some of the lumber. He might be underneath all that," Anika said, stepping around him and starting to move some of the more easy-to-reach pieces.

"Stay close to the wall," he said, making his way closer to the pallets, dodging heavy beams that lay like matchsticks all around him. He needed to assess the risk before diving in to look for whomever had been in the building—if the pallets were going to go off like Roman Candles like the ones on the other side of the warehouse, he and Anika might need to reassess their rescue plan.

His legs brushed against the wood several times, and he was grateful he'd worn jeans. Moving what timber he could as he made his way toward the pallets, he let out a little sigh of relief when he saw the reason they weren't catching fire like the others. Whoever had planned the explosion, probably hadn't counted on a shipment of ceramic plates to be stored underneath the target area. So while the packaging was burning, little else was catching fire.

Making his way back to Anika, Dominic shifted and moved a few more beams. "Can you see anything?" he shouted over the roar of the fire.

In response, Anika pointed. Following the line of her finger he saw the sole of a boot. Massive beams were scattered around it like a bizarre game of Pick-Up Sticks, and Dominic couldn't see more than just the sole, so it was anyone's guess as to whether it was attached to a human or not. But at least it was a place to start.

"I couldn't move the beams on my own," she said. Given the size and placement of them, the explanation as to why she hadn't started the recovery effort yet was unnecessary. Joining in her efforts, together they began lifting and shifting the timber the best they could while equipped with just a pair of leather gloves.

The closer they got the more they could see. The boot was attached to a denim-clad leg, and soon a torso came into view.

The man, whoever he was, was lying on his back which didn't bode well for his survival—the flames might not be as active in this part of the warehouse as they were in the other half of the building, but they were still burning their way through the available fuel. Having smoldering wood pressed on top of him couldn't be good, not to mention the fact he'd likely fallen at least twenty feet when the loft disintegrated.

"Can you grab his legs?" Dominic shouted to Anika, his question ending abruptly when he sputtered out a cough. Wiping his forearm across his eyes, he turned to look at her. Anika was coughing into her arm, but she was already squatting and reaching for the man's lower leg.

Dominic glanced around and found a piece of wood that looked mostly intact and reached for it. There was one big beam lying across the man's body that Dom needed to lift in a way that wouldn't involve using his bare arms. The piece of wood would, hopefully, give him the leverage he needed so that Anika could drag the man out. He jimmied his makeshift jack under the beam then used another to give him a fulcrum.

"On one," he shouted, and Anika nodded.

He called out the countdown and on one, he put all his weight onto the jack beam. It groaned and shifted and, when another pallet across the warehouse exploded into flames, he nearly lost his grip. Just as he thought he might need to stop and try again, the beam pining the man to the ground moved.

Putting everything he had into holding the wood that was his leverage, he ignored the searing heat and the sweat pouring down his back and chest. He looked down and Anika was slowly dragging the man out. Needing to focus on something other than the inch-by-inch progress Anika was making, Dominic raised his gaze and took in the warehouse. Flames were now crawling along the ceiling above them and more and more pallets were catching fire around them. He hadn't noticed until that moment that the smoke had also thickened, and it was becoming harder to see more than ten feet in front of them.

Fuck, they needed to get out.

He ducked his head and wiped his brow on his shirt sleeve, his back and shoulders protesting at the effort. Afraid of inhaling too much smoke by talking, he glanced down to see that Anika had the man nearly clear of the beam. The man's shirt was burned to his body and his face was almost unrecognizable, but there was enough left unburned that there was no question the man was, indeed, Patrick Dearil.

When just the hitman's arms were still under the beam, Dominic released his hold on the jack just enough to let him jimmy it a little farther under the beam. Then, gently releasing it more, the beam came to rest high enough off the ground that they could still get Dearil's arms out, but Dominic no longer needed to bear the weight.

Dropping to his haunches beside Anika, he grabbed a leg and together they pulled the man out the rest of the way. Once he was clear, Anika fell back, her body convulsing with a coughing fit. Wanting to go to her, to help her, but not having any practical way to do that, Dominic focused on what he could do.

Reaching down, trying to be as careful as possible about Dearil's burns, he checked for a pulse. When he felt the faint beat, Dom pulled the man up and hefted him into a fireman's hold.

"Can you lead the way?" he asked Anika.

She glanced up, taking in both him and the man he had slung over his shoulder, and nodded. Placing her hands on her knees, she pushed herself up then rose. Reaching out, she grabbed ahold of Dom's arm with one hand and Dearil's body with the other, steadying the hitman's body as Dom rose to his feet as well.

Smoke thickened around them as the fire made its way deeper into the part of the warehouse that still had a roof. With

Anika in the lead, they found their way to the wall that they'd followed in and began feeling their way out.

Ahead of him, Anika coughed again and paused. Dom's lungs burned, as did his eyes and muscles, but they couldn't stop. Rather than waste his breath on talking though, he nudged her forward. She hesitated, coughed again, then took a few steps. Though it was less than forty feet to the exit, it felt miles away and again, rather than focus on the details, Dominic turned his energy to counting each step. Each step that would bring them closer.

One. Two. Three...

Through the fog of his brain and the roar of the fire, he heard sirens. The sound was sweet but if they didn't get out of the building in the next minute, there was every possibility that the arrival of the fire department would be too late.

Suddenly, ahead of him, Anika stumbled and went down. His heart lurched at the sound of her coughing as she curled into the fetal position in an effort to avoid the smoke.

Dom didn't hesitate to slide Dearil from his shoulder and drop to Anika's side. He didn't want to lose Dearil as a suspect and a witness, but Anika was far more important.

"Go," Anika wheezed the word out. "Get Dearil out."

"Not happening, honey," Dominic managed to say. "I'm not leaving you." Almost blinded by smoke now, he reached for her hand and grabbed on. "We're crawling out."

"Dom."

Her voice was heavy and labored. But scariest of all, was the fatigue he heard. He was struggling with the lack of oxygen, but she was so much smaller than he was that she was reaching her limits sooner.

"I'm not leaving you here, Nik. I'm not leaving you behind," he hissed as a spark floated down and landed on his back.

"Stop arguing," she whispered. "Just go." She tried to curl into a tighter ball, and Dominic could all but feel the pull of darkness and sleep taking over her body. There was no way he was going to let that happen, not without a fight. He might not be able to save them, but he was going to damn well try.

Hooking an arm under hers, he crawled forward a step then pulled her alongside him. The sirens were louder now, and he knew the men and women outside would tell the firefighters they were in there, but Dominic wasn't going to rely on that to get them out. He crawled forward another few feet then pulled Anika along.

Dominic forced his arms and legs to comply and moved another few feet. Bracing himself to pull Anika alongside him, the first inklings that they might not make it out trickled up his spine. When they'd entered the building, it had been a consideration, but one he'd not let take root—you didn't go into a fight thinking you were going to lose.

But now, as his arm slipped and Anika's weight pulled him back, the possibility well and truly took root. He didn't want to die. He *really* didn't want Anika to die. But as a fit of coughing took hold of his body, the lure of sleep tugged and enticed him, too. Resting, even for a moment, was a death sentence. But it was hard, so very hard, to pull himself free of the promise of sleep—it would be so easy to cover Anika's body with his and hope that someone would find them in time.

Through the haze of his thinking, Dominic heard voices. Men shouting, the sound of metal ripping. The firefighters!

Digging deep for a filament of strength, Dominic once again gripped Anika's arm and pulled. Her body came along beside his and he crawled forward another few feet. Inching them both forward, his determination grew even as his body protested.

Then he caught scent of air. Still smoke filled, but lighter and cleaner. He gasped as oxygen filled his lungs. It wasn't enough to give him much more than a morale boost, but he'd take it— he'd take any grasp, any thread of hope he could.

"We're almost there, Nik," he muttered, more to himself than to her, though the silence that met his words worried him.

"Don't die on me, woman," he said, pulling them forward yet another few feet. Another tease of fresher air caressed his body and he convulsed into a fit of coughing. When he stopped, he found himself lying on the ground beside Anika with no idea of how he'd gone from being on all fours to being on his back.

Shoving aside the desire to close his eyes, Dom rolled to his belly and tried to push himself to his knees. Chancing a glance at the exit, he nearly wept at the sight. A firefighter, two of them, were visible in the smoky haze. Best of all, they were headed toward him and Anika.

Dominic tried to shout for them, but all that came out was a strangled noise. He raised an arm to catch their attention and when the two men pointed in his direction and picked up their pace, a wave of relief—which was such a paltry word for what he was experiencing—washed through him.

They were going to make it. Dominic forced himself to believe it. With that thought echoing in his mind, he did what he'd been wanting to do for what felt like so long. He curled his body around Anika's and held on.

A hand landed on his shoulder and another on his arm. He needed to let go of Anika if they were going to get out. Releasing her was the hardest thing he'd done since they'd entered the warehouse, but it was the only way to save them both.

"Take her," he mumbled to one of the firefighters.

"We'll take both of you," the man said back, his voice sounding distant and robotic.

"Her," Dom repeated. The firefighter standing over him nodded to the other man who swung Anika up into a fireman's hold. Two seconds later both were gone from Dominic's line of sight. A drop of moisture tracked down his face, and he wasn't sure if it was sweat or a tear, but in that moment when he saw

Anika being carried to safety, he let go. He closed his eyes and let sleep drag him down. He was comfortably drifting into darkness when he heard another explosion. A wave of heat roared across his body, and he jerked in response. The firefighter shouted something but pricks of fire were raining down on Dominic and making it hard to understand what the man was saying. Prying his eyes open, Dominic looked up.

Just in time to see a flaming beam above them swing down from the ceiling and pull the roof down with it.

CHAPTER TWENTY

Slowly, Anika became aware of little things—cool air against her skin, a lack of darkness on the other side of her eyelids, the muted sounds of voices and machines. More curious than anything else, she let these sensations wash over her until one voice grounded her with an intensity that had her heart jumping.

"Dominic is waking up," her brother, Brody said. "She'll want to know as soon as she's awake."

Anika forced her eyelids to open, then she blinked several times. A tube ran under her nose and it was clear to her now, that she was in the hospital. In a rush, it all came back to her. The explosion, pulling Patrick Dearil out from under the wreckage, the heat, the smoke, then the sense that Dominic was dragging her somewhere, though she couldn't tell where.

"Dominic," she croaked.

Her dad and brother spun to face her then rushed to her side.

"You want a little water, baby girl?" her dad asked.

Nodding, she didn't even protest the use of her dad's nickname for her. A straw appeared, and she leaned her head forward a little and took a sip. It was room temperature water, but it felt cool as it slid down her burning throat.

"Dominic?" she asked again after swallowing.

"He's waking up now. Similar injuries to yours, mostly smoke inhalation, but several embers fell on him as well and he has a few burns, mostly on his arms. But he'll be okay," Brody added quickly.

"He saved me," she managed to say before a coughing fit hit her. Her dad held out the cup and straw again and once she could, she took another few sips.

"The firefighter we talked to said you two weren't that far from the door when they found you." For maybe the second time in her life, Anika saw a sheen of tears in her dad's eyes. "Dominic insisted they take you first. There were two of them, so one grabbed you and ran. The other stayed to get Dominic, but they were far enough behind you that when the roof collapsed, they got caught in some of the debris."

"The roof collapsed?" she asked, her heart sinking. If they barely got her and Dominic out, that didn't bode well for Patrick Dearil. It was possible they might find some evidence tying him to the murders, but without him, the chances were slim.

Her dad and her brother shared a look. They knew her well enough to know she was more worried about her case than her own health. She was obviously fine, though—or was going to *be* fine—so to her way of thinking, there wasn't any point in dwelling on it.

"Can I see Dominic?" she asked, avoiding any further talk about what had happened at the warehouse.

Her dad gave a hesitant nod. "The doctor gave her okay to allow that once you woke. Jake's waiting outside and he can take you to him. James, Eva, and the rest of the family are also waiting to see you."

"You called them?" she asked, not bothering to hide the

twinge of surprise. Though why she should be surprised she didn't know. They *were* family.

Her dad frowned. "Of course I did. They care about you. They want to be a part of your life. They deserve the chance to do that unless you tell me otherwise."

Anika shook her head as she slid her legs from under the blanket and swung them over the side. "No, you're right. It's just that right now, I want to see Dominic. Can you ask Jake to come help me and then maybe let James and the family know I'll see them after I see Dom?"

"Of course," her brother answered, turning toward the door.

"You scared the shit out of us, Anika," her dad said once her brother had left the room.

She looked up at him, then rose and held out her arms. He stepped forward and engulfed her in a gentle bear hug—the kind of hug that always made her feel safe and stable and loved from the first time she'd experienced it.

"Scared me, too. We weren't expecting what ended up happening. I know they say to plan for the worst, and we were taking precautions thinking we might be encountering a hitman. We never considered someone else might be looking for him and would prefer to have him dead."

Her dad didn't have a chance to respond because Jake walked in, pushing a wheelchair, with her brother trailing behind.

"You doing okay?" he asked, the concern in his slate blue eyes warming her.

"I've been better, but I'll be okay. That my ride?" She pointed to the chair and when Jake nodded, her dad helped her lower herself onto the seat. Jake handed her the small oxygen tank attached to the hoses that ran under her nose while her dad tucked a blanket around her legs. When they were finally on their way, she turned and looked over her shoulder at Dominic's best friend.

"Is he really okay?" she asked. She hadn't wanted to press her dad and Brody—she hadn't been sure they'd even know or, if they did, if they'd tell her the full truth.

"Like you, he will be. He'll have some scarring on his arms, but that pretty mug of his somehow remained unscathed. He asked for you the moment he woke up. Alexis and Beni are in there trying to get him to talk them through what happened, but he's pretty distracted by not being able to see you. I think it will be better for the two of you to walk us through it together."

They turned a corner and passed through a set of swinging metal doors. A nurse smiled at them, but they didn't stop. Just as Jake slowed, she asked the question she hadn't wanted to ask, but desperately wanted the answer to. "Dearil?"

Jake shook his head and once again, her heart sank. "I don't know how he did it," Jake said, giving her pause. "He was knocked out in the initial blast and the doctor thinks he fell a fair distance resulting in a head injury. He'll also be blind in one eye and, judging by the injuries, unable to use one arm. But the son of a bitch somehow survived."

Anika blinked, not quite believing what she heard. "Say that again?"

Jake smiled. "Why don't we wait until we get inside and we can all go over it together? Damian is on his way over, too. He was hung up with Shah working on the potential plea deal for Dearil."

He didn't give her a chance to answer and instead, pushed through the door and into Dominic's room. Alexis and Beni turned when they entered, and Dominic started to throw the covers off but froze about halfway through the motion. Anika wasn't certain, but she'd bet the bandages around his arm and hand were giving him more trouble than he wanted to admit.

Grabbing the tank of oxygen, she rose from the chair and, with help from Alexis, walked to Dominic's side. Relief poured through her at seeing his green eyes staring back her, so full of life. So full of love. Her own emotions were in turmoil, and she wasn't quite sure what to do, so she stood there and stared. Until Dominic kicked the covers back, scooted over, and patted the bed.

She glanced at his colleagues, who were also friends, threw any professionalism out the window, and crawled in beside him. His injuries seemed to be more prevalent on his left arm, so she snuggled up against his right side and he wrapped his arm around her. Without comment, Alexis reached over and settled the blanket over both of them.

"How are you?" she and Beni asked at the same time.

Anika smiled. "Better now. Can anyone tell me anything about Dearil, though? Is he the one who killed Taglia, Khan, and Grant?"

"Why don't you tell us what happened at the warehouse before we get into Dearil," Beni said, then held up a hand to stave off Anika's objection. "We don't know a whole lot right now. He came out of surgery about ten minutes ago, but Damian is looking into a few things so by the time you finish telling us what happened, we might have more info to share."

"You're so fricken' practical, it's annoying sometimes, Beni," Anika grumbled, making the woman smile.

"You nearly burned to death; I figure someone has to be practical. And since Alexis will be the supportive one and Jake will be, well, Jake, that leaves *practical* to me. So why don't you walk us through it?"

So, they did. She and Dominic traded off telling his teammates what had happened, or at least what they each remembered. When they were done, both Alexis and Jake asked a few questions as Beni sent a few texts to, presumably, either Shah or Damian.

"So, what is this I hear about a plea deal?" Anika asked. She didn't like the idea of Dearil being able to plead out of the murders he'd committed. But since it sounded like the man was in no place to negotiate anything at the moment, she wasn't going to jump to conclusions.

Jake grinned. "Apparently, he was grumbling, a little incoherently—"

"A lot incoherently," Beni interjected, once again, being the practical one.

Jake waved her off. "He was mostly unconscious on the way to the hospital, but he managed to say a few things that caught the attention of the attending EMTs. None of it's admissible, of course, since he wasn't really aware of what he was saying, but it was enough to lead us to believe he *might* be interested in a plea. Especially since his days as a hitman are over and, so long as he doesn't rat out the family, then they'll protect him while he's in jail serving whatever reduced sentence the lawyers negotiate."

"I can't imagine what he managed to say," Dominic said. "He was out cold when we found him and stayed that way."

"That's the fun part," Jake said with a grin. "Apparently, he was ranting about how he shouldn't have taken the job. The money was good, and the connection came through the family, but he said he should've known it was a bad job when he was instructed to intentionally make the hits look less than professional. Apparently, he was very offended by that requirement."

"Offended?" Anika asked.

Jake shrugged. "I guess hitmen have standards they operate by, too."

"He said all this in the ambulance?" Dominic asked.

"Well, 'said' is a strong word," Beni said. Just as she finished speaking, Damian came striding into the room.

"You'll never guess what we locked down," he said, without preamble.

"A plea deal?" Anika asked somewhat sarcastically.

Damian stopped at the foot of the bed, took in the fact that she was curled up in Dominic's arms, then started talking. "No, Dearil isn't in a position to negotiate a plea yet, but all the evidence we had was circumstantial anyway. Until now," he added with a grin.

"You have something concrete?" Dominic asked, sitting up straighter in bed.

"We do. You know how Laura Gordon, Jason Grant's girlfriend, was insistent that he would never cheat on her?" Damian waited for them all to nod before continuing. "Well, it turns out she was right." He hit a button on his phone and held it out for Anika and Dominic to see. Alexis, Jake, and Beni crowded around as well.

What popped up was a video taken at the gas station near the private airfield portion of the airport. Laura Gordon arrived as a passenger in Patrick Dearil's car and while he filled the tank, she got out of the car and moved off screen. A few minutes later, she returned to view wearing a long black wig and large sunhat. Undoubtedly, the woman in the video with Jason Grant from the resort.

"What the actual fuck?" Jake muttered.

Damian grinned and pocketed his phone. "Shah's locating her now so we may need to head out any moment," he said, meeting Beni's gaze. "But we checked the incoming private flights and one landed from Miami just before this was taken. Our current thinking is that rather than stay at her friend's house for the night, she hopped on an arranged private flight, met up with Jason, participated, in some way, in his murder, then flew back to Miami to be at her friend's house by the time the good doctor got off work."

"But she and Jason have been together for nearly three years. Has she been planning something like this from the beginning or was it just an opportunity? Or maybe she was coerced?" Anika asked.

Damian shook his head. "We don't know for certain. But Taglia's and Khan's new jobs, and Laura and Grant's new relationship all happened at roughly the same time. I don't know what you all think, but that seems too orchestrated to me for it to be a coincidence."

"You really think they are playing the long game?" Alexis mused more than asked, as she moved to the window and gazed out.

"Of the big cases we've seen since we've been on Tildas, all of them seem to originate in the timeframe beginning from just before the last election to a year or so after," Beni said thoughtfully.

"Duncan Calloway's appointment as the project manager in the World Bank project happened just before the election," Damian said.

"The trafficking ring Serena was investigating came on to her radar shortly after," Alexis said.

"And the island that housed the drug lab was bought in that time frame," Jake added.

"If it's a long game, it's a coordinated and complex one," Beni said.

"I agree that the timing on all those is suspicious, but if this is all tied to The Summit, those things occurred, or were started, before Hemmeleigh was even selected as the location," Anika pointed out.

Damian made a noise, drawing everyone's attention. "I asked Charlotte about this once. Hemmeleigh might have been announced as the location just two years ago—a few months before the team was pulled together and after some of those activities took place—but she said it was a two-year selection process before that. Hemmeleigh, along with a resort in Singapore and one in South Africa, were shortlisted several months before the last election. And she said it was never really in doubt that Hemmeleigh would be chosen. Apparently, the resort in Singapore was big enough for the attendees but not their staff, and the one in South Africa was difficult to get to in any reliably safe way."

"That puts a new spin on things," Anika said.

"It does and it lends some support to the theory that the plan is a long-term investment, but the names that keep cropping up are Duncan Calloway and Calvin Matthews," Dominic said. "Are either of them capable of, well, hell, I'm not even sure what they'd be planning, but whatever it is, are they capable of planning such a long game? More to the point, I suppose, do either of them have the power to do things like ensure Joseph Taglia won that corporate contest or get a trafficking ring up and running?"

"Matthews is the Vice President of the United States, I imagine the power he is capable of wielding is far vaster than what we think," Anika said.

"But Duncan Calloway?" Dominic countered. "He's a friend of Matthews, or appears to be, but that, in and of itself doesn't come with much power."

"I beg to differ," Alexis interjected. "With so many years in politics, I think it's safe to say that Matthews *could* have the connections and power to do what we've seen. But if it's *not* Matthews, but someone wanting to make it look like him, then Calloway, who is someone who has access to and an apparent friendship with, the Vice President, would be an invaluable asset."

"I think either option is a solid possibility, but I also don't think we're going to solve this tonight," Jake said, rising from where he'd perched on Dominic's bedside. "Especially not with Dearil still out of it."

Damian's phone dinged and he read the text. "We won't solve it tonight, but I think we can make some good headway. Beni, you ready? Laura Gordon was spotted at the poolside bar of the hotel she's staying at."

Beni nodded, and the two left with little more than a promise to let them all know how the interview went. Anika was too exhausted to feel left out of the investigation. She—and

Dominic—would be back in fighting form eventually, but for now, they needed to let their bodies heal.

"So, you guys planning to lounge around for the rest of the day?" Jake asked, eliciting a punch in the arm from Alexis.

"I remember when a certain someone was in the hospital a few months ago and you didn't leave her side for *the entire day*," she said.

Jake shivered dramatically. "You're right. One of the most awful days of my life. Take your time, kids." The day Alexis referred to—the day Nia, the love of Jake's life, had been shot—had been an awful day for all of them. But with Dominic lying injured and bandaged beside her, Anika understood how these kinds of events took on a different meaning when they involved a loved one.

"We got this until you both are up on your feet," Alexis said. "That's what teams are for."

Dominic grunted. "I don't like it, but I get it. Not much I could do anyway given the painkillers they've given me. If only they'd been the tasty ones," he said with a grin, referring to the official drink of the Caribbean, the Painkiller.

"Humph," Anika grumbled. She agreed, she really did, but… "There's still one more hurdle we have though. Something we can't hand off to the team."

Dominic drew back enough to look down at her, a small frown playing on his lips. "What's that?"

She let out a dramatic sigh. "My family—both of them. They are all here, and since I'm not leaving your side, you'll have to survive it all with me."

Dominic's green eyes bore into hers, then he smiled. "I caught a hitman with you today. I crawled through a fire with you today. I survived an explosion with you today. I think I got this family thing covered."

CHAPTER TWENTY-ONE

Twenty-four hours later, Dominic walked into the FBI office with Anika at his side. The doctors hadn't really been on board about letting them go, but their lingering injuries weren't life threatening. The biggest threat was lung damage, due to smoke inhalation. But so long as they didn't tax their lungs, then they could recover at home as well as they could recover at the hospital. And with his team, and both of Anika's families, taking care of them, neither of them were going to be in danger of overtaxing themselves anytime soon.

"Just in time," Shah said, walking out of her office. "The rest of the team is in the conference room. Join us, there's a lot that's happened in the last day."

They followed her into the room where the rest of his team sat around the long table. A diagram that resembled an organizational chart on steroids was projected up on the screen on the wall.

"You guys want anything?" Alexis asked. "Juice? Coffee?"

Both he and Anika shook their heads. At this point, they just wanted to know where everything stood.

"Damian," Shah prompted.

Damian slid a laptop to Beni and rose to stand beside the image. "Just a few minutes ago, the attorneys for government and for Dearil signed a plea bargain. In exchange for a reduced sentence, Dearil gave us everything he knows about who hired him and why."

"He killed three people on my island, please tell me he's at least getting some jail time," Anika said. "I do not want to tell the family and friends of the victims that the man responsible for their loved one's death is walking scot free."

"Twenty years, no parole," Shah said. "Between the evidence we picked up from the CCTV and Laura's confession we had enough to tie him to Jason Grant's death. We also had enough to tie him to the attempt on your life, which, if you're curious, he said was just an opportunity to up the ante on the investigation by going after the lead detective and nothing personal."

"Oh well, I feel so much better now that I know it wasn't personal," Anika drawled.

Shah let a smile touch her lips before returning to the topic. "We only had circumstantial evidence on the other two murders, so we couldn't hold those over him. That said, we made it a condition of the bargain that he tell us everything, including the details about his orders to kill Joseph Taglia and Hameed Khan so we have closure on those victims as well."

Beside him, Anika let out a deep breath. It wasn't three life sentences coupled with the host of other charges they could have brought, but it wasn't a bad compromise. Dearil wasn't young, and in twenty years, between his age and the impact of the injuries from the explosion, he'd more or less be an invalid. A twenty-year sentence with no parole might as well be multiple life sentences.

"Thank you," Anika said.

Shah nodded then gestured for Damian to continue.

"What we have here," Damian said, pointing to the image beside him that began populating with names, "is what we believe is a conspiracy that involves Duncan Calloway, his half-sister, Georgina Grace, Ronald Lawlor, and several others, including Wainwright and Imperium Holdings."

As he spoke, all the boxes filled with names, and lines appeared connecting various names to others in the chart. When the graphic completed its task, what was left was a spider web of people, connected in various ways—through their industries, through politics, through family. As Dominic stared, he could see how the people they'd identified as being involved in the World Bank investigation connected with those they'd identified as being involved in the trafficking ring and the sale of the CIA asset identity. It was complex, and in some cases, the connections looked a bit tenuous, but it was a hell of a piece of work.

"You've been busy in the last day," Dominic said, his eyes still tracing the lines.

"With Dearil's information, everything started to fall into place and we began to see the whole picture," Beni responded.

"And the modeling and data visualization program Nia and I worked on did the rest," Jake said.

"But a conspiracy?" Anika asked. Statistically, true conspiracies were rare—they might be easy to initiate, but they were notoriously difficult to manage and usually devolved into a bunch of semi-connected, but individual crimes. That didn't mean they didn't exist, though.

Damian nodded in response to Anika's question. "It is a conspiracy. No one could do this without having the right factors in play." He pointed to Taglia's name then traced several lines. What the connections showed was a complex series of events that led to Taglia getting the new job in LA and, three years later, winning the random branding contest. If the data was right, Taglia's role had started with a friendship between Georgina Grace and Harold Kyper, owner of Loose Ends Studio.

"Or this," Beni said. Rising, she pointed to Serena's name, the CIA asset whose identity Angela Rosen had tried to sell to one of Duncan Calloway's contacts. Only the connections Beni was making weren't about Rosen and Calloway's activities, they were about the trafficking ring Serena had been investigating. A connection between one of Ronald Lawlor's informants and a very wealthy man in the Middle East—one who happened to also be on the board of Wainwright Holdings—appeared to be the origin.

"Okay, so there's some big conspiracy going on. But to what end?" Dominic asked.

"And did you get all this from Dearil?" Anika added.

Dominic turned toward her. She'd become so much a part of the fabric of his life that he'd forgotten she wouldn't know all the details of some of the other cases they'd worked since arriving on Tildas Island sixteen months ago.

"Some of those connections we knew," he said. "Like Lawlor and Calloway and Calloway's half-sister. We also knew several other names from when we investigated Imperium Holdings, though not their connections to each other," Dominic said.

"We've suspected something bigger was at play than the individual cases we were seeing and that it has to do with Calvin Matthews in some way. But the evidence we had was circumstantial and little more than suspicion. Until today, that is, when Dearil gave us what we needed to confirm it is, in fact, a conspiracy," Alexis said.

"What's that?" Anika asked.

"When Calloway hired him—and we do have confirmation it was Calloway," Damian said. "Dearil overheard a conversation between him and another man. Dearil didn't see who the man was, and he didn't speak, but he was in the room with Calloway. During the conversation, Calloway referred to the Fraternity and assured the man that everything was falling into place to restore the power."

"Nearly the exact words Gregor Lev used," Dominic said, referring to the lead chemist running the drug lab they'd shut down five months ago.

Damian nodded. "Then Dearil had his meeting with Calloway and Calloway was very insistent that Dearil not only complete the hits on the three victims, but that he make each look like it was done by a second-rate hitman."

"Did he say why it had to be done here on Tildas?" Anika asked.

Damian bobbed his head in "sort of" gesture. "He didn't know why Tildas, specifically, but the murders all had to happen in close enough proximity to each other so that law enforcement would make the DC Bank connection between the three. If they'd each been killed in their respective home cities, no one would connect them, and Calloway was insistent that they needed to be tied together."

"That makes sense, but again, to what end?" Dominic asked, but this time as it related to Dearil's specific orders rather than the end goal of the conspiracy itself.

"They wanted it to look like someone had hired a hitman, but whoever it was, didn't have the right connections to hire someone good," Beni answered. "So, someone connected into the world of organized crime, but not too well connected."

Anika frowned. "I'm missing something here."

As Dominic scanned the image, he thought about all the major investigations they'd undertaken in the past eighteen months. Anika's question echoed in his mind as he perused the lines and names, then, in blinding clarity, the light went on.

"Whoever is behind this—maybe Calloway or maybe someone else—doesn't care if any of these illegal ventures actually succeed," Dom said. "All that's important is that they happen, in some way. That there's some evidence, or implication, of wrongdoing."

Anika sucked in a breath. "Because even without proof,

implication—especially being implicated in the crimes you all have uncovered—can ruin a career."

His teammates all nodded.

"Do you think someone is trying to frame Calvin Matthews?" Anika asked.

At that question, Damian sighed and retook his seat, as did Beni. "That's the part we don't know," he said.

"Matthews is an obvious choice as someone to frame. He has connections to all the investigations we've run, and if someone succeeded in making him look like he was involved, it would definitely be the end of his career," Jake said.

"And if his career ends, the move to bipartisanship that we've seen during his and Cunningham's term comes to a screeching halt and the nation is divided once again," Dominic said.

"And a nation divided is easy prey which benefits the rich and powerful on both sides of the aisle," Anika added quietly.

The room fell silent for a moment before Alexis spoke. "But with Matthews at the center of everything, we don't want to overlook the possibility that he's running the show."

Dominic shook his head. "Why would Matthews frame himself? Because the more I process what I see there," he gestured to the projected image, "It does look like he's being set up to take the fall for all this."

"What happens if he is behind all this?" Alexis posited.

Anika jumped in before Dom could speak. "Almost the same thing than if he's framed. The country devolves back to its divisive politics that primarily benefit the rich and powerful. Matthews' career goes down in flames either way, but would he really do that to himself?" Anika asked.

Jake wagged his head. "Initially, Matthews will go down either way and if he's being framed, he'll always have a cloud of doubt hanging over him. But if he's behind it, I'd bet dollars to donuts that he has some 'evidence' that will clear his name."

"And then once he's vindicated, he can play the survivor card and his political star skyrockets," Dominic finished Jake's train of thought and the team nodded.

"So, what you're saying is that, at this point, we don't know if he's being framed by someone else or if he's framing himself," Anika said. "If the former, then the people who will benefit the most—people like those people," she said, gesturing to the image and the plethora of names on it, "are probably behind it. If it's the latter, he'll take a hit initially, but in the long run, he has an opportunity to grab power in a way he doesn't have with the two-party ticket."

"The key is here," Damian said, highlighting the link between Calloway and Matthews. "Calloway is doing someone's dirty work. Whether it's Matthews' or someone else's is what we need to figure out."

"Either way, Calloway seems like someone we might want to keep close tabs on," Dominic said. "I know we've been investigating him, but honestly, if he were that central to a conspiracy *I* was invested in, he'd be the loose end I'd eventually want to clean up."

Shah nodded and spoke for the first time since they'd sat down. "I've brought in a few specialists to keep an eye on him, because you're right. Whether it's Matthews or someone else behind this, it's unlikely Calloway is intended to survive to the end game. He's currently visiting some friends in the UK but is scheduled to return to DC in two days."

Dominic let that sink in before speaking again. "So, what now?"

Shah rose as she answered. "For the record, I agree with you Dominic. I don't believe Matthews knows a thing about what we've been uncovering in our investigations. But to Alexis' point, we need to be sure. I have a few more calls I need to make this evening, but for now, you and Detective Anderson go get some rest. We're at a tipping point here, we either slide back into darkness or we move toward the light. I know the analogy isn't great, but based on my experience that's where we're at—we find what we need to in order to solve this, or it slips through our fingers. I hired each of you because of your independence, intelligence, skills, and, contrary to what the Bureau thought, because of your ability to work as a team. I think we can all agree that whatever is being planned is meant to blow up during The Summit, so we have less than five weeks to make sure that doesn't happen. Tonight may be the last good night's sleep you all get and I want you to take it."

Dominic shared a look with his teammates. He, Damian, and Beni had all been military before joining the FBI, and they recognized a mission when they saw one, even if it came with a different title. The kind of vigilance and hours Shah was talking about were very familiar to him.

"Oh, and Detective Anderson," Shah said, pausing in the doorway.

"Yes?"

"Should you choose to accept the invitation, you will be temporarily reassigned as the official FBI Tildas Island Police Liaison through the end of The Summit."

Anika stilled but didn't hesitate. "It would be an honor, Director Shah."

Shah let her eyes linger on the group, then she nodded and walked out, leaving them all in a weighted silence.

"So," Jake drawled the word. "Anyone up for a drink at The Shack? You know, before we basically move in here for the next five weeks?"

"Took the words right out of my mouth," Damian said.

"Hell, yes," Beni added.

"I'll call Isiah and have him get our table ready," Alexis said.

"And as the newest member of your team—and given the fact that Dominic and I almost died yesterday—first round's on me," Anika interjected to a round of "woohoos" and "yesses."

"Dom, you up for a drink? Or twelve?" Jake asked.

Dominic looked around the table, his gaze lingering on Anika. The next five weeks were going to be hell, there was no way around that. Whatever train wreck was coming, it was in their hands to stop. If they didn't, and the political structure imploded, the effects could reach well beyond US borders. He'd been on a lot of missions before, with a lot at stake, but nothing quite like this. Looking at each person around the table he felt the weight of the responsibility, but it wasn't his alone. No, they might be going into Hell, but there wasn't anyone else he'd rather have with him.

He flashed his trademark grin, making Beni and Anika groan. "Really, Jake," he said. "Do you even have to ask?"

EPILOGUE

Beni lifted her rum and took a sip, the cool liquid burning a trail down her throat. The sun hadn't set yet, and the view from the veranda at The Shack was magnificent. The aqua blue of the Caribbean stretched out from the lush green of Tildas Island. Between where she and her team sat perched on the hillside, valleys filled with ferns, palms, and brightly flowered flamboyant trees carved their way down toward the ocean.

The task ahead of them was almost overwhelming in its complexity and importance. But like always, she didn't plan to fail. Whoever was framing Calvin Matthews would *not* have the satisfaction of bringing either him, or the political civility he and President Ann-Marie Cunningham had brought back to the US, down. She understood why some of her teammates might be considering the idea Matthews himself was behind the whole thing, but she knew better. For good or for bad, she knew better.

"I don't want to think Matthews has played the American people so much," Damian said, then took a sip of his beer. Neither his wife, Charlotte, nor Jake's partner, Nia, were present, so with just the addition of Anika and Isiah, who'd been considered a consultant to their team for eight months, they could still speak freely about the investigation.

"No one does," Anika said. "He and President Cunningham were a breath of fresh air when they ticketed up. I can't remember the last time we've had a political team in office that genuinely seems committed to the people of the United States."

"But power and money do funny things to people," Alexis said. And she'd know. Her parents were powerful people. Not politically, but in the world of music and entertainment, Jasper and Vera Wright were royalty. Years ago, in a quest for money, someone had preyed on them, and Alexis had been the one to suffer.

"Uh, yeah, I can vouch for that," Jake added then took a large swallow of his rum. Yeah, that little revelation about his family being part of one of the larger mafia families in the US had been quite a surprise.

"He's not involved," Beni said, stepping into the conversation.

Everyone looked at her.

"I don't want to think he is either, Beni, but Shah is right, we have to consider it," Dominic said. "The elite in both parties benefit when the country is divided, and with his connections, there's no doubt that he'd be one of them."

Beni took another sip of her drink then shook her head. "We'll do what we need to, but I'm telling you, he's not involved. Matthews is…" Is what? What could she say that wouldn't take the conversation down a path she didn't want to go down? "Have you seen his record? There's no way he would have invested in the work that he invested in and fought the fights he fought for those unable to fight for themselves, if he didn't believe in what he was doing. His life's work is completely antithetical to everything we've investigated. Human trafficking rings by a man who singlehandedly brought about the regulation and protection of sex workers in Chicago? Or a drug lab from a man who, when mayor of Chicago, fought for drug clinics and rehabilitation centers that reduced the number of drug related crime and deaths dramatically?" She shook her head. "I'll do what I have to do, but I don't believe anything that points to Matthews being involved."

When she finished speaking, she took a sip of her drink, finishing it off. She'd said too much, but it needed to be said. After a beat, she realized no one had responded. She looked around the table to see everyone staring at something behind her. The hairs on the back of her neck went on end and a shiver crawled up her spine. Slowly, she turned.

"I can't tell you how glad I am to hear you don't doubt me, Benita." And there he stood. All six-foot-two, blond-haired, blue-eyed specimen of a man. The man who'd all but broken her heart years ago. Calvin Matthews.

"Cal," she managed to say, then raised her glass to her lips to find it empty. Not knowing what else to do, she rose from her seat and faced him. "What are you doing here?"

"I received an interesting call from Director Shah this morning. Thought I'd come down and talk to her myself. We had a very informative discussion about an hour ago. Then she told me you'd be here. So, I'm here."

"Where's your Secret Service?" It was an inane question, but it was all she had at the moment.

He grinned, his left cheek dimpling. "Worried about me?"

She rolled her eyes, feeling a little bit of the shock at seeing him ease from her body. Though the happiness at seeing him again that replaced the shock wasn't any more welcome. "You're second in line to leading this great country we call our own. Yeah, I'm worried."

His grin turned into a smile. "I figure with five FBI agents, a retired Navy SEAL, and one of Tildas Island's finest—not to mention the two CIA spooks behind the bar—that I'm pretty safe here. But they're outside, watching the entrance and exits," he added. Then before she could say anything, he moved into her space and stole the breath from her lungs. "I've missed you Benita," he added quietly.

She didn't know what to say to that. She didn't know what she *could* say to that. She'd left him all those years ago because he was going on to bigger and better things and she was the housekeeper's daughter who was enlisting in the military. She'd never doubted her decision to leave him—even if how she'd done it hadn't been her best day. He *had* gone on to bigger and better things. There were, literally, thousands of people's lives that were better because of the man standing in front of her.

But she'd missed him, too. God how she'd missed.

"I—" She started to say something, but he cut her off. Sliding his hand behind her neck, he pulled her forward, slanted his mouth over hers, and kissed her. He kissed her with everything he had, trying to wipe away the nearly twenty years they'd been apart.

And god help her, she kissed him back.

She had no idea how much time had passed when her senses started to come back to her, and abruptly, she pulled away. Cal didn't let her go far though. His blue eyes burned into hers as he held her tight, one hand still at her neck, the other at her waist.

"I let you go once before, Benita Ricci," he said. "You can be damn sure I'm not going to do it again."

THE END

Thank you for reading THIS SIDE OF MIDNIGHT! I hope you enjoyed Anika & Dominic's story. Have you read the first 3 books of the TILDAS ISLAND SERIES?

. . .

Check out A FIERY WHISPER (Charlotte & Damian's story), NIGHT DECEPTION (Alexis & Isiah's story), as well as A TOUCH OF LIGHT AND DARK (Nia & Jake's story)!

If you've read the complete series already, stay tuned for the grand finale in book number 5 - EIGHT MINUTES TO SUNRISE (Beni & Cal's story) will be coming soon!

In the meantime, you can also dive into my WINDSOR SERIES, beginning with book 1, A TAINTED MIND. And here's a little fun connection, Charlotte & Damian both appear several times in the Windsor series.

EXTRACT OF
A TAINTED MIND

#1 Windsor Series

CHAPTER 1

Vivienne DeMarco guided her car onto the shoulder of the country road and peered out through the windshield into the black night. Her eyes skirted to the side windows as she tried to see something, anything. When that failed, she turned her gaze to the rearview mirror then let out a long, slow breath. There was nothing. Nothing but the darkness and the deafening sound of rain hammering her car.

It was a dark and stormy night, she thought to herself with a rueful sort of inevitability as she loosened her grip on the steering wheel. Here she was alone, in the dark, on a deserted road, and in the middle of a torrential spring downpour. Her life had become a series of clichés lately and tonight was no different. As if in a bad movie, she'd been felled by a simple flat tire.

She craned her head forward and looked up through the windshield again, debating whether or not to risk the pelting rain. She knew storms like this moved on as fast as they came in. And so, after listening to rain drops the size of New Hampshire lash at her car, Vivi put her faith in experience and opted to wait.

CHAPTER 1

Still, as she sat listening to the metallic sound of her roof taking a beating, the cliché-ness of the situation—of the past year—did not escape her. She was just a woman who'd thrown herself into her job after a searing loss—a job that had propelled her to the brink and finally catalyzed a meltdown of epic proportions. A meltdown that drove her away from everything she knew in an effort to find herself again. Honestly, all Vivi needed now was the urban legend hitchhiker scratching his hook along her window. But at least the hitchhiker would make a good story. As it was, her life story was all so prosaic that, if it were a book, it would never make it past an agent's slush pile.

With a sigh, she pulled her mind from her uninspiring existence and glanced at her GPS. Judging by the tiny map, she wasn't all that far from her destination, a place her aunt had been telling her about for years. Windsor, New York, was a small town in the Hudson Valley and, having been in her fair share of small towns, Vivi figured that if she saw anyone on this night, he or she was more likely to stop and help than to stop and slit her throat. But either way, the storm was letting up and she wasn't going to sit around and wait for help, or anything else, that may or may not come. She knew how to change her own tire.

However in the dark and wet, what should have taken her no more than twenty minutes took forty and, after tightening the last bolt, she needed to stand and stretch out the kinks in her back and shoulders. The now gentle rainfall had soaked her clothes, and water was running under her jacket's hood, down her neck, and onto her back. At least the job was done.

With the smell of wet earth hanging in the humidity, Vivi paused. Taking a deep breath of the heavy air, she inhaled the cleanness of it, the purity of the scent. No pollution, no smells of the dead and decomposing. And knowing Windsor would have somewhere she could stay for the night, Vivi ignored how

CHAPTER 1

uncomfortable she was for a moment and savored the peace as a sense of calm settled over her.

But as if to object to her enjoying such a small luxury, an owl screeched in the night, jarring Vivi back to the here and now. Gathering her flashlight and tools, she tossed the jack into the car, wiped the grease from her hands with a wet rag, and shut the trunk. She turned toward the driver's door as a sound behind her, muffled by the dense air, caught her attention. Vivi stilled and cocked her head. It wasn't a car and it hadn't sounded like footsteps either.

There, she heard it again. Vivi frowned. Judging by the gentle thuds and cracks, it was nothing but a few rocks tumbling down the shoulder behind her. But there wasn't much wind to speak of now that the storm had reduced to a drizzle, nothing strong enough to move rocks around. Shining her flashlight onto the water-soaked road, she realized that it was possible the runoff from the storm was stronger than she thought and that the rain had dumped enough water to loosen the soil under the asphalt. Or maybe there was something else causing the disruption.

This thought came out of nowhere and disturbed her more than the sound itself. Despite her experiences, despite her job, she was *not* one of those people who saw danger or evil everywhere she looked. And, more to the point, she didn't ever *want* to be one of them. So, forcing herself to come up with some alternate logic for her errant thought, she remembered her aunt telling her that bears were endemic to the area. Maybe one had come out for the night, dislodging the earth as it made its way into the field across the road?

Yes, a bear—or maybe even a deer or a fox. That made more sense than anything else out here on this quiet road. This option gave her a small sense of relief until she realized that, while she might know how to change a tire, she knew nothing about bears. What did someone do when encountering a bear? Run? Stay still? Vivi's mind had just started spinning when she

CHAPTER 1

brought it to a purposeful halt. She was getting ahead of herself. She had no idea what, if anything, was out there. And so, with some trepidation, she made a half turn and swept her flashlight across the road. Nothing.

She glanced to her left. A forest of elm and birch trees lined the road. Even if she shined her flashlight in that direction, which she did, she couldn't see more than a few feet into the dense woods. To her right, and steeper than she had originally thought, the side of the road dropped down about ten feet before leveling out onto a cornfield filled with stalks about a foot high. Curiosity got the better of her, and she moved a step away from her car. She'd seen lots of deer in her time, but she had never seen a bear, or even a fox, in the wild. As long as she knew an animal wasn't right next to her, she wouldn't mind catching a glimpse of one moving about in nature.

She pointed her light along the line of corn at the edge of the field, looking for some sign an animal had disturbed the crops. After two passes, the only thing she saw were neat rows of baby stalks, their tops and leaves battered by the heavy rain. Vivi should have felt comforted by the lack of wildlife, but she didn't.

As she took another step away from her car, the night encompassed her. Steamy fog was rising from the road, casting eerie shadows that drifted in the weighty air and made the hairs on her neck stand up. She thought about getting in her car and driving away; she hadn't gathered up the courage a few weeks ago to take a much-needed leave of absence from all the violence of her work only to step right back into the thing she was trying to get away from.

But it wasn't in her makeup to let fear guide her response, so Vivi took a deep breath, moved away from her car toward where she thought the sound had originated, and stopped. Standing silent and still, she let the night become familiar. After a few moments of hearing nothing but cicadas and frogs, Vivi directed her beam down the edge of the road as far as the light would go. But the fog and shadows blended with the black of the night and the darkened roadway, so it was hard to see much of anything.

Rather than move farther along the road, she redirected the light down the side of the slope to the field's edge, the contrast of the lighter dirt making it easier, just a bit, to see any anomalies. Starting below where she stood, she swept an area in a straight line away from her as far as the beam would go. Then, shifting it up a foot or two, she brought it back toward her, searching the area in a grid-like way, looking for what might have made the noise.

Standing on the side of the road, wet and exposed, combing the area for something unknown, Vivi couldn't ignore the reality that, to her dismay, she *had* become one of those people —one of those people she never wanted to be. She no more expected to find a simple little rock slide than she expected to see Santa Claus. The pain and death and evil she worked with every day had filtered into her life and colored her experiences.

The irony of her situation did not escape her. Whatever was compelling her to stay and find answers on the side of this country road was the same thing that had gotten her here in the first place. She didn't like to let things go, and because she couldn't let things go, she had almost destroyed herself with her last case. She'd taken to the road to escape, maybe to find some balance. If she were to hazard a guess, though, she'd say that whatever balance she'd found in the past few weeks was about to be tipped.

And, as if to give weight to the direction of her thoughts, about fifteen feet away from her position and about halfway down the embankment, her light landed on a small collection of rocks. No, not rocks, pieces of road that had broken away from the winter-weakened, rain-pummeled lane and tumbled down to rest a few feet away.

Vivi kept her beam trained on the pile as she walked closer.

CHAPTER 1

Tracing a line up the embankment, she could see an approximately two-foot by one-foot section of the road cracked and starting to cave in, the edge beginning to break away.

As she contemplated the small sinkhole illuminated by her flashlight, a gust of wind picked up. Her wet jeans pressed against her legs, her ponytail lifted, and her skin broke out in bumps from the sudden chill. Another piece of the road cracked and tumbled down the slope.

And there, at that crumbling edge, barely visible in the dark and shadows, was the unmistakable form of a human hand.

ALSO BY TAMSEN SCHULTZ

The Windsor Series

1) A Tainted Mind (Vivienne & Ian)
2) These Sorrows We See (Matty & Dash)
3) What Echos Render (Jesse & David)
4) The Frailty of Things (Kit & Garret)
5) An Inarticulate Sea (Carly & Drew)
6) A Darkness Black (Caleb & Cate)
7) Through The Night (Naomi & Jay)
8) Into The Dawn (Brian & Lucy)

Windsor Short Stories

Bacchara

Chimera

The Thing About London

The Tildas Island Series

1) A Fiery Whisper (Charlotte & Damian)
2) Night Deception (Alexis & Isiah)
3) A Touch of Light and Dark (Nia & Jake)
4) This Side of Midnight (Anika & Dominic)
5) Eight Minutes to Sunrise (Beni & Cal) *coming soon*

Printed in Great Britain
by Amazon